“Seeing you today, I’d say trick riding is every bit as dangerous as bull riding.”

“It’s not. I’m in constant control of a well-trained horse,” Kenna told him.

“How about when you’re hanging upside down off a horse? Where’s the control then?”

“I’m not being tossed about like a sneaker in a dryer. A sneaker that could land beneath an angry bull’s sharp hooves. And besides, standing up in the saddle is a relatively easy trick.”

“You were on a horse you’d never ridden before and performing a risky stunt that could have landed you in the hospital if something went wrong. I was impressed, Kenna.” His tone softened. “And scared for you.”

She would have responded except her throat had gone dry. Swallowing, she started over. “I might not have tried the hippodrome with someone else at the other end of the lunge line. You made me feel safe, Channing.”

“I’m glad it was me, too.”

Dear Reader,

I love friends-to-sweethearts stories—they're one of my favorites. I wanted to do something different with this book to give it a fresh twist that would make it stand out. I found it. Well, two things, I think.

Kenna is an accomplished trick rider. I admit to knowing little about this demanding sport and had a great time researching. My other fresh twist—Kenna's mom is marrying a man nineteen years her junior. I was able to explore how people feel about a large age gap between a woman and a man and, at times, took the story to an emotional place.

Mostly, however, I had fun getting Kenna and Channing to quit being so stubborn and realize they're not just friends—they're perfect for each other. I hope you enjoy their story and the second installment in my Wishing Well Springs series.

Warmest wishes,

Cathy McDavid

PS: I love connecting with readers. You can find me at:

CathyMcDavid.com

Facebook.com/CathyMcDavidBooks

Twitter: @CathyMcDavid

Instagram.com/CathyMcDavidWriter

HEARTWARMING

How to Marry a Cowboy

Cathy McDavid

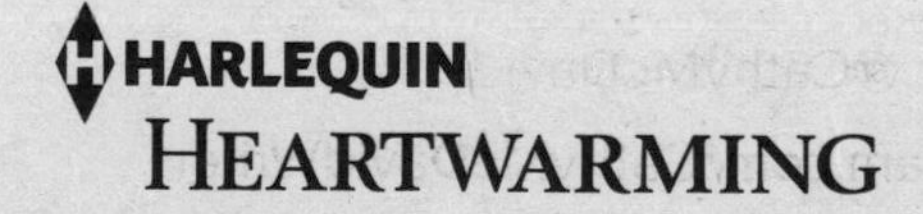

HARLEQUIN®
HEARTWARMING™

Recycling programs for this product may not exist in your area.

ISBN-13: 978-1-335-17982-1

How to Marry a Cowboy

This is a work of fiction. Names, characters, places and incidents are either the product of the author's imagination or are used fictitiously. Any resemblance to actual persons, living or dead, businesses, companies, events or locales is entirely coincidental.

This edition published by arrangement with Harlequin Books S.A.

For questions and comments about the quality of this book, please contact us at CustomerService@Harlequin.com.

Harlequin Enterprises ULC
22 Adelaide St. West, 40th Floor
Toronto, Ontario M5H 4E3, Canada
www.Harlequin.com

Printed in U.S.A.

Since 2006, *New York Times* bestselling author **Cathy McDavid** has been happily penning contemporary Westerns for Harlequin. Every day, she gets to write about handsome cowboys riding the range or busting a bronc. It's a tough job, but she's willing to make the sacrifice. Cathy shares her Arizona home with her own real-life sweetheart and a trio of odd pets. Her grown twins have left to embark on lives of their own, and she couldn't be prouder of their accomplishments.

Books by Cathy McDavid

Harlequin Heartwarming

Wishing Well Springs

The Cowboy's Holiday Bride

The Sweetheart Ranch

A Cowboy's Christmas Proposal
The Cowboy's Perfect Match
The Cowboy's Christmas Baby
Her Cowboy Sweetheart

Visit the Author Profile page at Harlequin.com for more titles.

To Stacy Connelly. Without you as a sounding board, this book might not have happened. Thanks, friend. When's our next brainstorming session?

CHAPTER ONE

WITH EACH STILTED step the big palomino took, anguish squeezed Kenna Hewitt's heart. She hated seeing her best friend, her constant companion and performance partner, in pain, but it couldn't be helped. She had to get Zenith to his stall at the Rim Country rodeo arena before the bull riding started.

"I know, boy. You're having a bad day. Me, too."

The horse came to an abrupt halt and squared off with Kenna. She tugged on the lead rope but to no avail. At a thousand pounds of pure stubbornness, there was nothing she could do to budge him.

"Come on. It's not far."

That was a lie. The twin rows of outdoor stalls were behind the livestock pens, a football field's length away.

"Snapple's in his stall already waiting for you."

Kenna had taken her other horse first, leaving Zenith in the trailer. Five hours on the road had aggravated the horse's acute arthritis despite several breaks. If she'd had any other choice, she wouldn't have subjected him to the ordeal. But her mother was getting married again—her third wedding in the last ten years. And, like every other time, Kenna had returned home to Payson in order to be her mom's maid of honor.

She doubted this marriage would last any longer than numbers two and three, or the countless previous relationships that had come and gone since Kenna's dad passed at an early age. This relationship might be the shortest of them all. The groom—Kenna couldn't bring herself to call him her stepdad—was nineteen years younger than her mother. A mere ten months older than Kenna.

Worse, Kenna was the one who'd introduced them. Worse even than that, he'd asked her out first before her mother. She'd declined, never guessing he'd dazzle her mom with his boyish charm and that they'd start dating. Then to get engaged and marry? No way! And yet, it was happening four weeks from yesterday at Wishing Well Springs.

Kenna kept hoping she'd awaken from this terrible nightmare and have a good, albeit shaky, laugh. Or maybe her mom would finally accept the improbability of meeting another man as wonderful as Kenna's late dad and stop trying to replace him with poor substitutes.

Shoving aside a tangle of emotions that ran

the gamut from frustration to consternation to grief, she drew in a breath and tried again to coax Zenith.

"There's a bucket of grain waiting for you at the stall."

Now *that* wasn't a lie.

"Come on, boy. We're blocking traffic."

He raised his head and whinnied at a passing horse and rider. Across the way, vehicles entered the public parking area in a steady stream. Doors opened and slammed shut and fans converged on the main entrance in their haste to purchase the best seats for the afternoon's event—Bring the Fury Professional Bull Riding. From the holding pens behind the arena, bulls grunted and bellowed and battled their pen mates for the best territory.

It was the same at every arena, regardless of the town or city. Rim Country, however, remained Kenna's favorite. This was where she'd learned to ride and competed in horse shows and where she'd discovered her passion for trick riding. Hoof Feats, her performance team and brainchild, had been formed on these very grounds.

"Need any help?"

At the sound of a familiar voice, Kenna whirled to see Channing Pearce approaching. She'd been expecting to run into him sooner or later; he was the arena owners' son and the reason she was boarding her horses at Rim Country. Being prepared didn't prevent a tiny spark of awareness from igniting at the sight of his confident stride and twinkling baby blues.

Understandable, she supposed. He'd been her first kiss, and a girl didn't forget those things.

We're just friends, she reminded herself before sending him a warm smile, dialed down from the dazzling one her mouth had initially tried to form.

"I won't say no. Zenith is being his usual contrary self."

"I could push. Put my shoulder into it," Channing teased and flashed the same dimpled grin that in the past always had her mooning over him rather than listening to their freshman social studies teacher.

Look away, look away.

"How 'bout I pull and you walk behind him," Kenna suggested and tightened her hold on Zenith's lead rope.

They took up their positions. At her signal, she tugged while Channing waved his arms and clucked. Eventually, the horse forfeited the power struggle and stumbled forward.

Five minutes later, Kenna thankfully led Zenith into his stall and removed his halter. He went right over to his neighbor—her other horse, Snapple—and sniffed the Appaloosa's nose. She poured the promised bucket of grain into Zenith's feed trough, relieved that he'd be able to rest at last. He immediately abandoned his buddy and shoved past her, burying his nose in the fragrant mixture. The metal feed trough clanged against the stall bars as he made quick work of his snack.

"I'm surprised to see you," Kenna said to Channing, exiting the stall and sliding shut the latch. "I figured you'd be at the arena. Isn't the bull riding about to start?"

"Everything's under control. Dad and Grumpy Joe are manning the announcer's booth. My sister's in the box office. The crew's overseeing the bucking stock until I get there."

Kenna didn't inquire about her mom's fiancé, Beau. He worked for Channing as a wrangler most days and as a bullfighter during rodeo events. Instead, she'd wait and get the lowdown from her mom. They were meeting shortly at the concession stand.

Channing rested his forearms on the stall railing and studied Zenith with the critical eye of someone who knew horses well. "What's his treatment and prognosis?"

Kenna hung the halter she'd been holding on the hook outside the stall. "He's on a regiment of meds and light exercise. Some days are better than others. But he'll never perform again."

"A shame he was afflicted so young."

"He's twenty, which is no spring chicken." A surge of fresh pain caused her voice to crack. "Still, I thought we'd have two or three more good years together."

Prematurely retiring Zenith had done more than wreak havoc with Hoof Feat's upcoming performance schedule; it had created a giant rift deep in Kenna's soul that nothing would mend.

"You've been together a long time," Channing said.

"Nearly ten years. I bought him right before I left home on my first tour." She still remembered the day. She'd been fresh-faced, naive, barely old enough to vote and mad as heck at her mom, who'd gotten married a week earlier to Kenna's first stepdad. "I trust Zenith with my life, which is more than I can say about most people. Replacing him won't be easy."

"You check out those pictures I sent yet?"

He'd texted Kenna while she was on the road this morning. His buddy had a horse for sale that he claimed was once used for trick riding.

"I did. He's a looker," Kenna conceded. "Guess I'll find out this week if he has any potential."

"You contacted the owner, then?"

"I talked to his wife and told her we'd set up a time for me to come out once I have a better idea of my schedule." There was an abundance of wedding-related activities planned for the weeks leading up to her mom's wedding, all requiring Kenna to muddle through with a smile on her face. "Any chance you'd go with me? I could use a second set of eyes."

"You bet. Afternoons are better for me."

"Mom has some stuff planned for us tomorrow—dress fittings, wedding shopping..." She tried to hide her done-this-twice-before lack of excitement. "What about the next day? Or Wednesday?"

"Tuesday works. Consider it a date."

A date. She tried not to react. Surely the two small words were a figure of speech and meant nothing.

In another life, had circumstance been different, their high school crush might have developed into something more. But it hadn't and their brief history was exactly that: history.

At least until recently it was. She and Channing had spent more time together than usual during her last few visits home. Kenna's mom had insisted Kenna accompany her to several events at the arena to watch Beau, and Channing happened to be there. Then there was that one time they'd all four gone to dinner. Being with him, sitting next to him at the table, had reminded her of what a great guy he was and how much she'd once liked him. Okay, *still* liked him.

"How are sign-ups coming along?" he asked.

"Good. I'm at my class size limit for the

twelve-and-under age group. And I'm pleased to say I have one boy registered. The thirteen-and-older group is about half-full. But there's still plenty of time."

In exchange for Zenith and Snapple's temporary accommodations, Kenna had agreed to give trick-riding lessons two weekends during her month long stay. The arrangement was a mutually beneficial one. Her horses would be well cared for and the arena received a cut of her fees.

The potential for publicity wouldn't hurt either of them. When Kenna left the morning after her mom's wedding—and she *would* leave then, make no mistake; Kenna refused to hang around and witness the inevitable train wreck—she'd hopefully have added one or two new names to Hoof Feat's client roster.

The next second her phone pinged, and she checked the screen. "Mom just pulled into the parking lot."

Kenna gave her horses a lingering last look, every cell in her body screaming at her to stay. During these few moments with them and Channing, she'd been able to pretend everything was fine and her mom wasn't courting yet another disaster.

Channing walked along beside her, briefly extending her reprieve. "You never said, why can't you use Snapple? He's young and healthy and seems docile enough."

"He's what I call a ninety-five-percenter," Kenna said. "Great ninety-five percent of the time. It's the remaining five percent you have to worry about. Every once in a while, for no apparent reason, he gets spooked and takes off running. I can't have that in a performance horse. My safety, and the safety of my teammates and my students, depends on it."

"What are you going to do with him?"

"I haven't decided."

The arena entrance came into sight. Channing took her through a side gate marked Employees Only. Inside, they navigated a narrow aisle that emptied into an open area swarming with activity. Warm April sunshine beat down on the noisy and restless crowd milling about or filling the stadium seats. The smell of livestock mingled with popcorn and people to create the unique rodeo scent Kenna would know anywhere.

"I may know a buyer for Snapple, if you're interested," Channing said.

"What kind of buyer?"

Kenna wouldn't sell the young gelding to just anyone. He needed a strong and experienced owner. He also needed someone patient with a gentle but firm hand who'd help him overcome his fears.

"The gal I'm thinking of is a competitive trail rider. You'd like her. If you want, I can put the two of you in touch."

"Let me think on that, if you don't mind."

"I'll text you her name and website. You can check her out."

Channing clearly understood Kenna's reservations without her having to go into detail. It was nice. Not for the first time, she wondered why no woman had snatched him up.

"Thanks for everything." She put a hand on his arm.

"Anytime."

It was, Kenna realized, their first physical contact in fourteen years—they hadn't touched even once since that high school dance and their kiss. He'd filled out, the muscles beneath his shirtsleeve more pronounced than she remembered. He'd grown taller, too. She had to raise her chin several notches to meet his gaze.

"There you are, kitten!"

Inwardly, she cringed at the childhood nickname. Outwardly, she manufactured a smile and pivoted. "Hi, Mom."

The smile faltered. Gracie Hewitt-Jacobson-Cordova-soon-to-be-Sutter—Kenna had to constantly remind herself of the many names or she'd lose track—wasn't alone. She came toward them, balancing Beau's eight-month-old daughter, Skye, on her hip. Yes, Kenna was about to become stepsister to a baby, one young enough to be her own child.

"We've been looking for you." Kenna's mom raised the baby's hand and shook it in something resembling a wave. "Say hi to your big sister. And Uncle Channing, too."

Uncle Channing?

"He was about to head to the livestock pens," Kenna said when her mom reached them. No way would she force him to stay.

He shrugged. "I'm in no hurry."

"Wonderful!" Kenna's mom beamed. "Me, my maid of honor and Beau's groomsman all together and watching my handsome fiancé."

Kenna blinked at her mom in disbelief. "Groomsman?"

"Channing. Can you believe it?"

She turned around to face him, attempting to mask her surprise. "*You're* in the wedding?"

"I thought you knew."

"No..." Her voice trailed off. "I didn't."

The news bothered her, even though it shouldn't. Maybe because she'd begun thinking of the time they'd spend together as a refuge from the constant chaos of her mom's wedding.

Well, obviously that wasn't going to happen. Just like her, he was smack-dab in the middle of things—for better or worse.

CHANNING STOOD BACK as Kenna's mom wrapped her in a fierce maternal embrace, narrowly avoiding being knocked over. The woman could be a force.

"I've missed you so much, kitten," Gracie cried. "I can't believe you're home for an entire month."

Frankly, Channing couldn't believe it, either. Kenna usually blew in and out of town like a bank robber on the run. If not for her horse being sidelined, this trip would be no different.

"I've missed you, too, Mom."

Channing swore he heard a trace of emotion in her voice. Interesting. Perhaps Kenna wasn't as cool and indifferent as she wanted people to think.

At a sharp squawk of alarm, Gracie extracted herself from the hug and peered down at baby Skye. "Oops! Sorry, cutie-pie. Are you okay? Didn't mean to trap you."

"Hey, you." Kenna aimed a bemused smile at her soon-to-be stepsister and reached out a hand. "Those are mine."

Skye had somehow managed to snatch Kenna's sunglasses during the hug and promptly stuck them in her mouth. Kenna gently pried them from the baby's tight grasp and, without missing a beat, wiped the drool off with the hem of her shirt.

"She's such a little dickens," Gracie said. "Just like you at that age."

Kenna rolled her eyes.

"What?" Gracie asked, dragging the word out.

Kenna slipped on her now-dry sunglasses. "No childhood stories. We had a deal."

"Well, you *were* a dickens. And utterly adorable. How can I not gush about you as a baby?"

It seemed to Channing that Gracie was trying a little too hard with Kenna. He knew from Beau how desperate she was for her daughter to accept him and Skye into the folds of their small family. According to Beau, that first conversation between Kenna and Gracie had gone something like this:

Gracie: "Kitten, I'm dating someone new."

Kenna: "No offense, Mom, you're always dating someone new."

Gracie: "It's Beau. The man you introduced me to at the rodeo arena."

Kenna: "Beau! He's, like, twenty years younger than you!"

Gracie: "Nineteen. And he's asked me to marry him."

Kenna: "Mom, are you crazy! It's only been what? Five months? Six?"

Gracie: "Yes, but we love each other. Oh, and you should know he has an eight-month-old daughter he just found out about."

Kenna: "A daughter!"

Gracie: "The mother practically abandoned her. What was he to do?"

Kenna: "I don't know, Mom. Postpone your wedding? Not marry you at all? Let's be honest, you have a terrible track record."

Gracie: "This time is different."

Kenna: "Are you ready to be a mother again at your age?"

Gracie: "My age! You make me sound ancient. I'm only forty-eight."

Kenna: "A baby is demanding. Plus, you work. Can you manage everything?"

Gracie: "You worry too much. Everything's going to be fine. Oh, and of course I want you to be my maid of honor."

Kenna: "If I say no, will you call off the wedding?"

Gracie: "You're so funny. See you soon. The wedding's April twenty-fifth."

While Channing hoped Kenna would give Beau a chance, he didn't blame her for how she felt. Gracie did have a long history of making poor relationship decisions after her first husband died, decisions resulting in two failed marriages. That had to be hard for Kenna to watch over and over. He'd immediately agreed to her suggestion of exchanging trick-riding classes for boarding her horses, not because it benefitted them both but because she could probably use a friend in the coming weeks.

There were times he wanted to be more than that to her and considered testing the waters. Then he'd shake off the impulse. Kenna's performance schedule kept her constantly traveling, and he had no interest in a long-distance relationship.

More than that, now wasn't the time; his parents were retiring soon, and the arena was having its worst ever year financially. He needed to stay focused, not be distracted worrying about what his girlfriend was up to during their lonely nights apart or taking weekends off to see her when he needed to be home attending to business.

"We'd better hustle," Gracie chirped. "The bull riding's about to start."

Kenna sent Channing an apologetic look. "Seriously. There's no need to tag along."

He grinned. "I'm your pass to the VIP section."

Gracie gave a whoop and lowered Skye into the stroller. "Did you hear that, cutie-pie? We get front row seats to watch Daddy."

"Thank you," Kenna added softly. She walked alongside her mom, who pushed the stroller.

Channing noticed Kenna dragging her feet, either from weariness—she had driven a long way from Kingman—or lack of enthusiasm. Both, possibly.

"We're going to have so much fun." Gracie paused from pushing the stroller long enough to sling an arm around Kenna's shoulders and give a squeeze. "Don't forget about the dress fitting tomorrow at Bellisima—that's the bridal shop at Wishing Well Springs. We can tour the wedding barn when we're done if you want. It's gorgeous. And the miniature Western town is simply charming. We're having our pictures taken there after the wedding."

"Sure, Mom. Whatever you want."

Channing had heard more enthusiasm from the crews dispatched to clean the livestock pens after a rodeo. In Kenna's defense, her dad had been one of the good ones, and she'd loved him with her whole heart.

He'd known Mr. Hewitt as well as a teenager could know the father of a girl who was always at his family's rodeo arena. The man had been easygoing, friendly, attentive to his wife and daughter, supportive of Kenna and well liked. When he got mad, he had good reason. He also wasn't so egotistical that he couldn't admit when he was wrong.

At fourteen, Channing hadn't appreciated those qualities in an individual like he did now. Gaining business experience, taking over more and more management responsibilities as his parents' retirement neared, had taught him a lot about people.

He wished he'd done more for Kenna when she lost her dad. They'd been in the beginnings of a high school romance. But she'd pulled away afterward, consumed by grief, and he, in his naivete, had failed to be there for her. As a result, they'd never gotten back to the place they once were.

At the entrance to the VIP section, Channing signaled the ticket monitor to admit them. The young woman nodded and swung open the gate.

"This way, ladies." He motioned to a small section of seats reserved for the family's use.

Gracie went first but then stopped. "I should probably sit on the end, what with the baby and stroller. You two go ahead." She moved to the side.

"After you." Channing waited for Kenna to precede him.

She had just passed him when Gracie said, "Channing, why don't you go in first? That way, Kenna and I can sit together."

The remark earned him another apologetic look from Kenna. "You mind?"

"Not in the least."

She backed up against the first seat in order for him to pass. There wasn't much room, and their knees bumped. At the last second, she raised her gaze to his. He wished he could see behind her sunglasses. What he did get was a close-up of her lovely Mona Lisa mouth, a glimpse of the gold charm dangling from a chain around her neck and a slight whiff of something flowery. Shampoo, maybe? Or lotion?

His senses went on high alert, and he became acutely aware of everything about her. Even in cowboy boots, the top of her head barely reached his chin. If she were to remove her ball cap, the black hair she'd shoved through the hole in the back would topple in thick waves to the middle of her back. The tank top she wore showed off tanned and toned arms with a hint of muscle from years of gymnastics and horse riding.

Kenna may not be girlie girl on the outside, but the peach lip gloss, gold charm and flowery scent told a different story.

A loud blare from a nearby speaker roused Channing from his Kenna-induced daze. Clearing his throat, he shuffled to his seat.

She followed, dropping down beside him. She brought that incredible scent with her. Channing decided it must be roses.

"These are great seats," she said. "Thanks."

"My pleasure." And it was.

He had to remind himself she'd be leaving in a month and not lose himself to the old attraction that resurfaced whenever they were together. For him, anyway. He wasn't entirely sure she reciprocated. Once in a while, he thought she did. She let her glance linger only to look away the next second.

Gracie unfastened the multitude of buckles securing Skye in the stroller and lifted the baby onto her lap. Snaking her hand into a large bag behind the stroller, she extracted a bottle filled with juice.

"Here you are, cutie-pie."

Skye grabbed the bottle with both hands and stuffed it in her mouth.

"You're good with her," Kenna said, watching her mom fuss over Skye.

"I've had plenty of practice with little girls, thanks to you. Here, want to hold her?"

Kenna stiffened. "No. That's okay."

Gracie ignored her protest and deposited the baby in Kenna's lap.

She held on—she didn't have a choice. Skye stared at Kenna over the bottle, her expression dubious.

"Has Beau heard from her mother lately?" Kenna asked, readjusting the baby to a less precarious position.

Gracie lifted a slim shoulder. "Not since last week. She insists she wants Beau to be Skye's primary caregiver."

"Have they signed an agreement yet? What about child support? Visitation?"

"They'll get around to that. Next time she's in town."

"Not before the wedding? You're going to be Skye's stepmom and her *co*-primary caregiver."

"There you go again." Gracie straightened and patted Kenna's leg. "Worrying over nothing."

While not exactly nothing, Channing took Gracie's remark to mean her choices were none of Kenna's business.

"Beau is a wonderful dad," She continued. "And I love babies." She turned toward the chutes and cheered with the rest of the crowd. "They're getting ready to start."

Clanging, banging and shouting accompanied the bulls being herded down the narrow passage and into the chutes. Long-legged cowboys with numbers pinned to their backs straddled fences or talked in small clusters. Others, the first to compete, checked safety equipment, evaluated the bulls and readied themselves to ride.

Kenna pulled Skye closer and hunkered down into her seat. Channing noticed her chewing on her lip and assumed the conversation with her mom was far from over.

He remembered the day almost four months ago when Beau called and asked for the day off. A barrel racer named Lora Leigh whom he'd briefly dated had appeared unannounced at his double-wide trailer. She had a baby in tow, and claimed Beau was the father. A week later, after the positive DNA test results were returned, she'd left without Skye. According to Beau, Lora Leigh had insisted she was on the road competing professionally and unable to provide their daughter with the stability and attention she needed. Beau had a job and a place to live.

He also had Gracie, though they'd only been dating a few months when Beau learned he was a dad. Honestly, Channing had figured Beau and Gracie were done for. Few women in her position would have stuck around. But she had, and that was the main reason Channing gave the two of them a fighting chance.

Grumpy Joe's booming voice carried across the arena. The arena's longtime announcer welcomed the crowd to Bring the Fury Bull Riding and explained the arena rules. "We're here to have fun, folks, so let's give these brave young men a round of applause."

Gracie suddenly leaped to her feet. "There's Beau!" She sat back down at Kenna's urging and reached for Skye's hand. Shaking it high over the baby's head, she said, "Wave to Daddy," in that high-pitched voice Channing often heard women use when talking to babies.

Beau entered the arena along with the other bullfighter. Both men wore colorful tie-dyed shirts and neon purple suspenders with ragged cut-off denim shorts. They'd stuck turkey feathers in the bands of their cowboy hats and painted their faces with clown makeup. Cheers rose from the stands—audiences loved the comical bullfighters' antics, which were used to minimize tense situations and keep riders safe by distracting the bull. It took courage and skill to avoid injury or worse. Channing had a lot of respect for them.

Beau didn't disappoint his fans and executed a wobbly bent-legged cartwheel on his way to the center of the arena. His cohort rolled a bright blue barrel with the bottom removed. They were joined by the cowboys, men on horseback tasked with herding the bulls out of the arena once the ride was over and, if needed, hauling the riders off the bull once their eight seconds were up.

Channing had seen hundreds, if not thousands, of rodeos in his career, so he let his attention shift to Kenna. At her curious glance, he nodded toward the baby.

"You're not so bad with her yourself."

"Kids are okay, I guess," she admitted.

"Just not when they're your stepsister?"

"I feel sorry for her. We're both in circumstances beyond our control."

He didn't worry about Gracie hearing them. Her attention was riveted on Beau, who, at that moment, was diving into the barrel in an effort to evade a charging bull.

"There are a bunch of reasons this..." Kenna paused and then whispered, "This marriage is doomed like the others."

"I agree they have some challenges."

"Challenges? They have mountains to climb of the Everest variety."

"Every couple does."

"They aren't every couple." Kenna absently removed the now empty bottle of juice from Skye's fingers.

Channing found himself fascinated by her and the baby. He wouldn't have pegged her as the maternal type. Yet, she obviously had the instincts, whether or not she wanted to admit it.

"They're in love," he said, leaning in to be heard over the cheering crowd. "Isn't that what really counts?"

Kenna withdrew as if he'd spewed fire at her and even went so far as to shield the baby.

"Are you saying you support this marriage?"

"Beau's my employee *and* my friend. Naturally, I support him."

She shook her head, her lovely mouth flattened into a thin line.

Channing said nothing. He knew when to continue pressing his point and when to shut up. This was clearly the latter.

CHAPTER TWO

KENNA STOOD OUTSIDE BELLISIMA, the designer wedding dress boutique at Wishing Well Springs, unsure if she should enter or wait for her mother.

Before she could make up her mind, Laurel Montgomery appeared, her cheery expression matching her tone. "Welcome, welcome." She beckoned Kenna inside. "This is your first visit here, isn't it?"

"Yes." Kenna's gaze traveled the elegant shop and all its delicate finery. "No. I mean, I've been to the house. And the ranch. Before all this." She indicated Bellisima and the business office across the entryway. "It was years ago. I was a kid. My parents bought my first horse from your grandfather."

"Did they?" Laurel smiled warmly. "I'm afraid I don't remember."

"It was twenty-something years ago. Your family had a lot of horses back then." Kenna grimaced. "Sorry. I didn't mean to..."

"It's okay. No worries. As you can see, we've rebounded nicely."

At one time, Laurel's family had owned the largest horse ranch in the county. Due to a string of misfortunes that started with health problems and ended with a tanking economy, they'd lost almost everything. Laurel's grandfather had left what little remained of the ranch to her and her brother. After a lengthy dry spell, they'd turned the main house and barn into Wishing Well Springs, now one of the most popular wedding venues in Arizona. Laurel, a talented wedding dress designer, owned and operated Bellisima.

Both the shop and the business offices occupied the first floor of the house. The wedding barn and newly constructed miniature Western town were a quarter mile up the road, nestled at the base of the hill.

"This is incredible." Kenna gawked at a rack containing a half-dozen or so stunning white gowns and another rack with twice as many bridesmaid dresses in an array of colors and styles. "You made all those?"

"I did." Laurel beamed with unabashed pride.

"I'm impressed. I can barely sew a button on a shirt."

"Well, I can barely stand on my head and you do that on a galloping horse, not to mention all the other incredible stuff."

"I'm giving some classes next week. How about I teach you?"

Laurel laughed. “I’d probably fall and break my neck. Better I stick to designing dresses, where the worst I can do is prick my finger.”

She escorted Kenna to a semicircle seating area that faced a trio of mirrors. “Why don’t we look at the dress your mom picked out for you while we wait. Make yourself comfortable. I’ll just be a minute. There’s snacks on the tray and sparkling cider chilling in the ice bucket.”

“Not champagne?”

“Your mom requested the cider. Said she’s driving.”

What about Dinah? Will she be here?”

Kenna liked her mom’s coworker and second bridesmaid. Though almost old enough to be Kenna’s grandmother, she was sharp as a tack, outrageously funny and very down-to-earth. Kenna and Dinah had yet to discuss the wedding, and she was eager to hear the older woman’s opinion.

“She stopped in Friday for her fitting. Something about covering for your mom today.”

“Oh, okay. I was looking forward to chatting with her. We’re cohosting the bridal shower.”

“I’m sure you’ll have plenty of opportunity,” Laurel said and disappeared into another part of the shop.

Kenna sat there, straining to hear the sound of her mom’s car. She’d come straight from the arena after saddling Snapple for a quick forty-minute workout in the practice ring, just enough to get the kinks out. Before that, she'd spent her morning administering Zenith's meds and taking him on a short walk of the grounds. To her vast relief, his limp had improved overnight.

Fortunately, she hadn't run into Channing, who must have been off somewhere on rodeo business. The bull-riding event yesterday hadn't ended as well as it started out for them. She was even considering not telling him about her appointment tomorrow to see the performance horse.

Silly, yes, and immature on her part. But he'd stunned her with his support of her mom's marriage to Beau. Granted, he and Beau were friends, and friends had each other's back. But surely Channing realized her mom and Beau's chances of success were one in a million. A friend might also advise another when they were potentially making a mistake.

What had he said? Oh, yeah. Her mom and Beau were in love. As if that alone was enough to overcome a huge age difference, the fact that Beau had a baby daughter, his sometimes dangerous profession—Kenna's mom had already lost one husband at a young age, and she didn't need to lose a second—his lack of ambition or desire to be more than a rodeo hand and, not the least as far as Kenna was concerned, they hardly knew each other.

Six months wasn't enough time to be absolutely certain the other person was the one. Yeah, yeah, falling for each other at first sight sounded romantic and straight out of a movie. Reality, however, was a different matter, as her mom's disastrous love life had proved.

Kenna had required only one broken heart to cure her of any relationship delusions. She and her former boyfriend had been together a whole year longer than Beau and her mom and had far fewer obstacles to overcome. Even so, they'd broken up, but not before things got messy. He'd accused her of fearing commitment—could she help it if she hadn't been ready to settle down? The arguments had become intense. He'd actually wanted her to not travel so much. Fed up with their arrangement and her unwillingness to compromise where work was concerned, he'd called it quits.

Just as well. Kenna figured it was for the best. Better to end things before she made the same kind of mistake her mom did, specifically marrying the wrong man.

She grabbed a stuffed green olive and popped it in her mouth, letting the sharp and pungent flavors help her refocus on the present.

Laurel appeared, holding a flowing creation

high in the air to prevent it from dragging on the floor. "Here we are," she sing-songed.

"It's, um, pink." Kenna gulped down the last bite of olive.

"The technique is called ombre. Very popular for spring weddings." Taking hold of the dress, Laurel spread the pleated bottom like a fan opening. "See how the color goes from light carnation on the top to pale magenta on the bottom."

"Yes." Still pink to Kenna.

"Your mother thought you might like this one-shoulder style."

"I do, actually." Truthfully, the bridesmaid dress wasn't as bad as the last two Kenna had worn. She suspected Laurel had influenced her mom. The dress designer seemed the type to expertly guide her clients toward the best choices.

She hung the dress on a stand by the mirrors and, checking her watch, joined Kenna on the sectional. "We'll wait for your mom before trying it on."

Kenna plucked a cheddar cube from the tray, thinking she should've stopped for a fast-food lunch on the drive over. "I guess she's running late."

"Your mom has a ton of stuff going on. I give her credit. Not many of us could arrange a wedding in six weeks. I'm so glad we had a cancellation with the barn and could accommodate her and Beau."

"What do you think of them?" Kenna blurted before she could stop herself. "As a…couple."

While she wasn't close to Laurel, they'd attended high school together and traveled in the same horse world until Kenna left Payson after graduation. Plus, she was Channing's sister, which made her a casual friend, and one of the few Kenna had in town these days. Other than Channing…but his status was currently in question.

"He adores her," Laurel said without hesitation. "And she him."

"Is that enough? I mean, they have some pretty significant challenges facing them. And I'd hate for Mom to get hurt again."

"Hey, I believe in happily-ever-afters. I'm in the wedding business." Laurel's smile spread across her entire face. "To me, challenges are relative. People who seem to have everything going for them can fail abysmally and those who, at first glance, appear ill-suited go on to celebrate a golden anniversary."

"I suppose."

A bell tinkled in the direction of the front door. Kenna's mom had arrived, and she'd been too engrossed with Laurel to notice.

"Hello, hello." Kenna's mom breezed into the

shop, her face flushed as pink as Kenna's bridesmaid dress and pushing a stroller. "You're both here!"

She'd brought Skye along. Kenna hadn't expected that. Didn't most kids attend day care or have a sitter? And what about Beau? Why wasn't he watching his daughter? Kenna's mom had a good job, far better than Beau's in fact. She managed a busy vacation rental business and put in long hours.

But Kenna knew the answer without needing to be reminded. Her mom was watching Skye for Beau, who probably hadn't even asked for the favor. That was what her mom did. She bent over backward for the men in her life. Not Kenna's dad—their marriage had been an equal partnership—but the ones since. It was as if she believed she could win and keep their affection by giving and giving and giving.

Kenna understood relationships required compromising and adapting and sometimes putting the other person first. In her opinion, her mom went too far, and Kenna worried it wasn't healthy.

"Oh, good." Laurel pushed off the sectional. "You brought Skye. We can try on the baby dress I have and see if it fits."

A dress fitting for Skye, too. All right, maybe Kenna had jumped too quickly to the wrong conclusion. While her mom did work overtime to please Beau, it seemed that wasn't the case today.

"Did Laurel show you the dress? Yes, there it is." Kenna's mom hugged her tight as if they hadn't seen each other this morning. "I've missed you so much."

Kenna ignored the surge of emotion squeezing her chest. She'd missed her mom, too, the one who wasn't completely smitten with her latest boyfriend or fiancé to the exclusion of everyone and everything else.

"I did see the dress," she said. "I haven't tried it on yet."

"Well, what are you waiting for?" Her mom bent and withdrew a rectangular box from beneath the stroller. "Here are the shoes. You still wear a size seven, right? We can return them if they don't fit."

Kenna accepted the box. Lifting the lid, she peeked inside and suppressed a groan. A pair of silver strappy sandals lay surrounded by tissue paper.

"I'm going to have to practice walking in these so I don't trip."

Her mom harrumphed. "The heels aren't *that* high."

As if offering her opinion, Skye squawked from the stroller and batted her pudgy little fists.

"Before you go change, say hi to your baby sister."

Kenna resisted her first impulse, which was to reiterate that she and Skye weren't sisters. Instead, she leaned down and tweaked the baby's cheek.

"Hey, squirt."

Skye broke into giggles, drool slobbering down her chin.

Kenna's mom produced a baby wipe from seemingly thin air and swabbed the baby's face. "She's teething."

"I'm surprised she's not in day care."

"I...ah, have her most afternoons." Kenna's mom became suddenly preoccupied with rummaging through the diaper bag.

"She goes to work with you?"

"No. I've cut back my hours."

"Temporarily, right? Because of the wedding?"

"Umm..."

"Mom! You love your job."

"This way I have more time at home with Beau and Skye."

Kenna gripped the shoebox to her middle and stared in shock. Maybe she hadn't been jumping too quickly to the wrong conclusion. "This isn't like you, Mom. You didn't quit or cut back on work with your last two marriages."

"I want this one to work." A flash of desperation appeared in her eyes.

Unfortunately, Laurel chose that moment to intervene. "Let me show you to the dressing room."

Kenna followed her, worry sitting like a heavy stone in her stomach. The last thing she saw before disappearing into the back of the shop was her mom perched on the sectional. With one hand, she wiggled a stuffed toy in front of Skye. With the other, she extracted the bottle of sparkling cider from the ice bucket.

Laurel swept aside the dressing room curtain. Reaching in, she hung the dress on a hook just inside the door. "Holler if you need anything."

Kenna gnawed her lower lip, wishing Laurel would leave her alone. The conversation with her mom had left Kenna disconcerted and distressed. On top of that, she wasn't a dress-and-glittery-sandals sort of girl. She much preferred jeans and boots or, when working out, athletic wear.

The last time she'd donned a dress had been for wedding number three. A blinding yellow number as she recalled. For wedding number two, she'd worn purple. Now pink. Kenna would forever associate her mom's weddings with the color of her dresses.

All right, this one did fit like a glove, she thought as she slid the dress up and over her hips. And the one-shoulder style complemented her figure, which, in Kenna's opinion, was a little too boyish. That was what years of trick riding and gymnastics training did to a gal.

The shoes also fit. Kenna studied herself in the dressing room mirror, not displeased with her reflection. Removing her ball cap, she let her long black hair cascade down past her shoulders in heavy waves. Pink, it turned out, went surprisingly well with her coloring.

"You're gorgeous!" her mom exclaimed when she returned to the viewing area and dabbed a tear away with a tissue.

Why did the best-looking bridesmaid dress so far have to be for the wedding with the least chance of lasting? Kenna mused.

Laurel circled her like an artist evaluating their latest sculpture. "It's a little long. Here, let's stand on the platform."

The platform was located in front of the three mirrors. While Laurel pinned the hem and took in the sides, Kenna's mom changed into her dress. She and Skye returned just as Laurel finished with Kenna.

"Be honest, don't you just love it?"

Kenna gawked at her mom. "White?" Her previous two dresses had been various shades of beige.

"Beau says I should wear what makes me happy."

The snug-fitting bodice with its daring neckline gave way to a full bottom and long train.

"It's a whole lot of dress," Kenna choked out.

"These days, many brides are choosing to wear white for their second wedding," Laurel said.

What about their fourth wedding? Kenna wanted to ask, but she kept quiet.

"Isn't Skye adorable?" Kenna's mom held up the baby.

"She is," Kenna agreed.

The baby wore a frilly white dress and lacy white ankle socks with black patent leather shoes.

"I want a picture of us three so I can see how we look together," Kenna's mom said and went for her purse on the sectional. She withdrew her phone and handed it to Laurel. "Would you mind?"

"Of course not." She snapped a few shots and then studied the results. "These are too dark. Let's go to the entryway where the lighting is better."

The four of them made the short trek to the entryway. Laurel positioned them facing the floor-to-ceiling windows bracketing the front door. Kenna's mom cradled Skye while Kenna tucked in close.

Laurel held out the phone in front of her.

"Okay, everyone. On the count of three. One, two, three—smile!"

Behind her, the door swung open, and Channing strode in, only to grind to an abrupt halt. Beneath the brim of his Stetson, his brows lifted in appreciation. "Wow. Look at you."

"Why, thank you, kind sir," Kenna's mom gushed and fanned her face with her free hand.

Except the remark had been directed at Kenna. She could tell from the way Channing's eyes bored into her with an intensity that left her feeling off-kilter, hyperaware and very pretty—three sensations she didn't normally experience.

"WHAT BRINGS YOU HERE?" Gracie thrust the baby into Kenna's arms and, collecting the folds of her dress, hurried forward to give Channing a hug and a peck on the cheek. "We don't have any wedding business for the guys."

He removed his cowboy hat, wishing it had been Kenna to kiss his cheek and hug him. She looked incredible with her hair spilling down around her shoulders and her luminous eyes going wide at the sight of him. His heart had tumbled hard when he first walked in and had yet to recover.

She wasn't having the same reaction to him and stood awkwardly to the side, bouncing Skye in her arms. When he tried to catch her gaze, she turned the other way.

His fault—he should have kept his mouth shut at the bull-riding event yesterday when the subject of her mom and Beau came up. He'd known she objected to the marriage; that had been abundantly clear. Instead of keeping quiet, he'd created a chasm between the two of them and wasn't sure how to bridge it.

He'd have to find a way. They were in the wedding together and she'd be at the arena most days. Most important, they were friends, and he didn't want to jeopardize that.

"I'm having lunch with Cash," he said.

"How nice." Gracie stepped lightly away. "A boys' outing."

"He's showing me the miniature Western town before we leave."

Laurel and her brother, Cash, co-owned Wishing Well Springs. It had been Cash's idea to expand the wedding barn side of the business by building a miniature Western town, complete with a bank, livery stable, jail and general store. Channing had heard the attraction was enormously popular, and a production company had even used it to film scenes for a short documentary.

Gracie clapped her hands together in excitement. "I'm taking Kenna on a tour, too. We should all go together!"

"Mom." Kenna spoke for the first time. "We're in wedding clothes." She shifted Skye to her other hip and carefully extracted a long strand of hair the baby had stuffed in her mouth.

Gracie pouted. "You'll wait for us to change clothes, won't you, Channing?"

"Absolutely."

Channing guessed from Kenna's fidgeting she wasn't keen on the idea. Too bad. He really wanted to apologize for yesterday and ease the awkwardness between them. Except now wasn't the time. Not in front of an audience—one that increased in size when Cash stepped out of the business offices and into the entryway.

"Hello, ladies." He released a low whistle of appreciation. "Don't you look stunning."

Gracie threw back her head and struck a pose. "Another gallant gentleman."

Channing noticed that his friend's glance landed briefly on Gracie before sliding over to Kenna, where it stayed. Juggling a baby didn't detract from her jaw-dropping appearance in that dress. Cash may be dating Phoebe, Wishing Well Springs' resident wedding coordinator and the love of Cash's life, but that apparently hadn't affected his ability to appreciate an attractive woman when he saw one.

Grumbling to himself, Channing fought the surge of annoyance at his friend. Potentially ex-friend. He had no claim on Kenna, and Cash was just looking. Still…

"We're going with you and Channing to tour the barn and Western town," Gracie told Cash.

"Great. The more the merrier."

"Mom." Kenna's tone hinted at impatience. "What about Skye?"

Gracie waved a hand. "We'll give her a bottle. She'll be fine." To Channing and Cash, she said, "Be right back. Promise me you handsome gentlemen won't abandon us."

"I'll help with your dresses," Laurel said and followed them toward the shop.

At the doorway, Gracie stopped and wagged a finger at Channing. "You'd better not be telling Beau anything about my gown, you hear me? Not one single detail. It's supposed to be a surprise."

"I won't." Channing didn't move until Kenna and her pink dress had disappeared inside the bridal shop.

Cash came over to stand beside him. "She's gorgeous."

"Yeah, she is."

"Gracie's not so bad, either."

Channing had to chuckle at that. Cash clapped him on the back, and the two men retreated to the client seating area in the business office to wait while the women changed.

"What's with you and Kenna?" Cash asked the moment they were sitting.

"Nothing."

"Ha! You were practically snarling."

Had he been that obvious? "We're old friends."

"Are you sure you don't mean *good* friends?"

"She's not interested."

"You know that for a fact?"

Channing thought about his misstep yesterday at the bull-riding event. Him being in favor of her mom marrying Beau was hardly an insurmountable difference. No, their problems ran deeper.

"She's on the road a lot with Hoof Feats, and now's a bad time for me to get involved."

"Not even with the right woman?"

He shook his head. "The folks are retiring soon and Dad's health isn't great. That leaves me with a lot on my plate. I can't afford to be chasing after some gal who's gone three out of four weeks."

What he didn't say to Cash was that if he failed to turn things around financially at the arena, they could go under. Channing refused to let that happen. He'd work around the clock if necessary.

"Kenna could always quit Hoof Feats," Cash said.

"I doubt that. The group was originally her

idea, and she cofounded it with her partner. They have appearances scheduled from now through the end of the year."

"Could one of the other members replace her?"

"She loves performing. I wouldn't ask her to give that up, and she shouldn't have to."

"Phoebe and I made a long-distance relationship work."

"Trust me, my friend. There are big differences between you and Phoebe and the rest of us. For starters, you made the trip here every weekend from Phoenix without fail. And didn't she sometimes drive to Phoenix midweek?"

"Once or twice…a month." Cash grinned.

"My point exactly. You two were seeing each other as often as people who live in the same town do. That wasn't long distance. And then you moved to Payson after a few months."

"Maybe all Kenna needs is a reason to stay," Cash suggested.

Channing shook his head. "Even if she quit performing, which I can't imagine, she doesn't put much stock in relationships lasting."

"Because of that horse trainer she dated?"

"In part. I heard they had a bad breakup." Channing remembered wanting to wring the guy's neck. He'd run into Kenna during one of her trips home and she'd been miserable—a paler, thinner, duller version of herself.

"From what I see, she pulled herself together and dusted herself off."

"She never got over the loss of her dad."

Channing hadn't heard of a brain AVM before her dad died. Afterward, all anyone talked about was how the poor man hadn't stood a chance. Channing couldn't forget Kenna's first day back at school after the funeral and how she quietly cried in class.

"You think she's sour on marriage because she's afraid of losing the person she loves?" Cash asked.

"She and her dad were close. But it's more than that. Gracie goes through men at the same rate some people go through paper towels. Kenna has little faith in the institution of marriage. And none in Gracie's marriage to Beau."

"Do you?" Cash asked. "Seriously, there's a mighty significant age gap between him and Gracie."

"Beau's in love. He can't think straight, she's got him wound so tight around her finger."

"Marriages fail for all kinds of reasons that have nothing to do with love. Just look at my parents. Casualties of the trickle-down effect. When Grandpa lost the horse ranch and filed bankruptcy, my parents' marriage took a big hit. Too big for them to survive."

"My parents have faced some huge obstacles and probably wanted to kill each other at more than one point, but they're still together after thirty-three years." Channing wondered if Kenna's dad had lived, if she'd seen that kind of lasting relationship, would she be more open and optimistic?

"Well—" Cash shrugged "—like you said, not the right time."

"I wish we were faring as well with the arena as you are with Wishing Well Springs. Profits keep sliding. Dad's worried sick and threatening to postpone retiring."

"Would it matter if he didn't?"

"He's not as well as he'd like people to believe. The doctor's warned him about too much stress bringing on another heart attack. But getting him to slow down is like pulling teeth. I think secretly he feels responsible for the arena's trouble."

"How's that?"

"He wasn't feeling well for a long while," Channing said. "Didn't pay attention like he should have. Then he was off work for a month recovering after the heart attack. Now he feels like he's to blame and should be the one to resolve the arena's financial troubles."

"But you can help."

"He doesn't trust me." Channing refused to let on how much his dad's lack of trust in him hurt. "Whenever I suggest something new to generate income, like renting the arena out for band concerts or RV shows, he launches into a speech about how we are and have always been a rodeo arena and horse facility. Period. Not a concert venue, not a sales lot."

"Hey, money's money."

"You don't have to tell me that." Channing shook his head. "He won't listen to any of my ideas. Especially after the women's breakaway-roping event I convinced him to host barely broke even."

"Really? I hear women's rodeo is getting really popular. Aren't they having national championships in Vegas these days?"

"They are. For barrel racing, breakaway roping and team roping. With our proximity to Vegas, we'd be a perfect arena to host qualifying rodeos. The sport of women's bull and bronc riding is also growing. That's where the real money is."

"What's there to object to?" Cash asked.

"Dad is a traditionalist. Hard-core. He thinks women don't belong in rodeo." He lowered his voice and grumbled, imitating his dad. "It's a man's sport."

"Yeah, but he's a business owner. He should appreciate the necessity of changing with the times."

"I couldn't agree more," Channing said. "If Rim Country is going to continue for another generation, we have to adapt. We can't remain stagnant."

Channing's great-grandfather had built the rodeo arena on land his father before him had purchased around the turn of the last century. Each generation since had taken over management from the previous one, usually expanding or making improvements. In his dad's case, he'd torn down the rickety wooden bucking chutes and replaced them with state-of-the-art ones. He'd also completely remodeled the concession stand.

What he'd refused to do was alter the way he operated the arena—Burle Pearce believed in continuing to run things the way his father and grandfather had. Channing struggled with his dad's stubbornness and shortsightedness. It was the cause of increasing strife between them.

Having a legacy to maintain also put added pressure on Channing. He didn't want to be the Pearce who drove the hundred-year-old family business into the ground.

At the sound of voices in the entryway, both Channing and Cash pushed up from the couch and sauntered out to greet Kenna and Gracie. Channing noticed immediately that Kenna wore her usual jeans and tank top. Her glorious hair, no longer falling loose, had been gathered into a ponytail and stuffed through the hole in the back of her ball cap.

Even so, she took his breath away with her natural prettiness and athletic grace. With great effort, he forced himself to stop staring.

Beside him, Cash leaned in and murmured, "What was that you were saying about not wanting to get involved with anyone right now?"

CHAPTER THREE

KENNA MADE A beeline straight from the porch to her mom's car parked out front—she'd opted to ride with her mom and the baby on the short drive to the wedding barn. Not that she was avoiding Channing or anything. Really, she wasn't.

He and Cash were taking the golf cart, Wishing Well Springs' mode of client transportation, and there wasn't enough room for her. That was her story, and she was sticking to it.

"Meet you at the barn," her mom called to Channing once the baby and stroller were loaded into her car.

Kenna didn't wave. Instead, she sat stiff and closemouthed in the passenger seat. Neither did she glance behind them to see if Channing and Cash were following.

At the barn, Kenna and her mom unloaded Skye and placed her in the stroller. The baby had fallen asleep instantly on the five-minute drive and didn't wake up when moved. Kenna adjusted the shade so that the sun didn't shine in the baby's face.

"Where'd you learn to do that?" her mom asked with a smile.

"I don't know. Around. Some of my friends on the rodeo circuit have babies."

Her mom's smile grew. "Or it comes naturally."

"Don't get your hopes up."

"That's like asking the stars not to shine."

They started toward the barn's looming front entrance, her mom pushing the stroller. To Kenna's vast relief, they parted from Channing and Cash, who continued on the path's left fork to the miniature Western town. Apparently, Cash was considering building an office there for his new architectural practice and wanted to show Channing.

Once inside the barn, Kenna's mom chatted nonstop about the various amenities and how she planned to decorate for the wedding.

"Are you free tomorrow for a trip to the party store?" she asked.

"Not in the morning."

Kenna thought of her appointment to see the performance horse and whether or not she'd tell Channing. Being in his company had become increasingly disconcerting of late. Their difference of opinion regarding her mom's wedding to Beau was only partially responsible. Her feelings for Channing were changing.

"Afternoons are better for me, anyway," her mom said.

Because she'd be at home with the baby. Kenna bit her tongue rather than respond.

"We can stop at that new bakery after the party store and check out their sample cakes," her mom continued. "And drop by the inn. Though that might have to wait for another day. We're having the rehearsal dinner there on the Thursday before the wedding. They're also catering the reception. Did I tell you we're having it outside in front of the barn? It'll be so pretty with the lights strung overhead."

Kenna's mom sought her input on every detail, big or small. Kenna kept her comments to a minimum, unable to stop thinking about her mom working less at the office in order to babysit Skye.

Try as she might, she couldn't keep quiet. "Not that it's any of my business, Mom, but can you afford to cut your hours?"

"I'll be fine. We'll be fine. Beau has his job."

Kenna didn't think he earned that much as a rodeo hand and occasional bullfighter. "I assume he and Skye are moving in with you."

Her mom laughed. "We can't all live in his double-wide trailer. He's going to rent it out after the wedding for extra income."

Kenna tried another approach. "Won't you miss your job? And what about benefits? Will you lose them going to part-time?"

"My, my. You really are a nosy Nancy today."

"I just want to make sure you've considered everything before..."

"Before what?"

Before it's too late and you end up hurt again. "The wedding."

"I have. Quit worrying." Her mom changed the subject. "Now, what about Madison? You talk to her yet?"

Kenna sighed. "About the wedding? Yes."

"Is she coming? Please say yes."

"She is."

Madison was Kenna's best friend and the co-founder of Hoof Feats.

Kenna's mom bumped shoulders with her. "I'm so glad."

"If all goes according to plan, she'll be here Tuesday afternoon."

"Good. She can come to the rehearsal dinner Thursday night."

"Ah, sure. I guess. I'll mention it."

"You could introduce her to Channing, since you say you're not interested in him."

Kenna refused to take the bait her mom dangled. "They've met already," she replied neutrally.

"And?"

"No sparks."

Her mom giggled. "Then you still have a chance."

Kenna crossed her arms over her middle.

Her mom continued with the wedding venue tour, showing Kenna the bride and groom dressing rooms. It was hard for Kenna to muster a lot of enthusiasm for something she'd been through twice before *and* for a marriage she doubted would last two years.

"Have you ever seen anything so beautiful?" Gracie gestured as she pushed the stroller with a sleeping Skye down the center aisle. "Look at the fresh flowers on the altar table. And the ribbons on the back of the chairs. And isn't the hayloft quaint? Maybe we could get a couple people to shoot off confetti cannons from up there after the wedding."

Kenna had to admit, the rustic-and-glamorous-rolled-into-one barn was nice. She could picture herself getting married here if the day ever came. If she met a wonderful man like her dad. If she ever quit Hoof Feats, which was unlikely. If, if, if.

"Beau wanted us to ride up on horses, but I told him absolutely not. No way am I getting on a horse in that gorgeous dress." Kenna's mom turned the stroller toward the door. "Let's head over to the miniature Western town and find the guys. Skye won't sleep much longer, and I want to take advantage of the lull."

Outside, they turned left. Around the corner of the barn, the miniature Western town came into sight. Kenna stopped to stare, utterly enchanted despite herself.

The entire structure stretched thirty yards from one end to the other, and not a single detail had been spared. The wooden boardwalk resembled those in an old West town. Iron bars in the jail's window kept any pretend prisoners from escaping. Bales of straw sat outside the livery stables and an old-fashioned scale hung from the ceiling behind the counter in the general store.

"Isn't this just adorable?" Kenna's mom raved. "You can see why we're taking our post-wedding pictures here."

Kenna could see. The attraction *was* adorable and an ideal spot for wedding pictures.

Her mom insisted on getting some of what she called practice shots and recruited Kenna to be her model.

"To test out different backgrounds," she explained.

Kenna reluctantly obliged.

"Smile," her mom cajoled. "Your face won't break."

Kenna sensed Channing's gaze on her but refrained from looking in his direction. After a moment, when his gaze didn't waver, heat flooded her cheeks. What on earth was he staring at?

"You're still not smiling," her mom complained.

Kenna forced the corners of her mouth up.

"Now let's get one with the two of you," her mom said and motioned for Channing to join Kenna in front of the general store.

He covered the distance in three long strides.

"Don't you have enough pictures?" Kenna choked out as he sidled up beside her.

Her mom ignored her and lined up the shot on her phone. "I want one of my maid of honor and Beau's groomsman together."

"Fine."

"Closer," her mom instructed, studying the screen.

Channing shuffled his feet, reducing the distance between them. His warm breath caressed the skin on Kenna's bare neck and caused her knees to wobble.

"You don't have cooties," her mom said. "Put your arms around each other."

Channing slipped an arm over Kenna's shoulders, the weight settling comfortably. She had to admit, it felt a little proprietary...but also pleasantly familiar. She waited for her defenses to kick in. She disliked it when men got all macho and possessive. Other men, apparently. With Channing, she had the wild and irrational desire to snuggle into the crook of his arm, where she felt…safe. Really?

He squeezed her tight. She snuck a peek at him beneath her lowered lashes, admiring his strong profile and attractive bristled jaw.

"Waiting on you, kitten," her mom chimed.

Reluctantly, Kenna circled Channing's waist with her arm and rested her hand on his belt.

"Was that so difficult?" he murmured, a chuckle in his voice.

Her resolve waned and, to her surprise, she started to relax. "No."

He turned his head and stared down at her. She tilted her face to his.

All at once, she was transported back in time fourteen years to that high school dance and their first kiss. It had been both the best night of her life and the worst. Best because of Channing and their kiss. Worst because, rather than her parents, the neighbors had been at home to greet her and tell Kenna that her dad had been taken to the hospital in an ambulance. She'd never see him alive again.

"Say cheese!" her mom called out.

Kenna and Channing both smiled on cue. Her mom snapped the picture while they were staring at each other, Kenna lost in her memories.

"What a fantastic shot!" her mom said, smiling at her phone. "You look great together."

Kenna withdrew her arm, suddenly shy and sad and with her heart aflutter all at the same time.

Little Skye chose that moment to wake up from her nap. Cash meandered over to say he needed to return to the office. Kenna realized she'd forgotten about everyone else. There'd been only her and Channing.

"You riding with me, pal?" Cash asked Channing.

"Will I see you at the house?" Channing didn't take his eyes off Kenna. "There's something I want to, need to, talk to you about. It's important."

"Um, okay." *Please,* she thought, *don't bring up Mom and Beau and the wedding.*

At the main house, Kenna climbed out of her mom's car and said goodbye. "I won't be late getting home."

"You like the dress, don't you?"

"Yeah, Mom. It's nice."

Relief spread across her mom's face. "Any requests for dinner? I have the fixings for spaghetti and salad."

"Sounds delicious."

"Beau will be over after work to eat with us."

"Sure." Kenna had figured as much. He'd be picking up Skye.

Channing was waiting for her by her truck, his expression serious. Her nerves hummed as she neared and not with the excitement she'd felt yesterday or the heart fluttering from their photo shoot.

"Hey," she said, infusing a lightness into her voice. "What's going on?"

"About yesterday." He removed his hat and combed his fingers through his dark blond hair. "What I said at the rodeo."

So he did want to discuss her mom and Beau. "It's all right, Channing. I get it. Beau works for you. And you're friends. Good ones."

"That's not why I support him marrying your mom."

She waited, her fingers clutching the door handle on her truck.

"I don't tell people how to run their lives," he said. "Just like I don't want them telling me how to run mine."

She nodded. "Okay."

"Beau's a decent guy. He may not be who you envisioned your mom with, but they make each other happy. Isn't that what you want for her?"

"They're moving awfully fast."

"Who are we to dictate their timing?"

Kenna clutched the door handle tighter, eager

to escape. "This is sounding a little like a lecture."

"Sorry." Channing retreated a step. "Not my intention."

"I don't want to argue," she said. "We'll be together a lot over the next month, and I prefer things don't get uncomfortable."

"All right." He gave her a more subdued version of the smile from the photograph her mom had taken. "See you tomorrow morning. You want to meet at the arena, say, around ten?"

"Ten?"

"To go see the horse. My buddy called earlier about our upcoming team penning and mentioned you and his wife had talked this morning."

She bit down hard. The decision on whether or not Channing would accompany her had been made without her. She either went along or created the kind of uncomfortable scene she'd just told him she'd rather avoid.

"Let's meet at the arena. In the parking lot. I'll drive." She opened her truck door and jumped in behind the wheel, glad to be putting distance between them.

Why did things with Channing always seem to go great one minute and terrible the next?

AT 9:55 A.M. on the dot, Channing rested a forearm on the parking lot's split rail fence and waited. Ten minutes later, Kenna had yet to appear. In truth, he half expected her to stand him up. For the second time in as many days, things between them had gotten strangely awkward. He still wasn't sure what had happened yesterday.

Apparently, any discussion of her mom and Beau pushed the wrong button. Though, in Channing's opinion, it was more than that. He and Kenna had veered off track yesterday earlier than their discussion, when Gracie took their picture in the miniature Western town. Yeah, Channing had lost himself a little in Kenna's eyes. Impossible not to, what with the way she'd gazed at him—as if she wanted to both kiss him and cry on his shoulder.

No, that wasn't right. The awkwardness had started earlier, when Channing walked into Wishing Well Springs' main house and interrupted the wedding outfit photo shoot. His expression must have given him away; he couldn't help himself that time, either. Kenna in a pink dress was a sight to behold. Never in his wildest imagination would he have pictured her looking so beautiful, and he'd been imagining her quite a bit since her return.

Why keep trying to fool himself? His former feelings for her had been steadily growing for months now, ever since they'd started spending more time together. She continually reminded him of why he liked her—namely her smarts, talent, fierce independence and ambition.

The sound of tires spitting gravel had him turning, and his muscles involuntarily relaxed. She'd come! She hadn't left to see the horse without him.

He raised his hand in greeting and smiled. Her white pickup resembled every other white pickup out there with one exception: vanity plates on the front and back read TRIKRDR. He smiled to himself. His vanity plates read RIMCNTY. Did she realize how much they had in common?

She braked to a stop beside him. He heard the door lock pop open as he reached for the handle. A sense of déjà vu struck him. This was pretty much where they'd left off yesterday. Would today end better? He hoped so.

"Morning," he said, climbing in.

"Hi." She waited while he buckled his seat belt. "Look, if you're busy, you don't have to come with me."

Ah. She was giving him an out. Possibly even making a suggestion. He didn't take it.

"Nope. I cleared my schedule for you."

"Hmm." She put the truck in Drive and executed a U-turn, leaving the parking lot the same way she'd entered.

She'd braided her hair today and left the baseball cap at home. Not the sunglasses. They remained firmly in place, denying him a glimpse of her eyes.

He didn't need to see them to know they flashed with emotion. Whatever had occurred the previous day continued to eat at her.

"I'm not mad," she said without taking her eyes off the road. "You can stop staring at me."

"I wasn't staring." Except he'd been doing precisely that, so he forced his glance toward the window.

"This wedding stuff is hard on me," she admitted. "I want to apologize for being…abrupt."

"Not necessary. I don't suppose it's easy."

"Did you know my mom started working half days at the office in order to spend more time with Beau and Skye?"

"Beau mentioned something."

"She loves her job and has always prided herself in being self-sufficient."

"From what I've seen, she's committed to making this marriage work."

Kenna stopped at the next intersection and shifted to meet his gaze. "Why should *she* have to be the one to sacrifice something she loves? Why not Beau?"

"My guess is she wants to."

"You didn't by chance refuse to give him time off?"

"Absolutely not. I swear, Kenna. If he had

asked, I'd've said yes. We always try to accommodate employees with families."

She scrunched her mouth in thought. "I just don't understand."

"Have you asked your mom?"

"She says the choice was hers."

"Is it possible you're putting yourself in your mom's place and thinking how you'd feel rather than accepting how she feels?"

"No doubt. It's hard not to."

Her honesty surprised him. He wondered how many of her life choices were intentionally the opposite of those her mom made. Maybe she was wondering the same thing.

"What are you looking for in a performance horse?" he asked.

The change in topic lightened Kenna's mood, and she launched into a list.

"Disposition, obviously. The quieter the better. Size and build. He needs to be strong, and a broad back helps with executing moves. He has to be smart and a quick learner. Completely trustworthy."

Her previous mood forgotten, Kenna and Channing talked at length about the right horse's potential until they arrived at his buddy's house. The man's wife, Rochelle, must have been watching for them, because she emerged from the house before Kenna shut off the engine.

"Hello, hello!" She met them in the driveway, a welcoming smile on her round cherub face. Introductions were made, and they all shook hands. "It's a real pleasure to meet you, Kenna. I saw you perform last year at the Double Sixes Rodeo in Flagstaff. Very impressive."

"Thank you."

"How long have you been trick riding?"

"I started when I was about twelve. I didn't get serious until a few years later."

Channing followed behind the two women, who were hitting it off like old friends. Rochelle took them around the house to the back where she and her husband had built an extensive horse facility that included a mini stable, round pen and covered roping arena. A livestock pen behind the arena housed a half-dozen calves of varying ages. Her husband, a serious team-penning competitor, had designed the facility to meet his exact specifications.

"Joe's sorry he couldn't be here," Rochelle said over her shoulder to Channing as they walked. "He's stuck at work, which he jokes is only so he can support all this." She hitched a thumb at the stable and arena.

"Sorry I missed him," Channing said.

"You'll see him next week at the team penning."

"Tell me about Rocket Man," Kenna said.

"What kind of trick riding have you done with him?"

"I personally haven't done any." Rochelle slapped her ample hips and gave a laugh. "Too much extra padding for me to try hanging off the side of a galloping horse. But Rocket Man's former owner put about six months of training into him before she got pregnant and quit. Not that she was very serious to start with. We wound up taking the horse to see if he had any talent for team penning. He doesn't," she added with another laugh. "We'd sure like to find him a decent home. He's a special guy, despite not having a lick of cow sense."

They entered the stables, and Channing gave a low whistle of appreciation at the shiny brass fixtures, fresh paint, spanking clean floor and enviable tack wall. "Nice place."

"I'll say." Kenna stared wide-eyed.

Rochelle gave a derisive snort. "I swear, these horses live better than we do."

Whinnies and snorts greeted them from the stables' eight occupants. Heads of all colors, shapes and sizes appeared over the stalls' half doors, including a small black nose that barely reached the top of the door. The kids' pony, Channing assumed. The farther inside the stables they went, the stronger the scent of fresh straw and leather.

"Is that Rocket Man?" Without waiting for a response, Kenna started toward the stall on the end, holding a large sorrel with a striking blaze down the center of his face.

"He's a real sociable fellow, that one." Rochelle remained behind.

Channing did, too, giving Kenna and the horse a moment alone.

"Hey, you." She reached up and stroked the side of his enormous head, letting her slim hand glide from there down his neck. A soft smile touched her lips. "What's up?"

Rocket Man pushed his nose into her hair, snuffling loudly, and then bobbed his head.

"Can I go in the stall?" she asked Rochelle.

"By all means. Or we can bring him out."

"That'd be great."

"I'll get a halter." Rochelle returned a moment later, her hand outstretched. "Here you go."

Channing liked how she let Kenna handle the horse rather than taking over. To him, it showed she had confidence in Rocket Man's docile nature. He was sure Kenna noticed the same thing.

She opened the stall door and went inside. The big horse stood quietly while she put on the halter and then followed her out, walking shoulder to shoulder rather than shoving or charging ahead. As far as first impressions went, Rocket

Man was making an excellent one. The true test, however, was coming.

"I'm assuming his former owner worked him on a lunge line," Kenna said as they left the stables and entered the bright sunshine where Rocket Man's four white stockings gleamed.

"We tried once." Rochelle came around to stand next to Kenna. "The horse did fine. Can't speak for his previous owner."

"Mind if I saddle him up?"

"Have at it."

Kenna walked Rocket Man to her truck, where, instead of tying him, she dropped the lead rope. Channing guessed that if Rocket Man could be relied on to stand untethered, he could be relied on to follow commands in the arena under more demanding circumstances where Kenna's safety, if not her life, depended on it.

From the bed of her truck, she removed a brush and gave Rocket Man a quick grooming that included cleaning his hooves. He did no more than investigate the side of the truck and the saddle blanket slung over the tailgate. Grooming accomplished, she placed the blanket on his back and, with both hands, lifted a saddle the likes of which Channing hadn't seen before from the truck bed.

"That's quite the contraption," Rochelle commented. "Custom-made?"

"From an outfit in San Antonio." Kenna hefted the saddle onto Rocket Man with some effort.

"Looks heavy."

"About eighty pounds."

Made of white leather, it bore silver and turquoise adornments. The horn in front had been replaced with a short post, and a handle was attached to the back of the seat. Channing had general notion of what purpose the multitude of straps and belts attached to the saddle served and figured he was about to learn more.

Slipping the bridle over the horse's head, Kenna adjusted the buckles for a secure fit. Lastly, she removed a lunge line and a long thin whip from the truck bed. After attaching the lunge line to Rocket Man's bit, she held out the whip to Channing.

"You willing to do the honors?"

"Let's go!"

Kenna led Rocket Man into the riding arena while Channing donned the pair of gloves he'd brought along. Finding a spot to her liking, she handed the excess line to him.

"Start with about fifteen feet," she told him. "See how that goes."

He gathered the lunge line in his left hand. In his right, he held the whip. Used solely to motivate and guide Rocket Man, the training tool would never come in contact with him. Like

Kenna, Channing was a believer in positive reinforcement, not negative.

"You nervous?" he asked.

"Naw." She scrunched her mouth and gave the horse a pat on the neck. "I'm excited. I have a good feeling about this guy."

"I'm glad. But be careful. He could still buck or run off on you."

She studied Channing intently, her voice taking on an intimate quality he hadn't heard before. "Thank you for worrying."

"You're important to me, and I'd hate to see you injured."

A moment turned into two. Channing thought she might respond, but then she grabbed the reins and placed a foot in the stirrup. The next instant, she was in the saddle, as light and nimble as a sprite.

"Ready?"

"As I'll ever be," he answered.

She swung Rocket Man's head to the right and clucked. He took off at a brisk walk, executing a perfect circle in response to the lunge line's light pull. Channing kept pace with horse and rider, the lunge line loose in his hand. No problems so far.

Once they'd executed three full circles, Kenna cued the horse into an easy trot, and then an equally easy lope. Twice he broke stride, and twice she nudged him back into the lope. When he remained steady for three full circles, she dropped the reins and stretched her arms out to the sides, perpendicular with her body.

"That's right," she cooed. "Steady does it."

Channing tightened his grip on the lunge line just in case. It wasn't necessary. Rocket Man continued to lope in a circle, his breathing strong and regular. Again, he broke stride and again Kenna returned him to a lope.

"Get ready," Kenna called out.

"For what?"

But she was already in motion. Lifting her legs high, she inserted her feet into a pair of straps on each side of the saddle near the front. With the easy effort of a person on solid ground, Kenna dropped the reins and raised herself up to a full standing position.

From the arena fence, Rochelle clapped. "Whoo-hoo!"

Channing stared, completely enthralled and more than a little impressed. She looked like a goddess riding a mythical creature. No, a warrior astride her valiant steed. Raising her chin and throwing back her shoulders, Kenna seemed to embrace the wind that tugged at her hair and clothes.

Channing had never seen anything more beautiful, and his heart soared. If he weren't careful, he could fall for her. Hard and fast. In truth, he already had fallen…and more than a little. He thought about how much he'd hate saying goodbye to her after the wedding and groaned under his breath as he continued watching her.

Rocket Man didn't falter a single step. The horse continued to lope, his pace steady, his attention focused in front of him. It was almost like he knew Kenna's safety depended entirely on him and he didn't want to fail her.

One more circle, and the spell Channing had been under abruptly broke when Kenna lowered herself into the saddle. She removed her feet from the straps and, legs dangling, picked up the reins. In response to a quick tug, Rocket Man slowed to a choppy walk.

"Attaboy." Bending forward, she patted his neck and pressed her face into his mane. "Well-done."

"That was amazing!" Rochelle hollered. "You rock."

Channing couldn't agree more. Kenna continued to walk the horse, the epitome of relaxed and comfortable, while Channing's hands shook from gripping the line so hard.

"That's enough for now," she said, reining Rocket Man to a stop. "I don't want to push my luck the first time out."

Channing dropped the whip and walked toward her, gathering the excess line. "I thought he did all right. What about you?" Reaching the horse, he unclipped the line from the bit.

"Not bad. He kept wanting to break stride, but we can fix that. He hasn't been used for trick riding in a while."

She nudged the horse into a walk, heading toward the arena fence. Channing returned to where he'd left the whip. Equipment in hand, he exited the arena to join Rochelle. They chatted about the team-penning event next week at Rim Country as they waited for Kenna to finish cooling down the horse. Kenna and Rocket Man came out five minutes later. She dismounted with the same nimbleness as earlier.

"Well?" Rochelle asked, her expression filled with expectancy.

"I was wondering," Kenna started. "Would you by chance let me take him to the arena and continue working with him for another week? Maybe two? He's showing potential, but I'm not ready to commit."

"I see no reason why you can't. Let me check with Joe first."

Rochelle fished her cell phone from her pocket and placed a call to her husband. From her end of the conversation and the smile she wore, it was clear he was agreeable. After disconnecting, she and Kenna hammered out a few more details and then shook hands.

"I'll come back this afternoon with my trailer," Kenna said.

A few more pleasantries were exchanged, and then she and Channing climbed into her truck. When they reached the road, she turned to him.

"About Rocket Man's board. I can put on an extra class—"

"I have a better idea," Channing said, cutting her short. "If you're game for it."

"For…what?" She stared at him, waiting.

He grinned in return, enjoying the expectant look on her face.

CHAPTER FOUR

"YOU WANT ME to be your sounding board?" Kenna asked, keeping one eye on the road as she drove. She hadn't been sure what to expect from Channing when he said he had a better idea. It certainly wasn't this.

"And to offer me your sage advice."

"On what?"

He shifted in the passenger seat, propping an elbow on the console. "You travel extensively, perform at rodeo arenas all over the country. I'd like you to tell me what they're doing."

"I don't understand."

"All right. The plan was for me to take over management of Rim Country when my parents retire in the fall."

Along with everyone in town, Kenna knew that his family's rodeo arena had been passed down from generation to generation since it was built over a hundred years ago.

"But Dad's reconsidering," Channing said. "Income's dropped the last eighteen months."

"Oh. I'm sorry to hear that." Being self-employed and dependent on rodeo arenas, Kenna knew this was troublesome. "Is it the economy?"

"Partly. Dad's heart attack is a big factor. It was a lot worse than he tells people. He nearly lost his life. The paramedics had to use the paddles twice on the ambulance ride to revive him."

Kenna gasped softly. "I had no idea."

"He's a prideful man and afraid people will see him as frail and weak."

"That's silly."

"To you and me. Not to him." Channing leaned back in the seat. "Turned out he hadn't been feeling well for a long time before the attack and let some things slide. We found out when he was in the hospital, and we had to take over for him. Now he's embarrassed and blames himself for the loss of income. He feels he has a responsibility to turn the finances around. Except he needs to retire. Or at least cut way back. His health will be in jeopardy if he doesn't. Whenever I insist I can turn the finances around and push for nontraditional events, he gets defensive."

"He may see your ideas as criticism."

"They aren't. The fact is, rodeo is changing, and Rim Country's not keeping current. There's a whole segment we're failing to tap into beyond PRCA and PBA rodeos."

"WPRA events?" Kenna guessed.

Channing smiled, his mood lightening. "Specifically women's bull and bronc riding and breakaway roping. I was wondering how much of that you're seeing at other arenas and what kind of crowds they draw."

Kenna considered his question. "Quite a bit, actually. Hoof Feats has performed at a few."

"What was the attendance like?"

"Not as many people as when the guys compete. But there's a loyal following, and I'm definitely seeing increased interest."

"That's encouraging." He nodded thoughtfully. "Thanks."

"Seriously, Channing. A ten-minute discussion isn't enough to compensate you for Rocket Man's boarding."

"Well, there's more I need from you." He slanted her a look.

"Okay..."

"How often do the smaller arenas host non-rodeo events? RV and camper shows. Automobile auctions. Band concerts. I'm not talking about giant facilities like state fairgrounds, but places the size of Rim Country."

Kenna shrugged. "All the time. At least, they advertise those types of events. An arena in Denver had a flower-and-garden show. And someplace—Lubbock, I think—had a tiny house expo. I personally haven't been to any events like that," she added, "so I can't speak to attendance."

"I've been checking out other arenas in the state similar in size and amenities to Rim Country. Flagstaff. Cave Creek. Show Low. They host a lot of non-rodeo events."

"Then they must be selling tickets," Kenna said, slowing down for the vehicle in front of her.

"That's what I say. The owners are responding to consumer demand or adapting to a changing world. I wish Dad would see that."

"I've always liked him and your mom. They were really nice to us when Dad died. They brought food by for weeks after the funeral, and your dad mowed our lawn."

"Yeah. He has his moments. He's also too stubborn for his own good. By not having women's rodeo events, we're losing out on a lot of potential income. It's not just ticket sales and concessions—there's merchandising, too. We do well leasing space to vendors."

"Okay, your dad's not a fan of women competing in rodeo. I'm guessing he believes it's too dangerous for the weaker sex," she said with a heavy dose of sarcasm. "But he's a businessman. A smart one. The problem could be you and your pitch, which is clearly not working."

"You're right." Channing chuckled, only to sober. "I'd probably have more luck convincing him if our women's breakaway-roping event last month had brought in more revenue."

“What went wrong?” She turned south at the light and onto the road that would take them to the arena two miles outside Payson. “Lack of interest?”

“Lack of promotion,” Channing countered. “And we didn’t have an additional draw. Big mistake. The other arenas I’ve researched all provided halftime entertainment. A high school marching band. A dog act. Trick riders.” He winked at Kenna.

“Plenty of local entertainment to tap in these parts.”

“I need to hire someone for my next event. Soon, too.”

“Which is what? And when?”

“Women’s bull riding. I’m thinking of hosting a non-sanctioned competition on the Friday night before the wedding. If that goes well, we can start hosting sanctioned WPRA events.”

“Wow.” Kenna drew back in shock. “That’s cutting it close. The wedding rehearsal and dinner are Thursday night. The wedding’s on Saturday.”

“We just got another booking,” Channing said. “Except for that weekend, we don’t have any available evenings. By June, it’s getting too hot for the bulls.”

“That’s less than four weeks away.” Kenna chewed her lower lip. “You’d need to begin advertising now. And put out the word to potential competitors. Update your website and social media page."

"I'll get my sister to do that. Right after I break the news to Dad."

"You haven't?"

"Not yet." Channing offered her a sheepish smile. "My pitch needs more work."

"Living dangerously?"

Kenna hadn't ever known Channing to lack courage. He'd been one of the most fearless bull riders she'd ever seen back when he competed.

"I think we're the same in that regard." His gaze on her intensified. "You enjoy living dangerously, too."

"Not like you."

"I disagree. Seeing you today, I'd say trick riding is every bit as dangerous as bull riding."

"It's not. I'm in constant control of a well-trained horse."

"How about when you're hanging upside down off a horse? Where's the control then?"

"I'm not being tossed around like a sneaker in a dryer. A sneaker that could land beneath an angry bull's sharp hooves. And besides, the hippodrome is a relatively easy trick."

"Hippodrome?" he asked.

"Standing up in the saddle."

"You were on a horse you'd never ridden before and performing a risky stunt that could have landed you in the hospital if something went wrong. I was impressed, Kenna." His tone softened. "And scared for you."

She would have responded except her throat had gone dry. Swallowing, she started over. "I might not have tried the hippodrome with someone else at the other end of the lunge line. You made me feel safe, Channing." She stopped at the intersection and turned toward him, gauging his reaction.

"I'm glad it was me, too." He reached over and skimmed his fingertips along her cheek. "And things worked out."

She went still for several seconds, enjoying the sensation of skin-to-skin contact and glad there wasn't a vehicle behind them. Sooner than she would have preferred, Channing withdrew his hand, ending their intimate connection. With some effort, she refocused her attention and eased on the gas. Thank goodness the entrance to the rodeo arena came into view a moment later—Kenna was uncertain where this conversation, or her sudden intense feelings, were leading.

"I think Rocket Man might be the horse for you," he said.

"Yeah. If the vet gives him a clean bill of health." *Stay focused.*

"You want me to go with you this afternoon to pick him up?"

"Thanks. I'll be fine." She slowed. "Where should I drop you?"

"In front of the main entrance. There's a stack of requisitions to review and billings to approve waiting for me in the office."

"What about talking to your dad?"

"That, too." He expelled a long breath.

"What does your sister think of your ideas?"

"She's my biggest supporter."

"Take her with you to meet with your dad."

"That's not bad advice."

Kenna braked to a stop across from the entrance. "If I can help with anything else, give me a holler."

"Are you serious?" A twinkle lit his blue eyes.

She sensed trouble but asked anyway. "What?"

"You could perform at the event. Be my additional draw. People will come just to see you perform."

"Um, yeah." She hesitated.

"If there's a conflict with the wedding..."

"It's not that." Kenna put the truck into Park. "I just don't know if I'll have a horse. Zenith can't perform, and using Snapple is out of the question. Rocket Man may not be ready." She debated a moment, not wanting to disappoint Channing. He was doing her a big favor by letting her board three horses at the arena. "Can you give me a week to decide?"

"I didn't mean to pressure you."

"You're not," she hurriedly assured him. "Worse-case scenario, my partner, Madison, can perform with her horse. She'll be in town for the wedding. I realize people aren't as familiar with her as they are with me, but we might be able to work out one doubles trick with Zenith. If he's having a good day."

"Again, no pressure," Channing said.

"I really want to help. And I'm all in when it comes to supporting women's rodeo."

Rather than get out of the truck, he settled into his seat. "I have more ideas I'd like to run by you."

"Tell me."

That sheepish smile of his reappeared. "You're going to think this sounds stupid."

"I'm not," she insisted.

After a moment, he asked, "Have you ever wondered what we do with our bucking horses once they're too old to use?"

"No." She'd heard what some rodeo arenas and bucking stock rental companies did and refused to think about that.

"We retire them," Channing said. "The horses spend the rest of their lives in a pasture, getting fat and lazy."

"That's kind of great." Her opinion of Channing and his family rose another notch. She intended on keeping Zenith despite his inability to perform.

"Some rodeo arenas and bucking stock outfits sell the occasional horse to places that use them for teens and adults learning to ride a bucking horse. They tend to want one a little less fired up."

"Interesting." Kenna hadn't heard of that.

"Some mares can be used for breeding. But the vast majority of retired bucking stock are considered untrainable and unsuitable for any other use. Few people want to spend the time and money rehabilitating them."

"Other than you?" Kenna asked, growing more and more intrigued.

"I'd like to try. Taught to buck isn't the same as being mean."

"But isn't the drive to buck bred into them?"

"That may prove to be my downfall. Then again, what harm can it do to try?"

"None!"

"I'm not saying I can turn a former bucking horse into a kid's mount, no way. A Western pleasure or trail horse? Maybe. A cutting horse or penning horse? Naw. A therapy horse?" He snorted. "If I wind up with a few extra pickup horses for the hands to ride, I'll be happy."

"I'm going out on a limb here, but I assume you've tried riding some of these retired bucking horses?"

"I have. I got thrown. But I also think a couple of them showed potential and acted like they might respond to a bit."

She could hear the excitement in his voice and her own excitement blossomed in response. "Rehabilitating former bucking horses would be good publicity for the arena."

"I'm way ahead of you." He leaned closer. "I'd like to put on an exhibit at the arena."

"That could be your entertainment at the women's bull riding."

She also leaned in, and the air between them snapped, crackled and popped with anticipation. Kenna went still as his gaze traveled her face.

"Would you...?" He paused, his hand poised as if to touch her again.

Do it, do it. "Would I what?" she breathed.

"Want to see the bucking horses? Work with me in rehabilitating them?"

She snapped up straight. "Yes! Are you kidding?"

"It could be dangerous." The corner of his mouth turned up.

"You just compared trick riding to bull riding."

He did reach for her then and, this time, instead of skimming his fingertips across her skin, he cradled her cheek. "I don't want anything to happen to you."

She closed her eyes for a second, feeling the heat from his palm. "I'll be fine."

"I worry about you." He narrowed the distance separating them by another few inches.

Was he going to kiss her? If he did, what would she do?

Kiss him back.

Not the smartest move. She knew it. He knew it, too, and the two of them stayed where they were, caught up in the spell the other cast.

Eventually, sadly, common sense prevailed. She took his hand in hers before gently pulling away. "This, um… We shouldn't."

He didn't disagree, and her heart sank a little. Squeezing her fingers, he released her. "Have I scared you off from helping me?"

"Absolutely not. I could use something to take my mind off Mom and the wedding." Spending time with Channing and fighting her attraction to him would accomplish that.

"Okay." He nodded.

"When do you want to show me the horses?"

"I'm slammed tomorrow and the next day."

"Me, too. Mom has trips planned to the party store and the bakery. Plus, I need to get ready for my class on Saturday and call Dinah about the bridal shower."

"Friday morning? We can at least visit the old folks and look them over. Narrow down our potential candidates."

She liked his nickname for the retired bucking horses. She also liked his use of the words *we* and *our*, as if she were a part of his team or the other half of their *couple*. "Friday works for me. Nine o'clock okay?"

"It's a date."

A date. That expression again. Kenna unfurled her toes. "See you then."

Channing jumped out of the truck—which suddenly felt big and empty without him sitting beside her.

KENNA PUT SNAPPLE in his stall and shut the door. He immediately inspected the feed trough, but a second breakfast hadn't been delivered while he was away having his early-morning exercise session.

"Sorry, pal. I'll stop by later with some treats."

These past few days, she'd increased her workouts with the stout Appaloosa, getting him in the best possible shape. The competitive trail rider Channing had put her in touch with was interested and coming to see Snapple early next week. Kenna had high hopes after talking with the woman and learning her approach to training. A few inquiries around the arena had further reassured Kenna. The woman was well liked and respected.

From her pocket, Kenna's phone beeped an alarm, encouraging her to hurry. Forty-five minutes until her trick-riding class started at 8:00 a.m. sharp. After a full morning, they'd break for lunch, and then work through until four o'clock. Rather than the main arena, the classes would take place in the shaded practice ring. By afternoon, they'd appreciate a reprieve from the relentless sun.

Kenna fetched Zenith from his stall. "You ready to strut your stuff, old man?"

Payson's drier climate had eased his arthritis, and she planned on using him today for backup and to demonstrate tricks from either a trot or a standstill. He'd be fine as long as she didn't overtax him. If necessary, she'd borrow a student's horse for more demanding tricks. They were each bringing their own mounts. Kenna didn't just teach the aspiring trick riders—she taught their horses, too.

Rocket Man bumped into the stall door, pawing the ground and huffing loudly.

"I know. I wish I could take you, too, but you're not ready yet."

He bumped the metal door again, causing the latch to rattle.

"Soon. I promise. Maybe by next Saturday's advanced class."

She'd been spending endless hours with the flashy gelding since picking him up at Rochelle's four days ago. Each time she rode him into the ring, they accomplished a little more, and her confidence in him increased. She'd scheduled a top-to-bottom exam with the vet on Monday. If he gave Rocket Man the all clear, Kenna would discuss the price with Rochelle.

"See you soon, boys."

After patting first Snapple and then Rocket Man's nose, she headed toward the practice ring. Zenith's hooves sounded a loud rhythm on the hard ground. He was glad to be unconfined, stretching his legs and checking out his surroundings.

Kenna noticed the trucks and trailers in the parking area across the way—horses being unloaded, youngsters scampering about, parents attempting to maintain order. Kenna led Zenith past them to her trailer, offering waves and repeating, "Good morning." The trailer's large storage compartment contained all her tack and everything she needed while on the road. The compact living quarters afforded her a place to sleep, eat and change into her colorful costumes.

Her partner Madison's grandmother sewed most of their outfits. Kenna's favorite was the electric-blue unitard with the gold lightning bolts down the sides. She always felt powerful and invincible when wearing it.

"Morning, kitten!"

Kenna glanced up from combing Zenith's tail. "Hi, Mom. Hey, squirt." She made a silly face at Skye and then added, "Beau." Her mom had said she'd drop by to watch the morning portion of Kenna's class. She should have guessed Beau and Skye would tag along. "You aren't working today?" she asked him.

"Got the day off." The dimpled grin that had won Kenna's mom's heart spread wide. "For a change."

"He and the boys are going to the tuxedo shop," her mom added, stooping and retrieving the plush toy Skye had dropped. "Why they waited until the last minute, I don't know." She brushed off the toy and returned it to Skye, who by then had lost all interest.

Three weeks before the wedding probably wasn't last minute, but Kenna didn't correct her mom. She supposed it was best the tuxes were ordered with time to spare should a problem arise. Since a tuxedo shop wasn't the best place for a baby, with Beau and the others occupied trying on suits and accessories, she assumed her mom was stuck watching Skye today.

Unless her mom *wanted* to watch Skye, as Channing had suggested, and wasn't just bending over backward in an effort to please Beau. It was something to think about. Kenna had always believed her mom changed in an attempt to win a man's love but what if, this time, Beau's love had changed her mom? Maybe the desperation Kenna thought she'd witnessed in her mom's eyes had been something else entirely?

"Is Channing going with you?" Kenna asked, attempting to sound casual and not let on that her heart fluttered at mentioning his name.

"He will." Beau glanced around. "If I can find him. Not sure where the rascal took off to. I'd better hunt him down."

He wrapped an arm around Kenna's mom's waist and anchored her against him. Staring into her eyes as if she were an ice-cream sundae complete with a cherry on top, he gave her a smacking kiss on the cheek. "Gonna miss you, darling."

Gracie giggled and pushed on his chest. "You won't be gone that long."

"A minute away from you is pure torture."

"Oh, Beau." She blushed. "You're the sweetest."

"Sweet on you."

Kenna might have gagged except, darn it, they really were kind of cute together. And then, to Kenna's surprise, Beau grabbed hold of the stroller handle.

"Come on, kiddo," he said to Skye. "Let's see

what kind of trouble we can get into while we find Uncle Channing." He sped up, steering the stroller in a winding pattern over the uneven ground and making zooming sounds.

Skye broke into high-pitched laughter.

Kenna stared. All right. He was better with the baby than she'd figured. Then again, Beau wasn't much more than a big kid himself, in a lot of ways.

While Kenna saddled Zenith, her mom babbled on and on about the wedding.

"I like that strawberry shortcake wedding cake we tasted at the bakery best, don't you? Strawberry is Beau's favorite. Oh, and I found a neat wedding supply website. Would you help me place an online order? They didn't have everything we needed at the party store." She paused to draw a breath. "Don't forget, we have the final dress fitting on Tuesday. Have you talked to Dinah yet? She said she'd call you."

"Yes, Mom, we've talked." Kenna finished bridling Zenith.

"Well? What did you decide?"

"Isn't the bridal shower supposed to be a surprise?"

"Oh, please." Her mom reapplied fresh lipstick using a strip of chrome on the trailer's side for a mirror. "Of course it's not a surprise."

"Fine, then. We've reserved a private room at

The Sip and Savor Bistro for Wednesday at six p.m. Dinah's excellent suggestion, I might add."

"I love that place! So quaint. Has everyone RSVP'd? I worry about the shower being on a weeknight, but, seeing as it's last minute, we didn't have much choice."

Rushed engagement, rushed wedding, rushed bridal shower. Kenna silently fretted. This wasn't new for her mom and hadn't ever ended well. Not just for Gracie but for Kenna, too. She doubted her mom knew how much her actions affected Kenna. How much being pushed away and virtually ignored hurt her.

If—when—Kenna met someone and decided to settle down, she'd do things differently.

Her thoughts ran headlong to Channing. He was such a terrific guy, and the attraction between them couldn't be denied. But there were no guarantees they wouldn't wind up unhappy. In facts, the odds were stacked against them. She traveled extensively for work, and he was busy with the arena, attempting to save the family business. If life had taught Kenna one thing, it was that love didn't last. Why set themselves up for misery?

Blinking herself back to the present, she said, "According to Dinah, most people have replied with a yes."

"You think the men will want to come, too?"

Gracie strolled alongside Kenna while she led Zenith to the practice ring, still talking. "I know we're having the shower at a bistro, not a sports bar, but men attend bridal showers these days."

"I have no idea, Mom." Kenna waved to the students gathering outside the ring. "It's your bridal shower. Invite whomever you want."

"Channing will come if you ask him." Her mom lowered her sunglasses and peered at Kenna over the rim. "You two have been getting awful cozy lately. I heard you're helping him with those old bucking horses. Training them or whatever."

"Hopefully rehabilitating them."

"Beau saw you in the pasture yesterday, heads bent together and holding hands."

"He helped me up after I tripped in a gopher hole."

"If that's what you say."

"We were deciding on the two bucking horses with the most potential. Channing's bringing them by after class today for our first session."

"That's good. He and the boys will be long done with the tux fittings by then."

Kenna's phone beeped a second alarm. "Look, Mom, I've got to run. Class is starting."

"Sure, sure. I'll just sit over there." She backwalked toward a row of wooden benches. "Don't worry if you look over and don't see me. I'm meeting Beau soon to fetch Skye."

Kenna mumbled a reply, her attention on the class. Entering the ring, she motioned to the group of students, horses and parents. Channing's mom had already checked them in and collected any outstanding registration fees.

"Good morning, people. Come on, don't be shy." Kenna mentally assessed each student as they filed in on their horses. Though they'd previously completed a questionnaire and stated their experience level, she relied heavily on initial impressions. "First things first, line up in a row."

When the students were done, she went down the line, Zenith in tow, and introduced herself, asking each student questions about their experience level and their horses. They ranged in age from nine to twelve, including the lone boy. Times were definitely changing. Women were participating in what had been traditionally men's rodeo events and now men, or boys, were participating in what was considered a woman's sport. Kenna approved.

She took a position in front of them. "All right. Who can tell me what step one is?"

"Warming up," a girl with short blond pigtails shouted.

"Before that."

"Put on your helmet," another said.

"Yes. Actually, a full equipment check. Trick riding can be dangerous. Your safety, that of your horse and the other riders is the most important thing."

They spent fifteen minutes meticulously inspecting their gear and tack. Only when Kenna was satisfied did they proceed.

Once everyone had warmed up their horses by walking, trotting and loping in large circles—more opportunity for Kenna to assess the students' abilities—she called out, "Who here can perform a layup?"

A flurry of hands shot into the air. No surprise—it was one of the simpler tricks.

"Okay, show me. Samantha, you first."

After each student had a turn, they advanced to more difficult moves, some of them performed on what Kenna called the Tin Man. Yesterday, Channing had helped her carry in the barrel mounted on four metal legs that she used to teach and practice new moves. Starting low to the ground and on a stationary vault was safer. It also alleviated fears and built confidence before attempting the same move on a horse in motion.

The hours flew by. Before Kenna knew it, they had to break for lunch. The afternoon passed just as quickly. Her students showed themselves to be hard workers and eager learners. Thankfully, there were no serious falls. A few tricks went wrong and students landed in the soft dirt with nothing injured save their pride.

Zenith performed like the pro he was, though, with these beginners, Kenna hadn't worked him hard. At four o'clock, she announced the end of class. Giving in to her students and their parents' pleas, Kenna put on a short demonstration. Launching Zenith into a fast lope around the ring, she executed a reverse neck layover, a backward bender and a sidesaddle layout. She finished to a round of applause.

"Thank you, everyone, for coming," she said, dismounting. "Be sure to practice at least three times a week."

"I'm tired," the boy complained on the way out of the ring.

"My legs hurt," chimed his friend.

"In a good way, though, right?" Kenna asked, following behind the students on foot.

They looked over their shoulders at her, making funny faces at her in response.

Kenna laughed. She had to admit, she was a little tired and sore herself. But the class had gone exceptionally well, and she couldn't be happier. She met briefly with each student and their parent or parents, thanking them for coming. Most inquired when she'd be returning to give another class, and Kenna advised them to keep updated through Hoof Feats' social media page.

The wooden benches had been deserted hours ago. Kenna's mom left well before lunch with Skye, off to wherever. As the last student headed to their vehicle, Kenna debated calling her mom and offering to pick up a pizza for dinner. She promptly forgot about calling when she noticed Channing approaching. Flanked by the pair of bucking horses they'd deemed most trainable, he strode toward her. A young wrangler brought up the rear, leading a third horse—this one a dependable gelding saddled and bridled for Channing to ride.

Kenna smiled in greeting. "Things go all right at the tuxedo shop?"

"We're all set."

She joined him and the wrangler and together the three of them entered the practice ring, Kenna staying a safe distance behind should the other horses decide they disliked Zenith.

"How was class?" Channing asked while she shut the gate.

"Fantastic! The students were really enthusiastic and a few of them were surprisingly talented."

"You're beaming."

"Am I?" She glanced away, suddenly self-conscious and unsure if her stellar day teaching or being with Channing was responsible.

"You ready for this?" A note of caution had crept into his voice. "These boys can be a handful."

They'd agreed yesterday that Channing would lead one of the bucking horses on his mount while Kenna rode Zenith on the other side, confining the bucking horse between them. They'd start out at a walk and, fingers crossed, advance to a trot and then a lope. Depending on how that went, they'd attempt to ride the horses during their next session.

"More than ready," she said.

"You've already put in a full day." He tied the bucking horses to the fence and fetched his horse from the worker. The young man left with instructions to return in an hour.

"I'm fine." Kenna's weariness had fled and her energy had soared the instant she'd seen Channing approach. Excitement about the bucking horses, she told herself.

They were done in less than an hour. Both bucking horses, named Sideways Sam and Hannibal, did relatively well, with only a few hops and kicks in the beginning. Being led around by a rider on horseback was nothing new to them.

The worker arrived and collected all three horses. Rather than leave with him, Channing accompanied Kenna to her trailer, where she unsaddled Zenith.

Channing's phone beeped, and he read the screen. "Mom's texting me. She's already gotten some feedback from your class." He grinned. "All positive."

"Cool." Exhilaration filled Kenna. "I do love teaching, and I'm always glad when my classes go well."

"You love it as much as performing?"

"Yes, but differently. Someday, when I'm ready to quit performing, I may take up teaching, if I can make a living at it."

"Have you considered training performance horses?"

"I kind of do that already. I incorporate a little of it into my classes." She gave Zenith a quick brushing down, removing the dirt and dried sweat. He'd earned himself a treat and a rest.

"I meant for clients," Channing said.

"Hmm. I wonder if there's enough demand."

His phone pinged again. He studied the text. "Sorry. I gotta run. There's a problem at the livestock pens. See you tomorrow?"

"I'll be here, as usual."

"Night, Kenna." He turned.

"Wait." She mustered her courage. "Mom wants to know if you'd like to come to the bridal shower. I doubt it's your idea of fun—"

"Sure. When and where?"

"Really?" Kenna felt ridiculously happy. "I'll text you the details."

"Sounds good."

He left after that. There'd been no moment between them like the other day in her truck, unfortunately.

The next instant, she chided herself. She was still leaving after the wedding. *Immediately* after. Wishing for moments with Channing was unfair and possibly risky for both of them.

She grabbed Zenith's lead rope. "Let's get you back to the stall, pal. Dinner's waiting."

She wound up making that phone call to her mom about picking up pizza. All during the errands and drive home, she contemplated Channing's suggestion of training horses for clients. Was it possible? Try as she might, she couldn't get the idea out of her head.

CHAPTER FIVE

As Kenna's eager student had shouted in class two days ago, warming up your horse before training sessions was an important step. When it came to trick riding, warming up oneself was equally important.

In addition to riding, Kenna had spent many of her teen years in gymnastics and dance classes. Nowadays, she kept in shape with a rigorous stretching and flexibility regime that incorporated both gymnastics and yoga. The stretches and poses kept her muscles limber and her joints flexible and maintained her strength.

She started out most days with a thirty-minute routine, which, depending on where she was staying, she performed in a variety of places: her mom's living room, the backyard at Madison's grandmother's house, a hotel room or a gym if one was available. Had Beau and Skye not shown up bright and early at her mom's house, Kenna would have worked out there. But their laughter and loud chattering and ridiculous carrying on while her mom fixed a big breakfast was simply too distracting, especially when her mom kept hollering to Kenna from the kitchen and Beau interrupted her to ask an irrelevant question.

As a result, she found herself in her horse trailer—her very *least* favorite place to work out—executing the crane pose on a yoga mat in the middle of the floor. She'd left the rear gate wide open so as not to feel penned in. Later, when she found a spare minute, she'd research what other options were available to her. If necessary, she'd buy a temporary pass to a gym or yoga studio.

Inhaling deeply, she tamped down her annoyance and attempted to clear her mind. She may not care to see Beau at the kitchen table every morning, but she had no right telling her mom whom she could have over or when. It was her house. And soon, Beau and Skye would be living there. Though it pained Kenna to admit it, technically, she was a guest. She'd given up her resident status a long time ago. Another deep breath pushed that thought away and enabled her to finally relax.

Her routine over, she lowered her behind onto the mat and sat in a classic yoga position with her feet tucked close to her body. Hands pressed together and in front of her, she continued her breathing, silently counting and expanding her lungs to their fullest capacity.

"Hi—oops, sorry. Didn't mean to disturb you."

She twisted to see Channing standing at the trailer's open rear gate. "Oh, hi! Is it nine already?"

"Five till." He retreated a step. "I'll come back."

"No, no." She unfurled her legs and stood. "I'm done."

"If you're sure." His gaze lingered.

Kenna was conscious of the strands of hair that had worked loose from her ponytail and the perspiration coating her skin. Her faded T-shirt and yoga pants had seen better days. This was hardly her best look. Yet, Channing's eyes followed her every move.

Kenna remembered seeing the same flash of interest in his eyes once before during their short-lived high school romance. Specifically, right before he kissed her.

Did he want to kiss her now? The butterflies in her stomach provided the answer. *Yes, he does*, they chorused.

She grabbed a hand towel from her tote bag sitting on the wheel well and wiped her face and neck, attempting to break the spell. She wasn't about to start something that had little chance of succeeding. Like her mom and Beau, Kenna and Channing had obstacles to overcome. More than that, Kenna wasn't sure she was ready or brave enough to take another chance.

"I usually work out somewhere that isn't my horse trailer," she said. "But Mom's house was like Grand Central Station this morning."

Smiling at Channing, she made her way down the trailer ramp, rolled up yoga mat in one hand and tote bag in the other. He accompanied her to the side of the trailer where Rocket Man waited, observing the subtle dynamics between the two humans with complete disinterest.

"Be back in a jiffy." She pointed to the door of her trailer's living quarters. "I'm just going to change."

"Take your time. I was early."

Channing's intense interest in her had dimmed. Though she knew it was for the best, Kenna felt a small stab of disappointment.

Giving the horse an I'm-behind-you pat on the rump, she went inside, where she washed up in the tiny sink before changing into her jeans, shirt, boots and a ball cap. While her usual clothes provided a level of comfort and security, like wearing a uniform or coat, she missed the impact her yoga pants and T-shirt had had on Channing.

When she emerged a short while later, she found him with his dad. Surprised, and sensing an undeniable tension, she said, "Oh, hi."

"Nice to see you, Kenna." Burle Pearce tugged on the brim of his old worn Stetson. "How are you?"

“Am I interrupting?”

“Not at all. Channing and I were just talking about the women’s bull riding.” He turned to his son. “I’ll see you later in my office. When you’re done here, we can continue our conversation.”

“Right.”

Whatever she’d interrupted must have been serious, given Channing’s grim, terse voice.

“Give your mom my best,” Burle said to Kenna before sauntering off.

“Everything okay?” she asked Channing when his dad was out of earshot.

“It’s nothing,” he insisted. “Ready?”

“You sure I’m not keeping you?”

It seemed like ever since she’d arrived, she’d been constantly distracting him from his job at the arena. He’d spent so much time assisting her with Rocket Man and her trick-riding classes, rehabilitating the bucking horses and dealing with various wedding activities.

“I’m sure,” he insisted.

“Your dad seemed kind of annoyed.”

“He was. And it had nothing to do with you.”

She thought he might be lying. “You’re busy.”

“Not that busy.”

Undoubtedly another lie. “I can get someone else to spot me. Rochelle, maybe.” Kenna lifted her saddle onto Rocket Man’s back.

“I like watching you.”

She liked watching him, too. Could he tell?

"Really," she said. "I don't want to cause a problem for you."

"For the last time, you're not."

"All right."

Kenna had to admit, Channing was her first choice for a spotter, and not because of his abilities. She enjoyed his company and, if she were honest, the way he looked at her. She may not be in the market for a romance, but that didn't mean she disliked a man's attention. Especially when that man was Channing.

Aware her thoughts were heading into dangerous waters, she said, "The vet's coming at noon for Rocket Man's health check. I'm a little concerned."

"Why?"

"I've noticed this little hitch in his step the last couple days. It happens after thirty or forty minutes of intense training, which is why I want to work him before the vet gets here."

"Could just be a misstep or a quirk."

"Or his personality. He gets excited." They headed across the rodeo arena grounds to the practice ring, their pace unhurried. "In any case, I'd like the vet to have a look. Rule out a pinched nerve or an old injury acting up."

"You can't be too safe."

No, she couldn't. Unnecessary risks weren't

an option when her well-being and Rocket Man's were both depending on his soundness.

In the distance, Kenna noticed Channing's sister, Jocelyn, putting out a sandwich board sign near the office.

"Is that what I think it is?" she asked.

Channing followed the direction of her gaze. "Yep. Signs for the women's bull riding."

"Your dad agreed?"

"He didn't squash the idea. Yet."

That must have been what they were discussing. "You're making progress. That's great. Is it still the night before the wedding?"

"Yeah. Dad wasn't too happy about that. I had to do some hard selling. But my sister, Jocelyn, updated the website and our social media pages as of yesterday. We've already had a few registrations. Hard for Dad to argue with that."

"I'm impressed."

He shrugged off her praise. "Now we just need to sell a decent number of tickets. If not, I'll be eating humble pie."

"Will the bucking horses be ready by then? Have you advertised a trick-riding exhibition? I talked to Madison yesterday about it."

"Yeah, we advertised the trick riding. I was waiting to talk with you before committing to the bucking horses."

"I can't answer that until you let me ride them."

"You certain?" he asked. "I know you take a lot of risks with the trick riding, but these guys, old and out of shape as they are, could buck you off like *that*." He snapped his fingers. "You'd go sailing."

"I've been bucked plenty. And we'll go slow."

"I want to ride them first. I'd hate for something to happen to you."

"I was thinking, I could ride one of them into the arena before the start of the bull-riding event. Maybe hold the flag." Trick riders often opened rodeos by carrying American and state flags around the arena while the national anthem played.

"Sideways Sam is the better choice. Hannibal isn't there yet."

Kenna had decided the names were misnomers. When not in the ring, the former bucking horses were relatively calm. "I agree. Sam's the better choice. He's gotten overweight in his retirement, and that will slow him down."

"Trust me, a few extra pounds won't slow that fellow down one lick. He can send you sprawling if he has a mind to."

"Relax, Channing." She reached over and for a quick moment linked arms with him.

"I'd ride him, but the audience would much rather see a pretty gal than ugly old me."

"You're not ugly."

"No?"

"Not too ugly," she joked and then averted her gaze, worried she'd give herself away. "Let's give Sam a try today. After my vet appointment for Rocket Man. If he doesn't pass the exam with flying colors, I'll be back to square one. Hoof Feats' sponsors won't like me taking off longer than I already am, which means I'll be busy looking for a new performance horse and won't have any free time for the old folks."

They reached the practice ring and went inside. Rocket Man had done this enough by now that he knew the drill frontward and backward. Channing sat on the fence, checking his phone, making a call and waiting while Kenna warmed up the horse.

Once she signaled him that she was ready, he hopped down and took up his position in the center of the practice ring. His primary job was to watch for any trouble. A loose strap. A worrisome move from Rocket Man, like the hitch Kenna had noticed. Outside interference that might spook the horse and cause him to bolt.

Channing was also there to intervene if, by some chance, Kenna found herself in a dangerous situation. A foot or hand caught. A loss of balance. Rocket Man deciding to run off. A fall. A stumble.

Her luck held, and the next hour progressed

well with no problems other than the tiny hitch in Rocket Man's gait Kenna had previously noticed. Feeling optimistic, she decided to attempt one last new trick before quitting. Until now, she'd been sticking to the easier and less risky moves.

Rocket Man pawed the ground, his energy level high.

"I'm going to try a side backbend," she called to Channing. "Heads-up."

She didn't give him a chance to respond before she cued Rocket Man into a lope. The horse hugged the fence as he circled the ring, adhering to his training.

Kenna cleared her mind and tuned into her senses. When the moment felt right, she raised her right leg and inserted her foot in the thick strap near the saddle seat. Her left foot remained in the stirrup. Rolling over, she dropped off the saddle and hung upside down, using only her lower limbs to anchor herself to Rocket Man's side. When he continued loping as if nothing about this was unusual, she arched her back into a deep curve and extended her hands as far as they would reach, her fingers curling gracefully.

"Attaboy." Her head hovered alongside Rocket Man's and bounced in rhythm to his gait. "Easy does it."

She supposed some might think it ludicrous, talking to her horse while she hung upside down off his side, a mere eighteen inches from the ground. But Kenna knew the sound of her voice soothed and steadied him.

A moment later, she rolled over and hoisted herself up and back into the saddle. Removing her foot from the strap, she let her leg dangle.

"Good boy." She patted Rocket Man's neck, reining him to a trot.

"Whoo-hoo!" Channing applauded and cheered. "Very impressive."

"Not too bad." Pleasure and satisfaction spilled over her. Rocket Man had performed flawlessly.

She slowed him to a walk and circled the ring twice more before jumping down and joining Channing at the gate.

"I'll finish his cooldown on foot—"

She didn't get the rest of her sentence out because Channing swept her up into a hug, lifting her off the ground.

"What's going on?" Unable to help herself, she laughed.

He put her down and brought his face close to hers. "You could have broken your neck."

"I perform far more dangerous tricks."

"Warn me next time. My heart almost stopped." He started to release her. At the last second, he closed the small distance between them and brushed her lips lightly with his. "Congratulations. I think you found your performance horse."

Kenna swallowed a soft gasp. Had Channing just kissed her? Her tingling toes said yes.

"We'll, um, see." She managed just barely to regain her bearings. "There's still the vet's exam."

"Call me later with the results. Beau texted me with a problem. The tractor won't start."

"Um...bye," she muttered, but he was already gone. She stared after him until he disappeared around the corner.

Kenna managed to pull herself together before the vet arrived. As hoped, Rocket Man passed the health exam. According to the vet, the tiny hitch was indeed no more than a quirk. Kenna paid the woman, whose tanned and weathered complexion conveyed a story of decades spent outdoors.

"Good luck to you," the vet said, stowing her gear in her truck. "You found yourself a fine horse. I suppose you'll be back on the road before long."

"Yeah. I guess."

Kenna lifted a hand in farewell. Now that she had a new performance horse, there was no reason whatsoever to remain in Payson.

Recalling Channing's kiss, she touched her lips, swearing she could still detect the light caress. It meant nothing. A spontaneous response to high spirits and passing danger.

She spent the next several hours attempting to convince herself of that and failing miserably.

KENNA COUNTED TO herself over a bite of toast, which she chased with a sip of hot coffee. On the beat of four, the kitchen door flew open.

"Morning!" Beau entered, Skye balanced in his arms, and boomed, "Where's my bride-to-be?"

In all fairness, Kenna wasn't a psychic. She'd seen Beau through the front window on her way from the bedroom to the kitchen. After a week and a half at her mom's, she knew exactly how long it took him to unload Skye, her diaper bag, toys and whatever else, and make it to the house. Enough time for Kenna to pour a cup of coffee and consume half a slice of toast.

"Coming!" Her mom appeared. Beaming like a…well, like a bride-to-be, she rushed over to Beau and Skye. "There you are."

She folded the pair into a group hug. Skye babbled her version of hello.

"Woman," Beau said, giving Kenna's mom a lingering up and down, "has anyone told you yet this morning how gorgeous you are?" He kissed her hard while Skye flailed her fists.

Kenna turned her head and finished her toast.

When she next looked, Beau was dropping Skye into the high chair beside her at the table.

He grinned. “Say hello.”

Was he talking to her or Skye?

Kenna mustered a weak smile. “Hey.”

Skye compensated for Kenna’s lack of exuberance. She slapped the high-chair tray with her open hands and cried out, “Ba, da, da, de.”

“Morning people.” Kenna feigned grumpiness. “I hate them.” But the instant Beau retreated, she reached over and pinched Skye’s cheek. “Hiya, squirt. I love your pony shirt.”

A sippy cup of juice appeared in front of Skye, courtesy of Kenna’s mom. Kenna added a small piece of toast crust.

“Here you go.”

Skye grabbed both items—cup in one fist, crust in the other—and held them high as if they were trophies.

Kenna pretended not to be amused while she sent a reminder text to the competitive trail rider interested in buying Snapple. She was meeting the woman at the rodeo arena around eleven o’clock. Kenna planned to get there early and give Snapple a quick workout, followed by a bath and grooming. He’d be spent and clean, and hopefully he’d make an excellent impression.

After the meeting, she might try to squeeze in some time with Sideways Sam, if Channing was agreeable. She'd yet to ride the chunky buckskin, though Channing had twice already. He'd let her watch and help groom and saddle Sam so he'd become accustomed to her. There'd been no mishaps and no injuries. No bites, no kicks, no bucks. Nothing to raise a single concern.

Today, Kenna thought she'd walk Sam around the grounds on foot. If that went well, she'd take him into the practice ring and lead him through a series of figure eights and serpentine patterns and then zigzag through the pylons. After that, she'd try to convince Channing to let her ride Sam.

"See you tonight at the bridal shower, darling. I should be back in town by three and unloaded by four."

Beau's words roused Kenna from her musings. "You leaving?"

He usually drove Skye to Grandma Malone's, the retired teacher who watched the baby in the mornings along with three other children.

"Yep." He hitched up his jeans. "Making a run to Marana for a load of hay."

"I love you, baby," her mom said. "Stay safe."

He swept her into his arms for another kiss. "You girls have a good day and stay out of trouble," he said before heading out the door.

Kenna kept her mouth shut while Beau was there, but now she did. "Marana's a six-hour round trip. What if he doesn't make it back in time for the shower?"

"He will. Beau's very dependable." Her mom set a paper plate with scrambled eggs in front of Skye, who ate them with her fingers.

"And you're left taking Skye to day care." Kenna doubted this was the first time Beau had left her mom with the responsibility of dropping Skye off.

"Actually..." Kenna's mom patted the baby's head. "Skye's not going to day care today. The facility is being fumigated. We were told about it a couple weeks ago."

"You're staying home with her?"

"That was the plan. But now I can't. I have software training at the office today from eight to five. They moved it up from next week. I just found out thirty minutes ago when my boss called." She hesitated, chewed her lower lip. "Attendance is mandatory."

Kenna shut her eyes, already anticipating what was coming next. "I can't babysit Skye. Maybe this afternoon for a couple hours. Not all day."

"She's hardly any trouble. And she adores you."

Skye chose that moment to throw a piece of egg at Kenna.

"I have an appointment this morning," Kenna protested.

"Can you reschedule?"

"At the last minute? No way. The woman squeezed me in as it was."

"Please, kitten. Beau will be here as soon as he unloads the hay at the arena, and the three of you can go to The Sip and Savor Bistro together for the bridal shower. I'll join you the minute training is over."

Kenna wanted to say that Skye was Beau's responsibility, not her mom's. She wanted to beg her mom to quit attempting to please and impress Beau by proving herself indispensable. That if he didn't love her for herself and not for what she could do for him, he wasn't worthy of her love. Kenna wanted to ask if Beau even knew she wasn't staying home today with Skye.

Instead, all she said was, "Why can't he go to Marana tomorrow?"

"The truck isn't available."

"You're asking a lot of me." Kenna sighed, a nostalgic sadness pressing down on her.

She suddenly missed her mom desperately. Her old mom. The confident, strong, intelligent, caring woman who'd been married to Kenna's father. This version acted younger in an attempt to make herself more appealing to a man nineteen years her junior. She twisted herself into knots in an attempt to accommodate others. She buried her insecurities rather than address them.

Kenna pushed at the sadness, willing it away. No relationship was worth losing herself. She'd spend the rest of her life alone first. Wasn't that better than this?

She stared down at Skye, who grinned at her with dimples identical to Beau's. The kid was going to be a real looker one day, once she learned to wipe food off her face.

"There are times Beau takes advantage of you, Mom."

"He does not."

"And you let him."

"I don't."

The half-hearted circular conversation would go nowhere. Kenna gave up. If she battled with her mom on the day of the bridal shower, she might cause a rift between them. Her only option was to give in. Could she manage her day with a baby for a sidekick? Working with Sideways Sam was out of the question. As far as getting Snapple ready, she'd think of something. Fingers crossed that the potential buyer was understanding.

"Where's the stroller?" Kenna grumbled.

Her mom let out an "Eek! Thank you, thank you, kitten!"

Kenna endured a similar hug to the one her mom had given Beau and Skye earlier. Together, they loaded Skye, the car seat, stroller and her enormous supply of baby paraphernalia into

Kenna's truck. Kenna kept up a constant chatter with the baby over her shoulder as they drove to the arena.

In place of a quick workout, she decided she'd take Snapple through his paces on a lunge line in the practice ring. It was better than nothing, she told herself, and would at least get the kinks out. The last thing Kenna wanted was for Snapple to act up because he had an excess supply of energy.

"How exactly are we going to manage this?" she asked Skye.

She parked the stroller outside the stall while she haltered Snapple. Getting both him and the baby to the practice ring would be a challenge. Snapple walked well, but he was a lot of horse and Skye a tiny baby. Not the best combination.

"Never again, Mom," Kenna grumbled and, checking the time, let out a frustrated groan.

"What's wrong?"

She spun, relief flooding her. Was it possible help had arrived?

Well aware she was pulling him away from his job yet again, she asked, "Channing! Are you by chance free? Ten minutes—that's all I need. I promise."

"As it happens, I'm on my morning coffee break."

He wasn't holding a coffee cup and neither were they anywhere in the vicinity of a coffee-pot. He really was a good guy, always willing to help a friend.

Or is it you *he's always willing to help?* a small voice asked.

"Can you take Snapple to the practice ring for me? I want to work him on the lunge line before Maia gets here," she said, referring to the potential buyer. "That way I can push the stroller."

"Happy to." He took the big gelding from her.

Kenna got the stroller, and they walked side by side. Skye was fascinated with Snapple and couldn't stop staring at him. She kept twisting in her seat to see better.

"Where's your mom?" Channing asked.

"At work." Kenna sighed. "She's in an all-day training session and can't watch Skye. And the babysitter's house is being fumigated."

"So you volunteered?"

"Grudgingly. Apparently, Beau had to pick up hay in Marana."

Channing looked apologetic. "I had no idea that would cause a problem with Skye's day care. Beau didn't say a word to me when I talked to him about it."

"Not that I'm his biggest fan, but, in his defense, I doubt my mom told him. Not until after I agreed to babysit."

"I see how that would bother you. Beau, too.

He should be kept informed when it comes to his daughter."

Channing maintained a tight grip on Snapple's lead rope. Kenna appreciated his concern for the baby and the extra caution he exercised. In his other hand, he carried Kenna's lunge line and lunge whip.

"I agree. But try telling that to Mom. She's so busy tripping over herself to please Beau, she won't listen."

"Why do you think that is?"

"Truthfully, I'm beginning to think she's terrified Beau will leave her someday for a younger woman. By being indispensable to him and Skye, she lessens the chance."

"Beau doesn't care about the age difference."

"If you believe that, you're fooling yourself." At the practice ring, Kenna pushed the stroller to a shady spot and applied the brake while Channing waited. "He may say the age difference isn't important to him, but he's well aware she's considerably older than him. People remind him. His family, for instance. They have their reservations."

"He told me they like her."

"They like her as a person, but not as his wife. Apparently his mom is lamenting that he won't be having any more children because my mom is forty-eight." Kenna's mom had been barely twenty when she gave birth to Kenna, a year after eloping with Kenna's dad.

"They could adopt," Channing suggested. "And for all we know, Beau may be fine with only having Skye."

"Mom said they haven't really discussed children. Don't you think they should before they get married?"

He shrugged. "I won't argue with you on that. But..."

"Right. Not my business. Not my life. I get it," she said on a wistful breath.

"You can't fix everyone's problems, Kenna. Sometimes you just have to let go and have faith they'll work it out."

"Why do you always have to make so much sense?" She smiled up at him, her insides going soft as his gaze roamed her face.

"Go on. I'll watch Skye while you give Snapple his workout."

"You're always rescuing me. If we're not careful, I might get used to it."

"Would that be so bad?"

He reached up, and his fingers traced the length of her jawline. She could think of a thousand reasons to sink into his touch and a thousand and one reasons to draw back. Kenna wouldn't follow in her mom's footsteps, making a series of wrong decisions that resulted in hurting herself and someone she cared about all because of a hard-to-resist attraction.

"Channing. I…I'm not sure. I'm leaving soon. And you need to stay."

You deserve someone less damaged than me. Less afraid.

His hand fell away. "Yeah."

Snapple pawed the ground, eager for his workout and giving Kenna the excuse she needed.

"We'd better go," she said, taking the lunge line from Channing.

The discussion would have to wait for another time. But they really should address their growing feelings and where they couldn't, wouldn't, shouldn't lead them.

CHAPTER SIX

IT WASN'T EASY for Channing, but he stayed out of the meeting between Kenna and his friend Maia. Sitting in the VIP section of the empty rodeo arena, he bounced Skye on his lap and watched the two women discuss the tall gelding.

Maia had ridden him a full hour in the arena, including five straight minutes at a full lope. To test his stamina, Channing assumed. A competitive trail rider's mounts had to be in prime physical condition and capable of exerting themselves for long periods of time. The sport wasn't for weaklings, either horses or riders.

She'd also put Snapple through reining maneuvers that tested his response to commands, ending with in-and-out poles and a pair of cavalletti jumps. In the mountains, where Maia rode and competed, she encountered all manner of obstacles, both natural and man-made. She needed to be confident of her horse's calm reaction.

During the entire hour, Kenna had run here and there, setting up the poles and the low jumps, timing Snapple when Maia asked, and fetching equipment she requested. During the times Kenna wasn't needed, she'd fussed and paced with palpable anxiety.

"Maia likes the horse," Channing told the baby, noting the tall slender woman's meticulous examination of the horse's feet and legs. For such large, strong animals, horses possessed surprisingly delicate limbs that were prone to injury. "Know how I can tell? She's trying hard to appear cool and unemotional."

Skye plucked the bottle from her mouth and held it straight out as if pointing, then told Channing in her baby talk that she agreed with his observation. At least, that was what he chose to think.

Channing pulled her cap down to shade her eyes, something he knew how to do only because he'd watched Kenna. She may not admit it, but she was good with her future stepsister. He suspected that deep down, she liked kids a lot, and babies in particular.

"I'm glad Snapple behaved himself," he told Skye. "Kenna was honest with Maia about his tendency to run off now and again. And if anyone can train a bad habit out of a horse, it's Maia. But it was better he behaved himself, right?"

Skye arched her back and kicked her feet.

"Bored?" Channing asked. "They won't be much longer. The deal looks to be closing."

Indeed, Kenna and Maia were suddenly all smiles. The next instant, they hugged. Kenna then threw her arms around Snapple and buried her face in his neck for a full minute before pulling slowly away.

"Snapple's going to a new home," Channing noted with satisfaction. "A good one."

Maia rather than Kenna led the horse from the arena. *Ah*, thought Channing, she'd already taken ownership. He stood and deposited Skye in the stroller. She burst into a loud wail, expressing her dislike that playtime was over.

"Sorry, kiddo. Them's the breaks."

Outside the arena, Kenna and Maia parted, with the endurance rider taking Snapple to her truck and trailer. Channing waved and hollered, "Congratulations."

"Thanks again, Channing." Maia waved back, Snapple plodding along obediently.

"Don't be a stranger."

Kenna walked toward him and Skye, trying hard to hide her tears behind her sunglasses. "I'm sorry this took so long."

"He's going to be fine, hon. Maia will treat him well."

"I know. She's amazing." Kenna sniffed. "You are, too. Now I get to add babysitting to the list of everything you do for me."

"Babysitting?" He winked at Skye. "We're just two buds hanging out."

Skye squealed and shouted, "Buh, buh, buh."

"See?" Channing grinned.

"She's not seriously talking, is she?" Kenna said but laughed anyway.

"Mind if I ask, did you get the price you were hoping for?"

"I had to come down a little, which was fine. I like Maia, and I'm happy Snapple will be used for something he's more suited to than trick riding. She said she'd trained horses like him before and has some techniques that should stop him from running off."

"I figured she did."

"I owe you big-time, Channing."

"You can repay me by buying me lunch."

"Really?"

He grinned. "That's my final offer. It's almost one. Skye and I are starving."

"Oh, gosh!" Kenna pulled out her phone and pressed the button to switch it off silent mode. "Mom's been calling and texting. I didn't want to answer until Maia and I finished. Let me report in to her and then, yes, I'll buy you lunch. Where did you have in mind? Someplace that's kid-friendly."

"I'm fine with fast food."

"You sure?"

"Maybe another time you'll let *me* buy *you* lunch somewhere nicer. When you're not baby-sitting." Dinner would be better, he thought. That seafood place, the two of them sharing a dark cozy booth and a bottle of wine.

"I...ah..."

"Next time you're in town," he added and wished she hadn't looked so relieved. He took hold of the stroller handle, though taking hold of her hand would have been much nicer. "In the meantime, feed us. Our stomachs are growling."

"You got it."

She called her mom as they walked to her truck. Gracie must have been in the training session, because she didn't answer. Kenna left a message saying she, Skye and Channing were going to lunch.

At her vehicle, Kenna checked Skye's diaper situation, making a quick change in the back seat while Channing stowed the stroller. Skye nodded off the instant they were on the road, her head lolling to the side. Keeping their voices low, Channing and Kenna discussed the bridal shower scheduled for that evening, the progress they were making with Sideways Sam, the women's bull-riding event—happily, tickets were selling—and the latest trick Kenna had attempted with Rocket Man.

The fast-food restaurant wasn't crowded, the

lunch rush having ended. They placed their orders and Channing carried the trays while Kenna pushed the stroller.

"Okay if we sit there?" She pointed to a corner table.

"Lead the way." Not a dark cozy booth. *Too bad*, he thought.

In between bites of her own meal, Kenna fed Skye a truly awful-looking strained meal from a jar. The baby whined and fussed—she'd been out of sorts since they woke her from her short nap—and Kenna did her best to soothe her. They were halfway through eating when Kenna's phone rang. She glanced at the screen.

"It's Mom. They must be on break." She put the phone to her ear. "How's the training session?"

Channing half listened to her side of the conversation as he finished his burger.

"She's crying because she's tired. She didn't nap long enough." Kenna shot him a glance. "No, actually, Channing watched her during the appointment." There was a long pause. "She's fine, Mom, I promise. He didn't drop her on her head or let her play with a choking hazard." Another, shorter, pause. "I didn't have much choice. I had a meeting and, besides, Channing's kind of a really good babysitter." She stabbed a fry in a puddle of ketchup but didn't eat the fry. "No, we're heading back to the arena after lunch. I'll see you tonight. Yeah, at the shower. I'll call before then."

Disconnecting, she let out a low groan and pushed the remainder of her meal aside.

"Everything okay?" Channing asked.

"She didn't like me pawning off Skye on you, which is ironic when you think about it since that's exactly what she did—pawned Skye off on me. Personally, I think it was her guilt talking." Kenna gave the baby a sad and affectionate look. "Poor kid. Constantly being shuffled around."

"You care about her."

"I feel sorry for her. She has a mom who thinks only of herself and puts her barrel-racing career ahead of her own child, a dad who gladly lets others perform a large portion of the caregiving duties and a soon-to-be stepmom who recruits the nearest available person to watch her. And I'm no better." Kenna's eyes glistened as if she might cry. "I recruited you."

"I didn't mind."

"Frankly, I'm surprised the kid's so good-natured. She's probably going to grow up with all kinds of issues."

"You can look at it that way." Channing shrugged. "Or, the more people who love her, the better adjusted she'll be. What's that old saying about it takes a village?"

"Kids need stability and to have confidence

their parents will put them first. I'm not convinced that's the case with Skye."

They both stared at the baby, who sat crookedly in the stroller, her eyelids drooping. Kenna reached down and lowered the seat back to a near-reclining position, her movements gentle, her gaze warm.

Channing assumed the baby would be asleep in minutes, if not seconds, and he was right.

"She reminds me of me," Kenna said wistfully, still staring.

"How's that?"

"I got pawned off, too. Ignored, I guess, is a better word. After my dad died, Mom retreated. Emotionally and physically. She used to send me to stay with my grandparents or a friend or the neighbors every chance she got so she could be alone in her misery. She was depressed and grieving, I know that now, but I didn't then. All I felt was abandoned." She took a moment to compose herself. "The pattern continued. Each time Mom met someone new, each time they broke up, I was pushed aside. It's already happening with Beau." She wiped her eyes with a paper napkin. "I sound childish. Sorry."

"You don't." Channing had remained silent until now, giving her the time she needed to compose herself. She'd been having an emotional day. First, selling Snapple and now this. "You sound like someone who's had a rough go of it."

"I hate that I'm constantly venting to you."

"That's what friends are for." Or maybe more than friends…if their circumstances ever changed.

Kenna sipped her soda. "I just wish Mom and Beau weren't rushing into marriage without first resolving their problems. It might save them some heartache down the road. Ending an engagement is much easier than divorcing."

"For some people, marriage can be a motive to stay together." Channing was thinking of his own parents. "When there's more at stake, they try harder."

"Marriage is risky. Over half fail. Some end in tragedy."

She was referring to her dad, of course. The wound clearly hadn't healed.

Channing went out on a limb. And why not? He had little to lose. "Have you been talking about your mom and Beau…or yourself?"

Kenna's head shot up and their gazes connected. When she opened her mouth to speak, he was certain she planned on telling him to shut up or mind his own business. Only, she didn't.

"Myself," she admitted softly.

"What are you really afraid of, Kenna?" Would she withdraw if he reached for her?

"Besides getting hurt?"

"Anything worthwhile is worth taking a chance."

"I'm okay with taking chances. Calculated chances," she emphasized. "When the odds are in my favor. When I've tried and tested and am fairly certain of the outcome."

Channing wanted to say, "I'm scared, too, but you and I are worth taking a chance on." He didn't. The timing wasn't right. And while he might be willing to take a chance, Kenna wasn't ready to lower her defenses and let him in. She might never be ready. Or willing.

"There are no guarantees in life," he said.

"You don't have to tell me. No one saw my dad dying at thirty-five from a tangle of abnormal blood vessels in his brain."

The hitch in her voice did him in. Let her raise her defenses all she wanted, Channing thought, and he covered her hand with his.

"I, um, liked you in high school," she said.

Her admission took him aback. They'd never talked about their past before, other than vague references. And certainly not about their former feelings. "I liked you, too."

"If my dad hadn't died, well, who knows? Or if you'd asked me out again later."

"I thought about it."

"Why didn't you?"

"I was young and an idiot." He shook his head. "I had no clue what to do or say."

"You were my first kiss," she said shyly.

"You were mine, too. Which I'm sure was obvious from my incredible lack of experience."

"You did all right."

"Feel free to kiss me anytime you want and compare."

She tilted her head slightly and evaluated him. "And what would happen then?"

"What would you like to happen?"

Answering a question with a question. *Way to duck and dodge, buddy*, he thought.

Kenna removed her hand from beneath his. "I'm leaving after the wedding."

"Right." There was his answer. She wouldn't start something she couldn't finish.

"But if I weren't..." She let the sentence dangle.

"If you weren't..."

He waited for her to say, *We could start dating*, or, *Then maybe I'd stop letting these stupid insecurities get in our way.*

Instead, she checked on Skye and rummaged through the diaper bag. "It's getting late—we should go."

Channing fought the urge to ask her to reconsider leaving after the wedding. To take a chance with him, on them. They could figure things out, he'd say. Find a way to make it work.

She stood, and his heart sank a little. But what had he expected?

Kenna had been running from relationships for the past ten years. She wasn't about to change because of one conversation with him, however revealing it had been. If he'd learned anything about her today, it was that she needed reassurances. Buckets of them. And he wasn't sure he could give them to her.

"I'll get this." He collected the trash and their trays, carrying both to the waste station.

Skye didn't wake up during the transfer from the stroller to her car seat or when they returned to the rodeo arena.

"You heading home?" Channing asked when they pulled in and parked.

"Yeah. Reluctantly. I'd originally planned to exercise Rocket Man and Zenith. I can't now, not with Skye."

"I'll watch her. She's sleeping, anyway."

"Not for long. And I refuse to burden you with babysitting again. Don't lie—you must have work to do. Besides, I have errands to run before the bridal shower tonight. Pick up the cake and balloons. Wrap Mom's gift. And change before Beau arrives. Dinah's bringing the games, thank goodness. You'd think with two other bridal showers under my belt, I'd be an expert. I'm not."

"If I have a few minutes," he said, "I can give the horses a walk around the grounds."

"I'll owe you another lunch at this rate."

"I'm also free for dinner."

"Uh..."

He let her off the hook. "Run your errands. I'll see you later at the shower."

"Beau wrangle you into coming?"

"I'm not going because of Beau, and I think you know that."

"Oh." Understanding dawned in her eyes.

He got out of the truck and shut the door. He'd taken a step, albeit a small one. Whatever happened next was up to her. Depending on what that was, they'd both know where she stood.

KENNA RARELY DRESSED with a man in mind. She wore whatever struck her fancy and was comfortable. Yet, she found herself staring at her reflection in the guest bedroom mirror and wondering if Channing would like her in this outfit. Or maybe that one lying on the bed. Or the one she'd tried on first. She didn't have a lot to choose from besides jeans, yoga pants and Hoof Feats costumes.

From her activity blanket on the floor, Skye offered her opinion. "Buh, buh."

Same thing she'd said at the restaurant in response to Channing. Was she thinking of him, too? Not that Kenna blamed the baby. The man practically demanded undivided attention.

"Can't go wrong with black slacks, right?" she asked.

Skye waved a rattle in the air.

"Turquoise top. I agree." She switched out blouses. "And earrings." She grabbed a pair from the small travel case she'd brought with her from the horse trailer's living quarters. Inserting the gold hoops, she swung her head from right to left in front of the mirror. When had she last worn these…or any jewelry for that matter?

"What's wrong with me?" Kenna sat on the bed, her feet at the edge of the activity blanket. "There's no point in trying to look nice for Channing," she told the baby. "Unless I'm ready to start something, which I'm not, we should remain strictly friends. No more flirting and cradling cheeks and staring. Though I do like those long stares."

Skye tossed the rattle at Kenna, and it bounced off her leg.

"Yes, he's a great guy, and I'd be a fool not to at least consider the possibilities." She sighed heavily. "But what if we start dating and things end badly? Channing's always been the one who got away. The perfect potential relationship that could never be because of circumstances beyond our control. I could lose that wonderful memory *and* our friendship, which is important to me." She pressed a hand to her middle and groaned. "Why is it every time I think about him, about us, I get all tingly inside? That is so teenage-girl-ish. I'm twenty-eight, for crying out loud."

Skye toppled over and onto her side.

"Careful, squirt. You'll wrinkle your dress."

In addition to getting herself ready for the bridal shower, Kenna had changed the baby into the adorable sundress and matching bloomers Gracie had left for her.

She bent over and took hold of Skye, lifting her into a sitting position. That earned her a gummy smile and a silly giggle.

"You're a little dickens, you know that?"

Kenna went still. Good grief. Had she just repeated what her mother said about her? *Please, God, no. Do not let me become my mother.*

A loud bang sounded from the other end of the house—the kitchen door opening and closing. It was followed by a, "Hello! Anybody home?"

Kenna poked the tip of Skye's button nose with her fingertip. "Your daddy's here. Guess he doesn't knock." Then again, this would soon be his home, too. Kenna picked up Skye and straightened, propping the baby on a hip. "Let's go." In the hall, she hollered, "Coming."

Beau waited for them in the kitchen. "There's my baby girl."

"How goes it?"

He must have showered and changed after delivering the trailer load of hay to the arena, for he wore clean jeans and a freshly laundered shirt.

Beaming a huge smile at Skye, he strode forward and held out his arms. "Gracie called me. Thanks for watching her today. I know you were busy." He took Skye from Kenna.

"No problem."

And it had been no problem, she realized. Plus, if she hadn't babysat Skye, then she wouldn't have gone to lunch with Channing, which, despite their at times uncomfortable conversation, had been fun. She truly did enjoy his company.

"You and Mom will probably need to find a backup babysitter after I leave."

"Yeah, we will. Today's just been too busy Too much going on at once." He grinned—not at Kenna, at Skye—his expression that of a father besotted with his baby daughter.

Had Kenna seen that grin before or simply missed it?

"We're ready to go," she said. "Let me grab the diaper bag. And my purse."

Another concession for the bridal shower. Kenna seldom carried a purse. She preferred to shove her phone and keys and what few items she needed into her pockets, leaving her hands free.

"Want me to drive?" Beau asked.

"I can. The car seat's already in my truck. We can swap it out at The Sip and Savor," Kenna offered, assuming Beau would return with her mom.

"You mind if I sit in the back?" he asked once they'd loaded Skye, the diaper bag and a foam seat in case the restaurant didn't have a high-chair.

"Nope. Doesn't bother me. You'll have to hold the cake and balloon bouquet, though."

"I think we can manage that, can't we, baby girl?" He kissed Skye's head.

Kenna moved her gift and the bags containing the decorations to the front seat. During the brief drive to The Sip and Savor, Beau entertained Skye with finger games and goofy faces. Kenna had to admit, he did have a way with her. And while he relied heavily on Kenna's mom for help, he hadn't shirked his paternal duties.

Skye truly was a cutie. Kenna understood why her mom had become smitten. Kenna felt a little smitten, too.

At the bistro, Kenna and Beau managed to carry everything in one trip, including Skye's foam seat. Both of them juggled their respective loads as they approached the entrance. Beau held Skye under his arm like a football, something she appeared to enjoy given her giggles.

A young smartly dressed man spotted them

and opened the glass door. "Welcome to The Sip and Savor."

At the podium, a hostess greeted them.

Kenna shifted the cake and smiled. "We're here for the Cordova bridal shower."

The young woman eyed the balloons. "Yes! Of course. If you and your husband will come with me." The hostess charged ahead. Over her shoulder, she said, "Your daughter is just precious."

"He's not… She's not—" Kenna didn't bother finishing. The hostess was already five steps ahead and not paying any attention.

Beau didn't correct her, either—it was possible he hadn't even heard her remarks. He followed behind Kenna, keeping up a constant conversation with Skye.

Relax, Kenna told herself. Who cares if the hostess misunderstood? They'd probably never see her again after tonight.

At the door to the private party room, the hostess paused before leading them inside. "Here we are," she sang out.

"Kitten! Beau!" Kenna's mom sprang up from her place of honor at the center of the long table and hurried toward them. "You made it."

"Now the party's complete." The hostess beamed. "Your daughter and her husband and your beautiful granddaughter are here."

Kenna started to object, but her mom beat her

to the punch. "Not *her* husband. *My* fiancé." She linked arms with Beau.

He leaned in and kissed her cheek. "Got that right, darling."

A stricken look passed over the young hostess's face. She couldn't have been more than seventeen or eighteen and was too inexperienced to gracefully cover her blunder.

"I'm sorry. I—I assumed. They came in together..." She faltered. "If you need anything, please let us know." With that, she executed a hasty retreat.

Kenna's mom ignored the hostess. Turning her attention to the gathering, she flashed a big smile—but not before Kenna noticed the tiny spark of pain.

Kenna gave her mom credit for not making a big deal of the hostess's slip. There probably wasn't a single person in the entire bistro who'd seen her, Beau and Skye and hadn't assumed they were a couple with their child.

Why hadn't Kenna corrected the hostess when she'd had the chance? If she had, none of this would have happened.

In the wake of the hostess's blunder, the room had gone silent, except for Beau, who made a production of sitting Skye in the foam seat and making sure she was secure.

Kenna's let her gaze discreetly travel the table.

Many of the dozen-plus guests wore stunned or sympathetic expressions. Some whispered, their heads bent together.

A mixture of emotions welled inside Kenna. Her mom and Beau would be facing this same situation for the rest of their lives. People were going to mistake Skye for her granddaughter. They may even mistake Beau for her son.

Kenna knew age shouldn't matter, but society hadn't yet caught up to her mom and Beau. And though she wished she could say it didn't matter, she feared it mattered greatly to her mom.

What would life for her and Beau be like in ten years? Or twenty, when the age difference became potentially more noticeable? Kenna's mom's insecurities already accounted for some of her over-the-top behavior. That could worsen.

Kenna's gaze landed on Channing sitting at the end of the table. He sent Kenna a warm smile that said none of what happened was her fault and to stop blaming herself. How did he know? She must be easy to read. Easy for *him* to read.

"Let's get the fun started!" Kenna's mom said, her bright smile still plastered on her face. "This bride-to-be is ready to eat and play some games. Is everyone here?" she asked Dinah.

"We're still waiting on Gail and Blythe."

Kenna prickled with concern at the mention of Beau's mom and sister. Thank goodness they'd missed the exchange with the hostess. Their reservations about the marriage would have only increased.

Would they try to talk to Kenna when they got here? Solicit her opinion on the marriage or attempt to make her their ally? She'd met Beau's family on her last visit to Payson and had liked them. His parents were down-to-earth, call-it-like-it-is people, and his sister was a hoot. They clearly liked Kenna's mom, just not as Beau's wife.

For the first time, Kenna felt a little sorry for Beau. It must be difficult, having your family unhappy about your choice of a life partner. Some people would fold under the pressure, but not Beau. Maybe he did love her mom *that much*.

"I saved you a seat."

She spun when Channing spoke close to her ear, and she smiled, ridiculously pleased to see him. "I need one after the last five minutes." She lifted the cake and boxes. "Let me take care of this stuff first."

"I'll help." He relieved her of the balloon bouquet.

"Thanks. That goes in the center of the table."

While he did as she asked, she set out the cake, paper plates, napkins and forks they'd bought in the colors her mom had chosen for the wedding.

Dinah materialized beside her. "What can I do?"

"Here." She handed the other woman the bag of decorations. "You can start on these. Are the games ready?"

"All set. I figured we'd play one after we order and the rest once we've eaten."

While they were draping streamers and arranging heart and flower ornaments at each place setting, Beau's mother and sister arrived. They went immediately to Skye, who relished the attention.

A waiter appeared as if summoned and took everyone's order. Kenna wasn't hungry. Between rushing to get here, the incident with the hostess and Channing's constant proximity, her stomach rebelled at the idea of food.

"You have to eat something," he told her when they were seated.

"I'll have a bowl of seafood chowder with sourdough bread on the side," she told the uniformed man, figuring she could get that much down.

To her vast relief, the party went well. After ordering, the guests played a game of wedding vow Mad Libs that had everyone laughing uproariously until the food arrived. Once the plates were cleared away, Dinah emceed a rousing round of newlywed trivia. Later, while she served the cake, Kenna's mom opened her gifts and Kenna kept a list of who gave what. They ended the party with a game of musical bouquet, a version of musical chairs but played with the bouquet made out of ribbons and bows from the gifts.

Kenna won the musical bouquet and was mercilessly teased that she was the next to get married. Despite that unlikelihood, numerous glances were cast at Channing and a few comments were made. But since they were both in the wedding, Kenna assumed remarks were expected.

The guests left one by one. Hugging Kenna's mom and Beau, they expressed their congratulations and eagerness to attend the wedding. All except Beau's mother and sister. They clutched Beau as if he were leaving to spend the next two years on a space station rather than getting married.

Eventually, only Channing remained. By now, Skye had become tired and cranky, and she was informing anyone within earshot.

"Channing," Kenna's mom said. "You mind taking Beau and Skye home? Kenna and I will stay and clean up."

"Not at all." He sent Kenna a glance. "You okay with that?"

"Fine by me," she said over Skye's grumpy

wails. "Thank you." She hoped he read more into the two measly words she'd spoken. *Thank you for coming. Thank you for your help, for your friendship and for being there when I needed you.* "I'll go with you and get the car seat."

At her truck, Channing held her fingers for several seconds when he took the car seat from her. "You did good, hon. Everyone enjoyed themselves."

"I was worried we'd have a major flop on our hands when the hostess made that remark about Skye being Mom's granddaughter."

"Your mom seemed to handle it well." He inched nearer. "You look good, by the way." His gaze took her in from head to toe.

"Thanks." She smiled shyly. So her silly efforts to choose the right outfit had paid off. "See you tomorrow."

"I'll bring the coffee."

"Okay." Coffee with Channing would be a nice way to start her day.

On the walk back into the restaurant, she forced herself to breathe deep. Channing had been right the other day. Yes, her mom and Beau faced some challenges, but they loved each other. And nothing Kenna did or didn't do would affect the ultimate success of their marriage.

But at the door to the private party room, she

was stopped by an unexpected sight. "Mom. Are you okay?" The next second, she hurried forward.

Her mom sat in one of the chairs, her face buried in her hands, sobbing.

CHAPTER SEVEN

"WHAT'S WRONG?" Kenna hovered over her mom's bent form, a hand on her shoulder. "Did something happen? Tell me."

"I'm fine." She collected herself and straightened, wiping at her damp cheeks.

Grabbing a chair, Kenna dragged it over and sat down so close their knees were touching. She reached for her mom's hands. "Obviously you're not."

"That hostess. When she called Beau your husband, it...hurt."

"I'm sure it did." Kenna wouldn't patronize her mom by offering a meaningless platitude or dismissing her feelings.

"His mother and sister... I overheard them talking. Gail said she's thinking of pretending to have a heart attack. That way, we'll postpone the wedding and, with luck, Beau will come to his senses."

"Oh." Kenna's heart went out to her mom. That must have been truly awful to hear, and on top of the hostess's blunder. "I'm sure Gail was joking. She doesn't strike me as the manipulative type."

"Yes, but still..." Her mom let go of Kenna's hands and reached for a napkin. "I know you're convinced Beau's the wrong man for me. That he's too young, too immature, has little ambition. And I won't lie—I have doubts, too." She sniffed and dabbed her nose. "Things like tonight are a reminder that everyone else is convinced we're a bad match, too."

Kenna straightened. "I'm glad you're being realistic and not pretending everything is rosy."

"Why is it okay for a man to marry a much younger woman but not the other way around?"

"My guess? Children. Just look at history. Men married younger women to give them healthy heirs."

Her mom rolled her eyes. "That's ridiculous. And so old-fashioned."

"I agree. But there's also the, well, physical side of it. Not that I have any experience," Kenna continued, "but I've heard it's generally harder for women in their forties to have a baby than for men to father one. Plus, and don't take this wrong, but...Mom, are you up to the task? Working weekday mornings and taking care of Skye afternoons and weekends when Beau's working? Sounds exhausting to me."

Her mom stiffened. “I get it. You don’t approve of me going to part-time at the office.”

“I know how much you love your job and how important being financially independent has always been to you. I worry you’ll regret giving that up.”

“I can always go back to full-time if I change my mind. My boss said so.”

Kenna was glad to hear that.

“And if we don’t have children.”

She struggled to swallow her surprise. “Are you and Beau considering children? Aren’t you postmenopausal?”

Her mom pushed at her short hair, once the same color as Kenna’s but now dyed several shades lighter to cover the gray. “Medical science has advanced in recent years. Women like me have babies all the time. And there are other ways. A surrogate, for instance.”

“Isn’t that expensive?” Kenna struggled to keep her voice neutral. Beau wasn’t a rich man, and her mom had recently taken a considerable pay cut.

“I think his family will be more accepting of me if I give them another grandchild.”

“Is that the best reason to have a baby?” Kenna vowed to herself that she’d have this conversation with her future husband well before the wedding. “What does Beau say?”

"He says it's up to me. Whatever I want."

"Mom, I would never tell you how to run your life, but I strongly suggest you give tremendous thought to having another child."

"I'm getting older by the day." She crumpled the napkin in her fist. "Skye's mom is twenty-four. How can I compete with that?"

Ah. Here, Kenna realized, was the crux of the matter.

"First off, Mom, you're not competing with Skye's mom. She's out of the picture for the most part."

"She comes back for visits."

"Does Beau flirt with her? Act interested? Talk about her in between visits? Express regrets?"

Her mom shook her head, her voice going soft. "No."

"Then you have no reason to fret where she's concerned."

"What about another woman? When I'm old and wrinkled and no longer attractive, Beau will still be a relatively young man. He may stray. Or worse…leave me."

"Having a baby with him is no guarantee those things won't happen."

Her mom started crying again, although not as hard.

"Mom, please. If you're this unsure, maybe you and Beau should wait."

Her mom spent several moments composing herself before saying, "Your dad was the love of my life, you know."

"I do."

"I've made so many mistakes since we lost him. I kept trying to replace him when he was irreplaceable. I chose the wrong man over and over." She squared her shoulders. "There'll never be anyone like him again, and a part of me will love him till the day I die."

Kenna felt the same. No one would ever replace her dad in her heart, either.

"But that doesn't mean I can't be happy again with someone else," her mom added.

"Of course not. And you should be. But, and don't be mad at me, you and Beau are moving at lightning speed. You've only known each other six months and you're making some very drastic changes. Going part-time at work. Taking care of Skye. Considering having another child. You just admitted you've made mistakes in the past and are having doubts about this marriage."

Her mom sighed. "When Beau and I are together, I don't notice any age difference. It's only when I see us through other people's eyes that I'm acutely aware. It makes me kind of irrational sometimes, and I go off the deep end."

"It's good you recognize that about yourself." Kenna gentled her tone. "Seriously, you don't have to get married in two weeks. You can postpone the wedding. Give yourselves another six months to test the relationship."

"What if he changes his mind?" her mom said in a squeak.

"Then he's not the man for you."

"I don't want to take the chance."

Kenna chose her words carefully. "Let me play devil's advocate for a minute. What's the worst that could happen?"

"I just said, Beau leaves me."

"He seems head over heels in love. But, again, playing devil's advocate, what if he grows to resent you because he feels trapped?"

A sob escaped. "With an old woman," her mom lamented.

"No. With someone who hurried into marriage and, maybe, had a child to ensure he wouldn't leave her."

"Can we please stop focusing on the negative?"

Kenna didn't mention her mom had started the conversation. "Have you talked to Beau about this?" she asked.

"Postponing the wedding? God, no!"

"Your concerns. Your doubts."

"I told you, I'm not doing or saying anything that might scare him off."

"Communication is important for any relationship to succeed."

Kenna's mom rose and started stacking the gifts into piles, her motions jerky, her features closed off.

"Mom," Kenna implored.

"I'll talk to Beau. When I'm ready and in my own way."

"Okay." Kenna also stood and began gathering trash. At that moment, the waiter appeared and asked if they needed anything. "We'll be done in a few minutes," she told him. "Thank you for everything. The food was fantastic."

The young man ducked out, leaving Kenna and her mom alone.

"You're a wonderful daughter." Her mom hugged her. "I love you."

"Love you, too, Mom."

"It means a lot to me, how much you care. I can't wait for you to find love." A twinkle lit her eyes. "Maybe with Channing? I saw the two of you sitting together."

"Don't hold your breath."

"Hmm. We'll see."

Kenna gathered all the bags and boxes and balloons. They'd need to make two or three trips to their vehicles. "I'm glad you're willing to consider postponing the wedding."

"Whatever gave you that idea?" She drew back

and crinkled her brow. "Beau and I are getting married."

Kenna clamped her mouth shut. Apparently, once again, she'd put herself in her mom's place and jumped to conclusions.

Rather than continue arguing, she pulled her mom into another hug. "I'll be at your wedding with bells on. And if Beau's family gives you grief, I'll defend you to the ends of the earth."

Her mom laughed, her previous distress vanishing. "You joke, but I may need that."

They carried the gifts and bags of leftovers to the parking lot. Kenna meant what she'd said—she'd support her mom fully and unconditionally.

Not because she believed this marriage would last longer than the previous two. Rather, if—when—it imploded, Kenna wanted to be at her mom's side to console her. That wouldn't happen if the two of them were estranged.

"WHERE YOU HEADED, SON?"

Channing paused at the sound of his dad's voice, his hand inches away from the doorknob. "On my way to meet Kenna."

"You have a spare second? We need to talk."

Swell. It appeared he wasn't getting out of the arena office this morning without a *little chat*, as his dad was fond of calling them. Most of the time, Channing didn't mind. Today, he was in a hurry.

"Just one," he said, turning. "I don't want to keep her waiting."

"You two getting together have anything to do with the old folks?"

"The plan is to work Sideways Sam in the round pen."

"You're working him and Kenna's watching." It wasn't a question.

He shoved his hands in his pockets, his defenses on the rise. His dad must have either heard from one of the wranglers or deduced that Kenna's involvement had been elevated from helper to more.

"Actually, if all goes well, she's going to ride him."

"That's not a good idea." His dad released a long frustrated breath. "She could get hurt, and we'd be liable."

"She's already signed a waiver for her classes and using the facilities. Just like any of our customers and competitors. We're covered."

"Nonetheless, I'd feel better if she stayed off the bucking stock. She's not trained to bronc ride."

His dad did have a point. Unlike professional rodeo competitors, she hadn't had the opportunity to practice and learn before entering the arena.

But his dad's objection went further. If he had his way, no women would *ever* ride Rim Country's bulls and broncs. Channing still couldn't believe his dad had relented about the women's bull riding. He suspected his mom might have something to do with it. Especially as she was eager for his dad to retire and for Channing to assume full management of the arena.

His sister, Jocelyn, sat at the desk in the reception area. She pretended to be on the computer, but her gaze continually darted toward Channing and their dad. She fully supported Channing's various endeavors at the arena and his ideas for the future when their dad retired. Except, as they both well knew Burle Pearce, was a force. Even at sixty-six, he easily intimidated souls far more hearty than gentle-natured Jocelyn, who didn't stand a fighting chance when he applied the pressure. Channing had inherited their dad's grit and determination and could, if needed, go toe-to-toe with him.

He shot his sister a look before addressing their dad. "Can we discuss this later? When I'm not in a rush?"

"Call Kenna. Tell her you're running late. And let's go to my office."

An official summons not to be refused. Jocelyn gave Channing a thumbs-up when he passed her desk, her subtle way of wishing him luck.

In his dad's office—the same office that he hoped would one day be his—Channing sat in the visitor chair and pulled out his phone. He composed a brief text to Kenna, informing her he'd be there in five minutes, ten at the most. Hitting Send, he sat back and waited.

"Look, son," his dad began. "I understand you wanting to rehabilitate the old folks. It's a good cause and could reflect well on the arena."

"It will. You'll see."

"Fine. But why involve Kenna?"

"Here's the thing..." Channing braced himself for the potential blowback. "She's going to ride Sideways Sam at the women's bull-riding event during the playing of the national anthem."

"What the...? You can't be serious! You're risking that poor girl's life! For what? Some publicity?"

Channing wished they'd shut the door behind them in case someone entered the front office. His sister was used to these heated exchanges. He preferred customers and employees not witness them. Or even worse, Kenna—there was a chance she'd decide to meet him here instead of waiting.

"Dad, in the first place, I would never risk her life. We're moving slowly with Sideways Sam. One small step at a time. If at any point he acts up or she appears in danger, we'll immediately stop. She's calling the shots. I'm asking no more of her than what she's comfortable and confident giving."

"You shouldn't have involved her."

"Her riding Sideways Sam at the bull riding isn't just good promotion for us," Channing said. "Hoof Feats will also benefit. And Kenna. Her performances are how she recruits new students for her classes and how Hoof Feats gets new contracts."

"I understand that. I do. But is the risk worth the reward?"

"She thinks it is, and that's what matters most."

"You sure you don't have another objective?"

"Meaning?" Channing asked.

"A personal interest in her, perhaps?"

Was his dad right? Did Channing have another objective, namely finding a way to spend more time with Kenna?

His gaze traveled the room he'd practically grown up in. Photographs of the arena at different stages of its existence lined the walls, going all the way back to his great-great-grandfather's time. Awards and plaques and trophies sat atop the credenza behind his dad's desk. More were mounted in a glass case. The large window provided a straight shot view of the arena, unobstructed when, like today, there was no event and no people.

Rodeo was in his blood—Channing felt excitement coursing through him every time he set foot on the grounds. He loved the arena and was determined to pass it on to his children and grandchildren. For that to happen, Rim Country had to grow. Change. Evolve.

"I enjoy working with Kenna," Channing admitted. "I won't lie. But I didn't invent this project just to spend time with her."

His dad pushed his coffee cup back and forth across his desk, something he did when agitated. "Doesn't alter the fact you're putting her in danger."

"She's a very experienced trick rider who's used to executing high-risk stunts with demanding precision. She knows the right way to fall." Channing repeated back the arguments Kenna had made to him when he'd questioned the wisdom of her participation.

"You're trying to convince me women have a place in rodeo and using Kenna to do it."

"That's true. I am trying to convince you. I have been for the last couple years. But I'm using the successful bull-riding event on Friday to do it, not Kenna. Registration and ticket sales are good. Excellent, in fact."

"Women's rodeo is a passing trend."

"No, it's the future. And we can either change with the times or wither and die."

His dad frowned. "You're exaggerating."

Channing had clearly struck a nerve. He attempted to backpedal rather than risk his dad shutting down completely.

"I hear your concerns, and I agree with them. The last thing I want is for Kenna, or any of the women bull riders, to get hurt."

"Will she be wearing safety equipment?"

"Yes. Absolutely."

"Won't prevent a broken neck."

Channing suppressed the urge to fire back. That would only widen the divide between them. "If I weren't confident in Kenna's abilities and in Sideways Sam's positive response to retraining, I'd nix the plan myself."

"It's an excellent idea, Dad," Jocelyn said from the doorway. "Give Channing a chance."

They both turned to see her standing with a shoulder propped on the jamb.

"This doesn't concern you, honey."

"No? Aren't I family? Don't I get a say in what happens around here?" she asked with surprising gumption.

"Of course you do."

"He's earned it. Besides," she added with a smile, "he's learned from the best."

Channing sent her a grateful nod and then picked up where she'd left off.

"I appreciate your belief in me even when you don't agree. Not everyone in your position would be supportive."

His dad harrumphed.

"Rather than take my word for it," Channing suggested, "talk to Kenna. If she expresses even one doubt or you get the feeling she's going along simply for my sake, then fine. She won't ride Sam."

"I might do that."

"Okay."

Jocelyn winked at Channing before scurrying off, the phone in the front office ringing. He'd have to thank her on his way out.

Ready to make his escape, he stood. "I really need to go."

"Come back here when you're done. I want to go over the estimates for the fencing repairs."

Did he? Channing guessed he wanted to hear about the practice session with Sideways Sam and Kenna.

"Will do," Channing said.

At that moment, the phone on his dad's desk buzzed.

"It's Hugh from the city council office," Jocelyn called from the other room.

"I have to take this. Can you shut the door behind you?"

Channing did as his dad requested. His dad had served on the city council for nearly two decades. Channing figured he'd take over his dad's seat there one day. Then he'd be taking the calls from Hugh.

Because Jocelyn was concentrating on the computer screen for real this time, Channing came up behind her and ruffled her carefully arranged hair.

"Hey! Quit it." She spun and gave him a teasing swat while feigning an indignant expression.

He ruffled her hair again, repeating an old joke between them. "What are you going to do? Tattle to Mom?"

As children, they'd bickered constantly. As adults, they were the best of friends. There was no one else he wanted to work alongside. More than once, he'd offered to comanage the arena with her, and every time she'd declined, stating she preferred having flexible hours that allowed her more time at home with her husband and young son.

"You look relatively unscathed." She gave Channing an up-and-down inspection. "Dad cave?"

"Not cave. Not come around, either. But he's

backed down a little, which is the best I can hope for."

Jocelyn glanced past Channing to their dad's closed office door. "It's the heart attack and retirement more than being set in his ways. He's hanging on to every last shred of control he can."

"He takes every suggestion I make as criticism."

"He feels personally responsible for the decrease in ticket sales over the last year and a half."

"The roller-coaster economy and rise in unemployment aren't his fault."

"No. But you're responding to outside forces in new and innovative ways. Which is good. That's what you, we, should be doing. Problem is, in Dad's mind, your attempts to promote change reflect poorly on him. And that makes him cling more strongly to those traditional beliefs even though, on some level, he knows they're hurting us."

"What do I do? How do I get him to see reason? We have to dig ourselves out of this financial hole."

"Continue with what you're doing. Present reasonable argument after reasonable argument. Remember, money talks."

Channing bent and gave her a peck on the top

of the head. “You’re too smart not to manage the arena with me.”

“Maybe I will.”

“Seriously?”

“The boys will be in preschool and first grade this fall. I’ll be ready to get out of the house more.”

“We’re going to talk about this. Soon.”

“Yes. I’d like that. But I wondering if we shouldn’t all talk.”

“Like with the folks?”

“Dad may need some convincing. It’s one thing for me to work in the office. Another to assume management responsibilities.”

“Let’s chat with Mom. Get her input.”

“Yeah. Let’s.” She shooed him away. “Now go meet Kenna. I really like her, by the way. I can see you do, too.”

Chuckling, Channing left the office. He did like Kenna—denying it with someone who knew him so well was a wasted effort.

He found Kenna tending Rocket Man and Zenith. They’d moved Sideways Sam from the old folks’ pasture and into one of the outdoor stalls. The relocation not only made the former bronc easier to catch when they were ready to work with him but, with luck, his well-behaved and docile neighbor horses would be a calming influence on him.

"Morning," Channing called as he neared. "Sorry I'm late."

She straightened from examining Rocket Man's legs for sensitivities and injuries, something he'd noticed she did daily. Rocket Man was more than a pet or a pleasure horse—Kenna made her living with him. His health and fitness, like Zenith's before him, were of paramount importance. She'd no sooner perform on a horse in less than peak physical condition than she would sporting a broken arm.

"Hiya. How goes it?" she asked.

"All right."

She met him at the stall door only to pull down her sunglasses and study his face. "What's wrong?"

"Why do you think something's wrong?"

"You're easy to read, Channing."

Was he? If that were entirely true, she'd have spotted his growing feelings for her. Then again, maybe she had. The thought intrigued him.

"I just came from meeting with my dad."

"Uh-oh." She slipped out from the stall and latched the door shut behind her. "Something you can share?"

"I told Dad about you riding Sideways Sam at the women's bull-riding event. Be warned, he may hunt you down for a chat."

"About what?"

"He thinks it's too dangerous," Channing explained as they strolled down the row of outdoor stalls to where Sideways Sam stood with his head in the corner, tail swishing and eyes half-closed.

"Let me guess." Kenna smiled. "He said something like, *You're not letting her ride that monster!*"

"Were you listening outside the window?"

"You did assure him I volunteered and have my own motives?"

Channing nodded. "But now I'm wondering if he's right. Are you sure about this, Kenna? Nothing matters more to me than your safety. Sam is a handful."

"Quit worrying," she insisted. "Sam and I will be fine and, I'm willing to bet, a huge hit at the bull riding."

"Promise me, if you have the slightest doubt or worry or hesitation, you'll tell me." He was sounding more and more like his dad by the minute. The thought unsettled him.

"I promise."

She took his hand in hers. The gesture, while innocent, felt intimate and natural and stirred memories from when they were in high school.

A moment later, she released him as they came to a stop. "We're here."

"Right." He grabbed the halter hanging beside the stall door.

"You're being overly cautious," Kenna accused when he refused to let her enter the stall with him.

Channing remained firm. "My way or the highway. Sam isn't some docile kid's mount. He's a bronc, taught to buck, and given the chance, he'll stomp you into the ground."

Sam stood patiently when Channing put the halter on him.

"See, I told you." Kenna beamed at him from the other side of the stall door. "He's a big baby."

"Don't be fooled. I've seen this innocent act before."

They led Sideways Sam the short distance to the horse barn. Inside, they tied him to the hitching post in front of the tack room.

"I noticed you pull in earlier," Channing commented as he gave Sam a brushing. He would only let Kenna near the horse's head, taking care of the hindquarters himself. "I figured you sleep in after the bridal shower last night. You must have been tired."

"I still am. It was a… We didn't have the best night after the shower."

"Everything okay?"

"Mom was upset about the hostess's remark. She held her feelings in until everyone left."

"I guess that wasn't entirely unexpected." Channing finished saddling Sam, whose one and only dangerous move was to shake his head when a pesky fly refused to leave him alone.

"No, it wasn't." Kenna gave him a brief rundown on what had happened, how she'd returned to the party room at the bistro and discovered her mom crying. "We talked. It was brutal for both of us."

"We can do this another day," he offered. "If you're not in the mood."

She shook her head. "Thanks, but I could use a distraction. And I've been looking forward to riding Sam for days."

"All right. Let's do it, then. Helmet and vest first."

She scurried into the tack room, returning a minute later with the equipment.

As they walked, tension gnawed at Channing's gut. Until the meeting with his dad, he'd been brimming with certainty. Now that certainty was waning. He really hoped they weren't making a mistake. Sam could change in an instant once he had a rider on his back.

Just outside the horse barn, they stopped short when they spotted Beau bounding toward them at breakneck speed, his normally happy-go-lucky features etched with worry.

"Kenna." He raised his arm and beckoned to her. "Can we talk? Please. It's important." He nodded to Channing when he got closer. "Sorry to interrupt, boss. But I'm really worried about Gracie. She's mighty upset, and I'm hoping Kenna can help me."

Kenna sent Channing a nervous glance before saying, "What's going on?"

CHAPTER EIGHT

KENNA HAD KNOWN Beau for as long as he'd worked at Rim Country. Longer than her mom knew him. In that time she'd never seen him frazzled. He defined *easygoing* and *laid-back*. For him to be in this state of agitation was disconcerting.

"What's wrong with Mom?" she asked.

"I think she may be getting cold feet."

Kenna took charge. "Let's head over there and get out of the sun." She indicated the hay barn across from the round pen, where six giant stacks of alfalfa, delivered and stored from Beau's recent trip to Marana, sat beneath the awning.

"I can take Sideways Sam and meet up with you later," Channing said.

"No," Beau said. "Stay. I can use all the advice I can get."

"If you're sure," Channing said.

"Course I'm sure."

Kenna wasn't easily upset, and heaven knew her mom could be a drama queen. But Beau's sorrowful expression, combined with his unusual agitation and announcement, had her concerned. She was glad he'd asked Channing to stay. She could use the support, too. For no other reason than they were friends, she told herself. No reason she'd admit to, anyway.

They made their way to the hay barn, where they ducked into the shade. Sweat lined Beau's skin and dampened his shirt. How far had he run to reach them?

Sideways Sam couldn't resist temptation. Lowering his head, he nibbled on the bits of hay scattered across the ground. Channing let out the lead rope an extra length.

"Breathe deep," Kenna said to Beau.

"I'm probably overreacting."

"What's happened to make you think she's getting cold feet?" Kenna was guessing it might have something to do with the bridal shower, her mom breaking down afterward, and their long talk.

"She was acting really strange this morning," Beau said.

"Strange how?"

"Crying when she thought I wasn't looking. Quiet, which ain't like her. Shooing me away and telling me to mind my own business."

"Did you ask her what's wrong?" Kenna hesitated, not wanting to say too much. It wasn't her place to repeat the conversation she'd had with her mom after the shower.

"I did," Beau insisted. "More'n once. She swears nothing's wrong. But she's lying. I can tell."

"Ask again. Mom clams up when she's upset."

"What do you think's the matter with her?"

Kenna considered how to give Beau a clue without overstepping. "She's getting married in a couple weeks. She's bound to have a lot on her mind."

"I reckon."

"She's stressed. Tired. Uncertain. Giving her some reassurance will help. Getting married's a big step." Kenna looked to Channing for confirmation.

"I imagine it's natural to be nervous," he agreed. "Aren't *you*?"

"Naw." Beau broke into his typical goofy grin. "Ain't nothing I want more than to marry Gracie. She's the love of my life."

"Tell her that," Kenna advised gently. "She'll like hearing it."

"I was thinking about flowers and a bottle of wine? She likes those, too."

"Good idea."

"You reckon this could this be on account of what happened at the restaurant? That gal mistaking you and me as being… Well, you were there."

He was more astute that Kenna had previously given him credit for, and her opinion of him raised another notch. And since he'd asked the question Kenna didn't feel disloyal in answering. "You might be onto something, Beau. I'd mention that to Mom if I were you. In a roundabout way. Don't bring up your age difference."

"I won't." His gaze turned thoughtful.

"The sooner the better."

"You mind if I take a long lunch, boss?"

"Not at all." Channing clapped him on the back with his free hand. "Good luck."

"Appreciate that." Beau beamed at Kenna. "And I appreciate the help, Kenna. I'm lucky to have you for a stepdaughter."

"Please don't call me that! Ever."

He laughed in response. "I won't. Not to your face."

She rolled her eyes, minding…but only a little. "One more thing. Stay after Mom. If she doesn't open up at first, push harder. Not a lot. A light nudge. She can be stubborn."

"Don't I know it." He grinned broadly. "I'd better hurry if I'm gonna stop on the way to the house and get those flowers and wine. She picks up Skye from day care around noon and should be home soon."

"Good luck." He'd impressed Kenna yet again with his insightfulness and determination. She'd certainly misjudged him.

"Catch you later. Thanks again. Both of y'all."

He sauntered off, a different man than the one who'd stopped Kenna and Channing a few minutes earlier. This one whistled a tune and had a spring to his step.

Channing pulled on Sideway Sam's lead rope. The old bronc reluctantly abandoned his foraging for tidbits. A horse was a horse, Kenna thought, regardless if it was a Shetland pony or a one-time fierce bucking champion. Food came first.

"You going to talk to your mom about this?" Channing asked as they continued to the round pen.

"No way. If she asks my opinion, like she did last night, I'll give it. That's as far as I go."

What Kenna didn't admit to Channing was how immersing herself in other people's troubles always forced her to examine her own—past, present and potential future ones. The exercise left her emotionally gutted and mentally drained. It was another reason why she didn't stick around after her mom's weddings or soured relationships. Pulling herself out of the resulting funk required weeks.

Reaching the round pen, Channing rechecked

Sideway Sam's girth, making sure it was tight. "Let me warm him up first."

Kenna smiled, happy to leave the subject of her mom and Beau—and herself—behind. "You're letting your dad get in your head."

"For once, I'm okay with that."

She could have insisted but chose not to. Better for them both that Channing trusted Sam to behave before she climbed on the horse's back.

Putting on the helmet and vest, she said, "I'll watch from here." Once she'd hauled herself to the top of the round pen fence, she swiveled and sat, her hands gripping the railing.

Channing gathered the reins in his left hand. Speaking quietly to Sam, he slowly raised his leg and put his boot in the stirrup. The horse swung his big head around to give Channing a what-are-you-doing look, but that was all. Kenna crossed her fingers.

"Easy, boy," he cooed. "That's right."

When nothing more happened, he hoisted himself up into the saddle. Sam shuffled in place for a few seconds and then rocked back and forth. Channing tightened his hold on the reins and brought the horse under control. Only when Sam stood motionless for a full minute did he cluck and jiggle the reins.

Sam started forward. Channing didn't cue the horse with his legs, Kenna noticed. That action was too similar to the repeated spurring Sam had gotten when he was ridden in competitions and encouraged to buck.

They walked two circuits of the round pen under a continued tight rein before Channing clucked again and shifted his weight. When Sam didn't start trotting, Channing applied a slight pressure with the inside of his calves. Sam lowered his head and began prancing.

Kenna swallowed a gasp. "Keep cool," she murmured, not certain if she was talking to Channing or Sam.

The old horse must have heard her, for nothing happened other than him breaking into a slow trot.

"That's right, old fellow," Channing said, his attention razor-sharp and focused on Sam.

After several minutes with the horse breaking stride only once, Channing attempted a controlled lope. Sam didn't pick up the correct lead, which was par for the course. Bucking broncs weren't trained in the finer points of reining. A small enclosure like the round pen could encourage a horse to pick up the correct lead. Other times, like today, that didn't happen.

"Whoa, boy." Channing returned Sam to a walk and tried again. This time, the horse started with the correct lead. He patted Sam's neck. "You're learning, boy."

More likely it was luck, Kenna mused.

Rider and horse completed a half-dozen more circuits without incident. Sam kept his head raised and his eyes straight ahead. A promising sign, as a horse readying to buck would lower his head for leverage.

"My turn," Kenna called to Channing on his next pass.

"Let me tire him out some more."

"Come on. He hasn't taken one wrong step."

Channing ignored her for another five minutes. She offered no more than a token objection, content to watch. He made a thrilling sight, sitting tall and straight in the saddle, confident and in command of a powerful animal. In response, her heart skipped several beats. She appreciated the skill required to gain that level of confidence.

She noted that the old horse eagerly moved out—before, he'd only plodded along. It seemed he liked to work and responded well to instruction. Who knew? They might make a Western pleasure horse out of him yet.

Finally, Channing brought Sam to a standstill.

"My turn." Kenna scrambled down the fence, dropping to the ground from the last rung. "Get off now, Channing," she insisted, expelling a long impatient breath when he took his time. "You're just stalling."

"Anyone ever mention you're a nag?" Dismounting at last, he held on to the reins and waited until Kenna joined him. "If he shows the slightest inclination to buck, you bail, you hear me?"

"Yes, sir."

"Kenna, I'm serious."

"Me, too. I'm no show-off."

"Says the person who makes her living showing off on horses."

"Seriously, Channing. I'll bail if necessary rather than get hurt." She grinned up at him. "And I'm talking about horses, not my love life."

He captured a wisp of stray hair and tucked it behind her ear, letting his hand linger while his thumb caressed her jaw. "The women's bull-riding event doesn't matter to me as much as you staying safe and sound."

Heat coiled through her, heading straight for her toes. Was that all he wanted? She almost asked but lost the courage, saying instead, "This is important. You have to show your dad that your ideas are good ones, that they're money-makers."

"What if you bust a leg? What about your career? Or your mom's wedding?"

"You're a sweet guy, Channing. And a wonderful friend."

He locked eyes with her and opened his mouth as if to… What? Object? Tell her they were much more than that? Kenna waited. But he stayed quiet—apparently, like her, he'd lost his courage or thought better of it.

Hiding a disappointment she shouldn't be feeling, she ruffled Sam's forelock. "Look at this guy. He's a teddy bear."

"A teddy bear silently contemplating how to fool the unsuspecting humans."

"Careful. He has a sensitive soul."

Channing pointed at the gate. "I'll be waiting right there. No tricks."

"Me?"

He grumbled under his breath while, together, they shortened the stirrups. Channing rechecked the girth a second time despite it having not loosened. When they were done, Kenna collected the reins and clambered onto Sam's back before Channing could try to stop her. The horse looked around again, that same what's-up expression on his face. Then he turned back as if completely disinterested.

She waited until Channing was safely outside the round pen before clucking and jiggling the reins like she'd seen him do. Sam immediately broke into a walk, a little faster than he had with Channing. No problem. Kenna could handle it.

"Slow him down," Channing said.

"He's just stretching his legs."

"I don't care. Slow him down."

She did. For now. She'd give the horse, and Channing, another few minutes to relax and see that she was in complete control. Then she'd ask more of Sam and test for herself what the horse was capable of. She made three more circuits before easing Sam into a jog, her confidence growing. He had a rocky gait, and Kenna struggled to keep herself planted firmly in the saddle. Maybe she'd been wrong before. With his thick, muscled body and big bones, Sam would never make a Western pleasure horse. But a decent ranch horse? Maybe.

"What do you think?" she asked, quite delighted with herself. "I could drop the reins and try a hippodrome."

"Don't you dare," Channing warned, his tone sharp.

Kenna had half a mind to do it. She didn't, however. She'd made Channing a promise. Besides, he was right about her not needing to get hurt.

"Kidding," she teased.

"You'd better be."

The next instant, Sam broke gait, dipped his head and gave a funny hop, kicking out with one back hoof. "What was that?" Kenna's stomach pitched, then settled when Sam did, too.

"I don't know." Alarm had filled Channing's voice. "I think you should quit."

"He seems fine now." After another circuit, Kenna relaxed when Sam's gait returned to its former easy and regular rhythm. "Must have been a fly bothering him again, or a muscle cramp. He's not used to this kind of workout."

"Careful."

"I'm going to try loping him."

Sam performed like a pro. On the third circuit, he repeated the head dip and funny hop.

"What was th—"

Kenna didn't finish. All at once, the world tilted on its axis. Head spinning, she watched as the horizon disappeared—replaced by the ground rushing up to meet her and colliding solidly with her left side. White and red starbursts filled her vision as all the air escaped from her lungs in a whoosh.

CHANNING BANGED OPEN the round pen gate and charged in. His blood pounded and his heart slammed violently into his rib cage. "Kenna! Kenna!"

Please, God, let her be all right. What had he been thinking? She had no business whatsoever riding a bucking horse. Reaching her side, he dropped to one knee. To his enormous relief, she was already hauling herself upright and re-adjusting her helmet.

"Easy, honey. Don't move." He placed a hand

on her shoulder, restraining her. "You could be hurt."

"I'm not. But my pride is. Okay, my left elbow is possibly sprained." She moved it and winced. "Ouch."

"Do you need to see a doctor?"

"Oh, for crying out loud, Channing. You're hovering. Give me some space." She shooed him away with her uninjured arm.

He reluctantly backed up. Three inches, to be exact.

She found her sunglasses in the dirt, tapped them on her knee to dislodge the dirt and then pushed them onto her face. Satisfied, she climbed to her feet, using the hand he offered for support. He was glad to observe that, while moving stiffly, nothing appeared broken. He'd bet money she'd be hobbling tomorrow during her class. That had been some tumble. He'd also bet she'd tough her way through it. Kenna wouldn't let a few bumps and bruises keep her down.

Swiping her hands together, she started toward Sam. The horse stood ten feet away, tail swishing and ears flicking—the picture of innocence. He hadn't even gone out the partially open gate.

"What are you doing?" Channing sprang to his feet when he realized her intentions. "You are not riding that horse again."

"Yes, I am."

"I'm serious, Kenna."

"Me, too. You know the old saying. When you fall off the horse, get right back on."

"Don't joke with me."

"Sam needs to know he can't get away with throwing me."

"I'll ride him." Channing caught up with, and then passed, her.

"'Fraid not." She snaked her arm around him and snatched the reins.

"Kenna. Honey."

"Five minutes. Just long enough for him to realize I'm the one in charge. Not him."

"He'll throw you again." Channing couldn't survive a second tumble. "He can't help himself."

"What happened was my fault," she insisted. "A case of overconfidence. That won't happen again." She turned and faced Channing, her hands on her hips. "And let's be honest. That wasn't much of a buck. If he really and truly meant to hurt me, he'd have tossed me over the side of the round pen. Zenith has sent me sailing far worse than this little whoops. The only reason I landed so hard was because I broke the cardinal rule of trick riding."

"Which is?"

"Concentration. But I've learned my lesson, and Sam will, too."

Every fiber of Channing's being rebelled, and

not just because his dad would have a fit if he found out. Given his choice, he'd tuck Kenna under his arm and carry her outside the round pen to safety. But she was right about getting on Sam again. Not just to teach the old horse a lesson—she needed to ride him in order to overcome her own fears. Kenna couldn't afford to let doubts and uncertainties creep in. Not in her profession. That, more than the likelihood of Sam bucking again, would get her hurt.

"I'm staying in here," he said. When she attempted to intimidate him with a look, he folded his arms over his chest. "It's that or you're not getting on the horse."

She groaned with frustration. "You're impossible."

"Take it or leave it." He had half a mind to never let her fifty feet near a bucking horse again. If she still insisted, he'd encase her in Bubble Wrap. Or keep her close to him and refuse to let her go.

Except that would be impossible. She was leaving. Soon. In just over two weeks. He didn't like thinking about that day.

As he watched her hop onto Sam's back, his hands balled into tight fists. He had to stop himself from stepping in front of Sam when she nudged him into a trot.

"You're killing me," he complained when Sam loped past.

"Chill, will you? You're making both of us nervous."

Them? What about him?

Five minutes, by Channing's calculations, was two seconds shy of an eternity. During that time, Sam behaved. Kenna had been right—he needed to realize who was in charge. For her part, she remained hyper-attentive the entire ride, as evidenced by her rigid posture. Channing was about to suggest she'd made her point and enough was enough when she slowed Sam to a walk. Two more circuits of the pen, then she pulled him to a stop.

"That should do it," she announced.

Channing walked toward her. As he neared, she suddenly dropped the reins and held her arms out perpendicular to her sides.

"Have you lost your mind?" He grabbed for the reins.

"Leave them," she ordered.

He did, though the effort cost him. Finally, she lowered her arms and retrieved the loose reins. Clutching the saddle horn with her other hand, she jumped down, landing lightly on her feet. Guess she wasn't that sore and bruised from earlier.

"It's a teaching exercise."

"It's a potential trip to the hospital." Channing felt the tension leave by small degrees. "What am I going to do with you?"

She smiled. "Next session, we try the flag."

"We'll see." The thing was, she'd practice with the flag whether he liked it or not. "On one condition," he said. "You wear a helmet and vest over your costume the night of the bull riding."

"We'll see," she echoed.

Channing ground his teeth. She did that to him, sent his emotions shooting all over the place. He told himself she was safe. In one piece. Unscathed. But it was as if his mind refused to accept the proof in front of his eyes and demanded he confirm for himself.

She turned toward the gate, Sideways Sam in tow. Channing moved, putting himself directly in her path, and she walked straight into his open arms.

"What's this?" she asked, surprise in her voice.

"Relax."

"Channing..."

"Humor me. I need a minute." Long enough to be assured she was okay.

She wrapped her free arm around his waist. His two arms circled her, and he rested his chin on the top of her head. It was nice how they fit together. He remembered that from their dance and kiss fourteen years ago.

"Channing," she repeated.

"Yes?"

"It's been *two* minutes."

"Time flies when you're having fun."

He drew back and stared down into her face, unable to release her.

"If we were in a movie," she said, "you'd kiss me now."

He'd been wanting to do precisely that for a long time now. Whenever she came home for a visit and they ran into each other. Constantly of late. Something had changed between them, and he was done resisting.

"I would."

"Then what are you waiting for?" She closed her eyes and lifted her lips in invitation.

Channing pulled her closer but stopped there. This moment would only ever happen once, and he wanted it to last.

She leaned into his embrace, which proved his undoing. He lowered his head and covered her mouth with his. The fireworks he'd imagined exploded between them. Her soft sigh said she felt them, too.

In the distance, a truck engine rumbled. A horse whinnied. Sam shook his head and snorted. Channing's phone pinged with a notification. He ignored all of that. Only Kenna and the fireworks between them existed. At some point—everything had become foggy—he pulled away. She stood on tiptoe and drew his head back down to her, kissing him anew. Okay by him. He could stay right here in this spot forever. No *problemo.*

Eventually, as was bound to happen, they parted. Cradling his face in her hands, she stared at him. No, *into* him. To the very center of his soul where he hid his dreams and secret desires and scars he'd rather no one saw.

"That was...um..." Channing faltered. He wasn't often at a loss for words.

A teasing light flickered in her eyes. "You weren't bragging the other day. You have gotten better at kissing since high school."

"I was nervous then."

"And now?"

"I like you, Kenna. A lot. I think that's obvious."

She suddenly sobered and withdrew her arms.

"Too much? Too soon?" he asked.

"I like you, too, Channing. Also a lot. It's just that..." The eyes she lifted to him now had gone from teasing to brimming with uncertainty.

"You're leaving after the wedding."

"I am." She smiled sadly. "I wish I could say I'm okay with getting together whenever I'm in town. But I'm not. I don't do casual hookups."

"Me, neither."

"My schedule is so busy. I can't say for certain when I'll next be in Payson."

Part of him longed to say he'd fly or drive to see her like some guys on the rodeo circuit did with their girlfriends. But he couldn't be away. Not until the arena was doing better and he'd proved to his dad—and himself—that he was capable of taking over management.

Failure wasn't an option. His entire family depended on their salaries from Rim Country. His parents were counting on drawing a monthly stipend to supplement their social security, and his sister needed the income for her two young sons. Channing could probably find employment elsewhere, but the arena was his life and, with luck, a legacy he'd pass on to future Pearce generations.

"I get it," he said, giving her an easy way out. "I shouldn't have...pressured you."

"It's not just my schedule," she said and led Sam through the gate, his big hooves shuffling along. Channing followed, latching the gate after them. "I'm kind of messed up when it comes to relationships."

"Maybe you just haven't found the right partner. Or aren't ready to settle down."

"Possibly." She removed the helmet and wiped her damp forehead with the back of her wrist. "Sometimes I think there's something wrong with me, like a flaw I developed when my dad died."

"There's nothing wrong with you, Kenna."

She sighed. "I fantasize about having a place to call home. Getting married. Having kids one day. But then I look at my mom and all the mistakes she's made and think, that could be me if I pick the wrong man. Heck, I did almost pick the wrong man." They reached the horse stables. At the entrance, she paused. "You're a real catch, Channing, and I'm not just saying that. Frankly, I'm surprised you've stayed single this long. It can't be for lack of prospects. This town is full of them and the arena is a magnet for women."

He attempted a grin. "What if I said I've been waiting for you?"

"We both know that isn't true."

"It's a little true, Kenna. I knew at fourteen how I felt about you. That hasn't changed."

"The timing's not right for us." She lifted her hand to his cheek. "I wish it were."

"Any chance it will be in the near future?"

"I can't answer that. Hoof Feats has contracts through December, and beyond that if we renew them. The decision to cancel isn't mine alone. Madison and the other teammates have a say."

"Understood." He cleared his throat, trying to conceal the tightness there. He didn't think he'd succeeded given Kenna's teary expression.

"I'm sorry," she murmured. "I shouldn't have kissed you. I gave you the wrong impression."

Her remorse hit Channing like a kick to the gut. He suddenly needed to put some distance between him and Kenna before he either kissed her again or pleaded with her to change her mind and give them a chance.

"I'll take Sam from here," he said, relieving her of the reins. "See you in the morning."

She didn't stop him or chase after him. When he reached the horse barn, he glanced back in the direction he'd come. By then, Kenna had disappeared.

CHAPTER NINE

EVERY BONE IN Kenna's body ached, and not just from the fall off Sideways Sam two days ago. She'd spent a full day teaching trick riding to her advanced students. They were good, the majority of them accomplished competitors, and considerably more demanding than her beginner students last weekend. Thanks to word of mouth, registration had picked up during the past week, and the class had reached maximum capacity.

With the higher level of skill and talent, Kenna had been required to demonstrate far more complex tricks. The hot shower and over-the-counter pain relievers she'd started her day with hadn't lasted long. By midday, she was hiding her limp, downing more pain relievers and slathering oodles of ointment on her elbow and side during a lunch break in her trailer's living quarters.

The only real escape from pain she enjoyed was during those frequent moments when she recalled kissing Channing. Yes, it was wrong. No, they shouldn't have done it—they were only setting themselves up for misery. Yes, she'd treasure the memory always. And, yes, if things were different, she'd… What?

Travel less? Stay in Payson? Take up horse training like Channing had suggested? Teach more than the occasional Saturdays class?

Stop! What was she thinking? Leaving Madison and her other teammates in the lurch in order to pursue a romance wasn't an option. Hoof Feats might—okay, would—eventually recover, but at a cost. Lost income for starters. Not to mention the hit to their reputation. Their sponsors had contracted with them expecting Kenna to be one of the two headliners.

Lost in thought, she exited the practice ring, Rocket Man ambling along beside her. She'd picked him rather than Zenith to use with the advanced students. Zenith's poor arthritic joints would have prevented him from keeping up with the intense physical demands.

As if knowing he'd locked in his position as her new performance partner—Kenna had delivered the check to Rochelle two days ago—Rocket Man had been nothing short of perfect today, exceeding all her expectations and proving she'd chosen wisely.

True, her heart ached a little at not being able to use her beloved Zenith anymore, but the old horse would travel with her until that became impossible. Eventually, someday, she'd find a nice place with open pastures where he could live out the remainder of his days in comfort. Here at Rim Country? Channing took excellent care of the old folks. He would take excellent care of Zenith, too.

Kenna pushed the thought away. She and her best equine buddy still had many months left to travel the country. Unless she stayed in Payson… which she wasn't doing. No point entertaining fanciful notions.

"Kenna! I just wanted to say thanks so much."

Rousing herself, she peered over Rocket Man's neck and spotted one of her students. "Hi, Piper. You're very welcome."

The high school senior caught up with her. "You have a minute to talk to me and my parents?"

"Sure." All Kenna wanted was to put Rocket Man away, limp home and hit the shower again. But business came first. Piper was a return student and had brought a friend along today. "Lead the way."

They met up with Piper's parents at their top-of-the-line SUV and all-the-bells-and-whistles horse trailer. Apparently, the couple had money. They'd certainly invested a considerable amount of their disposable income in their daughter's riding pursuits. Some parents, Kenna had learned, considered it money well spent, similar to high school athletics or dance and music lessons. They were committed to keeping their child engaged in a positive activity that challenged them and, hopefully, taught them worthwhile values.

Of course, there were always a few parents who lived vicariously through their children. Kenna had seen and dealt with her share. She'd been lucky growing up with two supportive parents who gave her what she needed to thrive without inserting themselves into her activities. After her dad died, her mom continued to see that Kenna got dance and gymnastic and riding lessons and was able to compete in horse shows to her heart's content.

At the time, Kenna had believed her mom was trying to help fill the giant hole in Kenna's life. But being repeatedly shuffled aside and excluded for over more than a decade had changed her opinion. She often wondered if her mom had merely been keeping Kenna busy and occupied so she wouldn't have to deal with the demands of a teenager, which then freed her to pursue new relationships.

Not a kind or flattering thought to have about her mom. Sadly, nothing over the years had changed Kenna's mind.

"Another great class," Piper's mom said, pulling Kenna back to the present. "Piper loves coming."

"Thank you, Mrs. Fensand. I always enjoy

having her. She's very talented and a hard worker."

"Well." Piper's dad wrapped an arm around his daughter's shoulders. Unlike his wife, he wasn't particularly tall, and he and Piper were almost the same height. "That's what we wanted to chat with you about."

"Okay." Kenna waited, smiling congenially. This was nothing new. Parents regularly sought her opinion on their child's potential, and Kenna endeavored to be honest while also encouraging.

"I want to be a professional trick rider like you," Piper blurted.

"Oh. All right."

"Do you think she has what it takes?" Mrs. Fensand asked. "I've heard the competition is tough."

"You heard right," Kenna agreed. "There are limited opportunities. Plus, like most sports, it requires determination and commitment and sacrifice. Piper is talented. No question. And an excellent athlete. Is she more talented than the rest? That needs to be tested."

"I'm willing." Piper clutched her hands together, eagerness lighting her face. "I'll do anything."

"She's excelled in local horse shows," her mom added. "Made it all the way to State the last three years."

"That's good, of course. Experience helps." Kenna thought for a moment. "Aren't you graduating next month?"

Piper nodded.

"What are your plans after that?"

"Piper's been accepted to three universities," her dad said, smiling with pride.

"Congratulations. Good for you."

"I'm taking a gap year," Piper interjected. "To try trick riding."

"She's *considering* taking a gap year," her mom corrected. "Which is why we're talking to you."

"That's a huge decision," Kenna cautioned both the girl and her parents. "Are you absolutely sure? College is important."

"That's what her dad and I say."

"Mom," Piper complained.

"I took a gap year, too," Kenna said.

"See." Piper puffed up as if proven right.

"To be honest, it was a decision I came to regret. One year turned into two and then four and then six. I did finally wind up taking online classes, but I can only fit in about three a year when my schedule allows."

Kenna had eventually enrolled at Eastern Arizona College. She was close to obtaining an associate degree in business admin, needing only fifteen more hours to graduate. She wanted a degree for her career, yes, but also for herself. If she were to stay in Payson, that was something she could accomplish in a couple semesters. Channing had also attended Eastern Arizona College. They'd share an alma mater.

Yeesh, everything did not need to connect to Channing. She forced her attention back on Piper.

"Another thing to consider..." Kenna said. "Professional athletes tend to retire young. They also sometimes get injured and have their careers ended prematurely. You need a fallback plan."

"College isn't for everyone," the teenager insisted.

"You won't know it isn't for you until you try," her mom said. She was an older version of her sweet-faced daughter, just with short-cropped hair and too much lipstick.

"What do you recommend?" Mr. Fensand asked.

Kenna recalled when she'd first started professionally trick riding. Back in those days, a mentor had given her a helping hand. Without it, Kenna wouldn't have succeeded, and she was a big believer in paying it forward.

"I have an idea," she said. "But I need to run it by my partner, Madison. I think you met her the last time I gave a class in Payson."

"We did," Mrs. Fensand said.

"She's coming to town in a week and a half for my mom's wedding—we could set up a meeting for while she's here. She and I will need to talk and iron out the details before then. But if she agrees, maybe Piper can spend a month or six weeks touring with Hoof Feats over the summer."

"Really!" Piper squealed with excitement and whirled to face her parents. "Mom, Dad, can I? Please?"

"This would be an unpaid internship, mind you," Kenna advised. "You'd have to cover your own expenses and those of your horse. Gas. Meals. Lodging, if necessary. You'd also need your own vehicle and horse trailer. And there are no guarantees you'd have any solo performances."

"I don't care."

"You'd be expected to work as hard as anyone else, even though you aren't getting paid and may not perform. We are a team."

"I will. I swear it."

"Up early. Long grueling days. Late nights."

Mr. Fensand laughed. "She's young. Every night's a late night for her."

They discussed more of the specifics. Ten minutes later, Kenna bid the Fensands goodbye with a final reminder. "Again, no promises. I still have to get my partner's consent and hear from the other teammates."

Kenna was suddenly knocked off balance when Piper smothered her in a hug. "You're the best."

Kenna's mood lifted after that. She liked Piper and believed the girl might have what it took to be a professional trick rider, though she still hated the idea of her postponing college. Six weeks traveling with Hoof Feats would either convince the teenager she'd made a terrible mistake or the opposite: introduce her to a lifelong passion as it had Kenna.

KENNA AND ROCKET MAN meandered along from her trailer to his stall, both of them drained. And the day wasn't over. She'd promised her mom she'd help make wedding favors this evening.

As they rounded the horse barn, Kenna's back pocket vibrated. She dug out her phone and, seeing Madison's number, answered with a bright, "Why, hello. You must be a mind reader. I was just talking about you."

"Oh, yeah? With whom?"

"The—" Kenna had been about to say the Fensands but decided to wait and ease into the subject of Piper's possible internship. "With one of my students."

"Ah. How'd class go?" her partner asked with her perpetual cheeriness.

"Fantastic. My best yet. These gals were off-the-charts talented. I even learned a thing or two."

"I find that hard to believe."

Kenna laughed. "It's true. A new way to pull out of a sidesaddle layout. I'll show you when you get here."

"This I have to see."

"Where are you?" she asked, changing the subject.

"An hour outside Lubbock. Everyone said to tell you hi and we miss you."

The Hoof Feats team members frequently traveled in a caravan. Though sometimes they went separately if one of them made a detour to visit family or friends or needed time off for personal reasons.

"I miss you all, too." And Kenna meant it. She loved performing and the camaraderie she enjoyed with all the Hoof Feats team members. "Tell me how it's going. Spare no details."

"San Antonio was a disaster. Carolyn got in a fight with her boyfriend right before we went on. Her mind was off in la-la land after that, and she dropped the banner. Every horse in line ran over it. Grandma's sewing us a replacement as we speak."

"No way!"

"And that was only the start of it." Madison groaned and went on to describe additional Carolyn-caused disasters. Turning the wrong way during a drill. Executing a move out of order. Missing her cue and coming in late. "We covered for her well enough. I don't suppose too many in the audience noticed the flubs, but I did."

Carolyn was their youngest team member, only a year older than Piper, in fact. She and her boyfriend often fought, the distance and time apart putting pressure on their relationship. Carolyn thought he might have a wandering eye that made the weeks apart all the harder.

Kenna contemplated her and Channing. While she doubted he was the cheating type, long-distance relationships often suffered temptation. She'd seen her share of painful breakups over the years for exactly this reason, and sometimes with couples she'd thought would be together forever.

"She says she's thinking of quitting," Madison continued, referring to Carolyn.

"Is she serious?"

"Oh, you know her. Serious one minute but not the next. I'll believe it when she packs her bags and hits the road."

"I may have a replacement for her if she does choose to leave."

“Who?”

“Do you remember Piper Fensand?”

Kenna and Rocket Man had reached his stall. Tucking her phone under her chin, Kenna opened the door. The hungry horse shoved past her and dove straight for his food trough. She had to fight him to get his halter off. Latching the door behind her, she went over to Zenith and gave him some loving while she conversed with Madison. He’d eaten earlier and was content to bask in her attention.

“I was talking with her and her parents after class today,” Kenna said. “You met them once.”

“Piper’s the tall gal? Freckles. Skinny as a broom stick?”

“That’s her.”

“She’s quite the go-getter as I recall.”

“The Fensands asked if I thought she had the potential to be a professional trick rider. She wants to take a gap year to give it a try before going to college.”

“I don’t know.” Doubt crept into Madison’s voice. “I’m not sure we can afford another member.”

“No, no. I suggested she join us for four or six weeks during the summer as an unpaid intern. She’d have to front her own expenses and provide her own vehicle and trailer.”

“Hmm.”

"I was thinking we could meet with Piper and her parents when you come to town for the wedding."

"Will we have time?"

"We can surely sneak away for an hour or two. Worst case, we can talk to them at the women's bull-riding event on Friday. After I ride Sideways Sam for the national anthem." She waited for her friend's reaction.

"Is that one of the former bucking horses? Oh, my God, that is so cool."

"Yeah. I'm excited. Though we still have some work to do. He threw me the other day."

"Are you all right?"

"Fine," Kenna insisted. "It was a minor power struggle, which I won. Channing and I are giving him another ride tomorrow morning before the team-penning competition starts. With me carrying the flag this time."

"Ooh. You and Channing," her friend singsonged. "How's that going? Evidently well since you mention him every phone call."

"I do not." But Kenna did. She'd tried to tamp down her feelings without any success. "We've been flirting a lot lately," she admitted. "And we've kissed."

"Like I'm surprised."

"Twice, though the first time was just a peck. Yesterday, however..."

"Was not a peck," Madison finished for her.

"Definitely not."

"You don't sound happy."

"I'm not *un*happy."

"Confused?" Eight hundred miles separating them and still her friend could get right to the core of the matter.

"Every time I think I've figured out how I feel, I change my mind. We're friends. We *were* friends and could potentially be more. Maybe we should stay friends. Safer that way. I'm just not sure."

"I'll clear up the confusion for you. Friends don't kiss."

"No, they don't."

"Was he any good?"

Kenna sighed. "What do you think?"

"And you totally enjoyed kissing him. Don't lie."

"Which is why we have to stop before one or both of us gets hurt."

"You don't know for sure that'll happen," Madison said.

"Even under the best of circumstances, Channing and I could only see each other two or three days every month. What kind of relationship is that?"

"Love will find a way."

"Ha! Look at Carolyn. I refuse to be like her,

where my conversations with my boyfriend are mostly phone calls and video chats that end in arguments. I doubt Channing would want that, either."

"Have you asked him?"

"He has a ton going on with the arena." She briefly explained the financial situation.

"That's a bummer," Madison said, her tone sympathetic.

"Yeah. And he doesn't need the complications of a long-distance relationship on top of that."

"Don't hate me or anything..."

"What?"

Madison drew in a breath. "It sounds a little like you're making excuses again. I mean, seeing as how you avoid commitment, a long-distance relationship is right up your alley. You could have a boyfriend but, at the same time, not have one."

Kenna frowned, disliking Madison's assessment of her. "I'm on the road. I avoid commitments because I don't do casual hookups."

"What came first, the chicken or the egg?"

"Excuse me?"

"I'll rephrase. Do you avoid commitment because you're on the road or are you on the road to avoid commitment?"

One more less-than-flattering assessment. Kenna's mood soured.

"My mom is perfectly fine putting herself out

there only to be knocked down and kicked in the ribs. Not me. I've had that happen twice before, and I'm in no way ready for round three."

She didn't have to explain herself to Madison, who knew Kenna was referring to her dad and Dennis, the horse trainer she'd thought she might be in love with and had considered marrying. Her dad's death had been much worse, but both experiences had devastated Kenna and left her leery of trying again.

"When are you going to stop letting the past shape your future?"

Another straight-to-the-core-of-the-matter question. Madison had a real knack for them.

"It's not like that," Kenna snapped. Except it was like that. It couldn't be any more like that.

"I'm sorry. I shouldn't have pushed. I can't help thinking Channing's such an amazing guy and he's clearly into you. It's a shame to let a few obstacles ruin what could be a glorious romance."

"The timing's not right." Wasn't that what she'd told Channing yesterday? "We both agreed we shouldn't have kissed. That it was a mistake."

Only they hadn't both agreed. Kenna had insisted, not him.

"What did he say today?" Madison asked.

"Actually, I haven't seen him. I had my class, and he didn't come around like usual."

"I suppose you have your answer," Madison speculated. "He's not interested enough to fight for the two of you. That, or you scared him off."

Was it true? Maybe Madison was right and Kenna had discouraged Channing. But that was what she'd wanted, wasn't it? So that neither of them got hurt?

"I swear, this trip home, nothing's been the same," she bemoaned. "Between mom's wedding and this intense attraction to Channing, I'm a total wreck."

"Well, yeah."

"Why now? It's not like I didn't see him every trip home."

"You're seeing him every day. Spending all that lovely time with him."

"The strain is killing me." Kenna rubbed her temple.

"Weddings are emotional. They lower a person's defenses. Make them weepy and vulnerable. Women, especially. Men, too, though they won't admit it. You should have seen my dad when my sister got married."

"This is ridiculous. For the last ten years, I've been content with my life. I have. Now it's as if the universe or fate is saying, silly you, that was merely an illusion."

"Could be fate showing you there's someone out there for you and his name is Channing."

"You're smiling," Kenna accused.

"A little."

"Look, I have to run. We're making wedding favors tonight at Mom's."

While true, they weren't making the favors for another two hours. But Kenna desperately needed to shower and decompress to clear her head.

"You okay?" Madison asked.

"Terrific."

"Are *we* okay?"

"We're fine."

Madison would have to do a lot more than speak a few painful truths for Kenna to get mad at her.

"Good. Then I have one last thing to tell you. Find Channing. Talk to him. Make sure the two of you are okay. You've been friends a long time. Plus, he's in the wedding."

"You're right. I will." They hung up, and Kenna bid the two four-legged males in her life good-night. Patting both Zenith and Rocket Man, she said, "Have a good night, boys. I love you."

By then, the rodeo grounds were deserted. Her students and their families were long gone. The wranglers had finished with the evening feeding and prepping for tomorrow's calf roping practice. A quiet and solitude Kenna had rarely seen fell over the arena. It was almost eerie.

On the other side of the horse barn, her gaze traveled to the entrance and office. An indistinguishable figure passed in front of a window. Someone was still working. Who, Kenna couldn't tell. Beyond the entrance, the parking area stretched for a hundred yards. A few lonely vehicles sat several spaces apart, including Kenna's and Channing's trucks. Her pulse raced in a combination of excitement and anticipation. Was he the someone pacing in the office?

Madison was right. Kenna should make sure things were okay between her and Channing. For the sake of the wedding if nothing else.

Mustering her courage, she strode purposefully toward the office, her boots kicking up little dust clouds on the dry ground. Reaching the entrance, she glimpsed the open sign posted in the window. She tested the knob and found it gave easily. Pushing open the door, she entered, glad to see the lights in the reception area were burning brightly.

Channing's sister wasn't sitting in her usual place at the front desk. Since it was well after five o'clock, she'd probably gone home to be with her family. Whomever Kenna had seen through the window was either Channing or one of his parents. She hoped the former. Otherwise, she'd have to admit to his mom or dad that she was looking for him, and they might ask why.

While Kenna was mentally concocting an excuse should one be required, she heard muted voices from down the hall. Two of them. Channing and his dad? She strained to hear better. Yeah, it was them. They were probably talking arena business.

Should she wait? Leave and go home? Hanging around felt a little like eavesdropping. Better she go back outside and sit on one of the benches. If Channing didn't appear after five or ten minutes, she'd hurry home for that shower and making wedding favors with her mom.

She turned when the voices suddenly rose in volume and intensity. Uh-oh. Channing and his dad were having a loud discussion. She could now hear some of what they were saying and winced.

"Women's bull riding…"

"…car show…"

"Why are you always being so stubborn?"

"…Sideways Sam."

"Kenna…"

Were they arguing about her and the fall from yesterday? Channing's dad hadn't been sold on the idea of her riding the former bucking horse, though he hadn't talked with her as Channing said he might.

Her nerves hummed. She'd inadvertently stumbled on a conversation between Channing and his dad that she wasn't meant to hear. One where she was a source of discourse between them.

Trembling slightly from embarrassment and guilt, she covered the remaining distance to the door. As her fingers closed on the knob, she heard a loud noise and froze. The next instant, footsteps echoed behind her. Try as she might, she couldn't escape fast enough.

"Kenna? Is that you?" Channing called.

"Sorry," she mumbled and ran out.

CHAPTER TEN

"WAIT!" CHANNING CALLED again and broke into a jog, catching up with Kenna near the main entrance.

As if the disagreement with his dad wasn't bad enough, now they'd upset her. His day could not get any worse.

She still refused to stop, charging ahead. Exactly how much of his argument with his dad had she overheard? Dumb question. Clearly enough not to want to talk with him.

"Hey. Hold up a sec." He reached for her arm and managed to waylay her. "Are you okay?"

She came to a reluctant stop. "Why is everyone asking me that?"

"Who's everyone?"

"Never mind. I'm fine. Just in a hurry." She glanced toward the parking lot. "Mom's waiting on me. We're supposed to make wedding favors tonight."

"Were you looking for me back there in the office?"

"No!"

"Then who?" he asked.

"I was… Forget it. Can I go now?"

"Whatever you heard, it's not what you think."

"I didn't hear anything."

Not true. Her stilted speech and flushed complexion gave her away.

"Dad and I don't always see eye to eye. You know that. Our debates can become lively." That was putting it mildly.

"I should have left when I realized… I'm sorry," she repeated.

He massaged his forehead, which had started to pound during the confrontation with his dad. "Quit apologizing. None of this is your fault."

"You were talking about me and Sideways Sam. I heard you. And you and your dad were talking about me the other day at my trailer, too, weren't you?"

"I promise, we weren't arguing about you. Not really. Dad's mad at me for negotiating with an auction company." Channing stopped short before saying, *He brought you up because he knows I care about you.* Instead, he said, "He brought you up because you're an easy button of mine to push. That's all."

She didn't appear convinced.

Grabbing her hand, Channing glanced around. "Come on. Let's get out of here and find someplace more private." He didn't want to be standing there with Kenna when his dad emerged from the office.

"Where are we going?" she asked, hurrying along beside him and, he was relieved to see, not resisting.

"I could use a cold drink. How about you?"

"I guess."

He took her around the corner of the building to the concession stand. Removing a ring of keys from his jeans pocket, he unlocked the employee and delivery entrance. Inside, warm stagnant air enveloped them. The concession stand was open and staffed only during public ticketed events. Not for practices, livestock groups, or classes like Kenna's. It had been sitting closed for the last several days, the windows shut and the air-conditioning turned off. It was, however, spanking clean and free of offensive odors, Channing noted. The crew was doing their job.

"This way," he said.

They passed a walk-in cooler, a storage closet, a dishwashing station and the prepping counter before entering the central area where meal assembly, beverage dispensing and selling was performed. A row of four customer service windows were sealed shut with the blinds drawn.

Channing wove in between the food warmers and a freestanding freezer containing ice-cream treats. At the beverage station, he yanked a couple cups free from the dispenser and filled them with ice.

"Diet cola?" He held the cup under the spout.

"Thanks."

"Two straws, right?"

Surprise lit her features. "Yeah."

She hadn't expected him to know her tastes so well. Well, she'd be surprised to learn how much attention he'd been paying to her since high school.

Removing two straws from the holder, he passed them to her along with her diet cola. She stubbed the straws on the counter, forcing the tops free of their wrapping. Stripping the remaining paper away, she stuck the straws in her cup.

The icy drink hit the spot, and Channing downed a large portion of his. Disagreements with his dad left him weary and parched. Setting his cup on the counter, he dragged two wobbly stools over from the corner for him and Kenna to sit on.

When they were both settled, he explained, "We're hosting a classic car auction in July. That's what the lively debate with Dad was about."

"An auction?"

"There'll be over a hundred cars from the 1970s and earlier. I just finalized the contract with the auction company today."

"Really?" The lines of worry on her face softened slightly. "That's cool."

"The timing couldn't be better. July is high tourist season in Payson. It's a two-night event, and a lot of people will travel from Phoenix and Tucson and maybe even California to get out of the heat. The local motels are reserving blocks of rooms in anticipation of reservations."

"And your dad's not happy about this?"

"Everything came together really quickly over the last few days. I contacted the chamber of commerce asking for some leads and they put me in contact with the auction company. I negotiated and signed the contract."

"Without telling your dad."

Channing thought he detected a hint disapproval in her tone. Then again, that could be his own guilt affecting his hearing.

"The company was looking at another venue. I needed to make a quick decision or they would have moved on. If I'd consulted Dad first, he would have dragged his feet if not brought the negotiation to a complete standstill."

"So you cut him out."

"Sounds worse when you say it."

She sent him the same exasperated look his mom used to when he was young.

"I figured once he heard about the contract, he'd be happy," Channing said. "I can't believe he didn't break out the champagne when I told him the terms."

"Really? Champagne?"

He chuckled. She had him there. "Okay, no. But the terms are *very* good. And the work involved for hosting a car auction doesn't come close to a horse event. We're going to make a tidy profit. He of all people should appreciate that."

"What about your dad? A car auction isn't a horse event."

"He hates that. He says Rim Country has a reputation of being one of the oldest rodeo arenas in the entire Southwest, and he won't risk seeing that change. According to him, some things are worth more than money."

"Honestly, I can't see the arena's reputation being damaged from hosting a classic car auction."

"Of course it won't be. He's making excuses rather than admitting what's really bothering him. That his heart attack left him feeling vulnerable and giving up control of the arena increases that feeling. Add to that he sees my successes as a reflection of his failures."

"It must be hard, having your kid take over from you and fix the screwups you blame yourself for."

"I haven't thought of it in exactly those terms. You're onto something." Channing polished off his soda. “Jocelyn and Mom are convinced we need to have a family intervention with Dad.”

“An intervention?” Kenna drew back. “That sounds serious.”

“My word. Mom called it a discussion. She’s worried that Dad’s going to have another heart attack if he doesn’t slow down. And then there’s Jocelyn’s news.”

“What news is that?”

“She’s considering working more hours and helping me manage the arena.”

“Good for her, but how do you think you dad’ll take that?”

“Not sure,” Channing admitted. “Mom wants me to wait on my latest news about Honky Tonk Nights until after the intervention so we don’t hit Dad with too much at once.”

“What’s Honky Tonk Nights?”

“Three popular country acts from the eighties and nineties. If we can come to terms, one of their tour dates in September will be here.”

“Channing.” She studied him as if seeing him for the first time. “I’m impressed. Classic car shows and country entertainment acts are just what people in Payson love. You’ll sell out.” She placed her hand on his knee. “Those are smart moves.”

“Thanks.” He enjoyed the feel of her hand on his knee and was sorry when she removed it.

"Did I tell you ticket sales for the women's bull riding have picked up this week? We're well past the total number we had for the women's breakaway calf roping, and there are still two weeks left before the event. If we keep going at this rate, we'll make more during that one night than the previous three weeks combined."

"Congratulations!"

"Some of those ticket sales are because of you and your trick riding. You're a big help. I owe you."

"No way. You've helped me—boarding my horses, agreeing whenever I ask a favor… You're far too generous."

He'd do more for her if he could. If she'd let him. "We make a good team, Kenna. We do. We think a lot alike."

She surprised him by laughing. "You're kidding."

"What?"

"Maybe we think alike on some things, like the qualities needed for a good performance horse. You were spot-on about Rocket Man. But you're as stubborn as you claim your dad is when it comes to other things."

"Me? No." He shook his head.

"You didn't want me to ride Sam yesterday. I practically had to run you over to get back on him."

"The horse threw you."

She laughed again. "Thirty years from now you'll be just as opposed to change as your dad."

He grumbled under his breath. "I don't like the direction this conversation has taken."

"Retiring is hard. Suffering a serious life-threatening health scare is harder. Cut your dad some slack," she advised.

"Jocelyn and I have been talking about this. She thinks Dad's afraid of becoming old and useless and unneeded, and that's why he's digging in his heels."

"I bet she's right," Kenna said. "Think about it. Retiring is a huge adjustment. Your dad will leave behind the life he's had since he was a kid. That has to be unsettling. And scary."

"True."

"First, he has a heart attack, which reminds him all too clearly of his mortality. Then, he's being pressured into retiring by your mom and his doctor. On top of that, you're making changes that go against a hundred-year tradition. Changes that are necessary to repair a problem he thinks he created. What's next? He gets old and sick and then dies? Nobody likes to consider *that* grim possibility."

"Hmm." Channing studied Kenna at length. "You're onto something. Especially the mortality part. Dad's always thought of himself as invincible."

"Who doesn't until something happens?"

"Not sure how I can combat that or convince him otherwise. If I say, hey, Dad, retiring doesn't mean you're a failure or gonna die soon, he'll deck me just to prove he's still as strong and virile as he used to be."

"You're joking."

"A little." Channing massaged his jaw.

"Ha ha. Is he retiring on a specific date or easing into it?"

"A combination. He's easing into it over the next couple months and supposedly retiring in full at the end of July." Channing shifted his weight on the stool. "I don't want his last few months managing the arena to be him and me at each other's throats day after day."

"What if he continued working part-time?"

Channing shook his head. "Mom won't have that and neither will his doctor. He's supposed to be taking it easy. The job of manager is physically demanding and stressful and probably led to his heart attack in the first place."

"Okay. I get that," Kenna said. "But what if he retained some duties that were less physically demanding and stressful? That he could accomplish in, say, ten or twelve hours a week. He'd have plenty of time left for the things your mom wants to do, like traveling and renovating the house. Plus, it would take a small burden off you."

Would his dad go for it? Would his mom?

"There's the monthly city council meetings. And working the booth at rodeos. Dad's always loved that, and I'd rather work the chutes and livestock, anyway."

"You'd have to spin it right." Kenna showered Channing with a bright smile that kicked his pulse up a beat and made him forget what they were talking about. "Tell him that he's taught you a lot, but that you're not quite ready to fly solo without his sage advice."

"Way ahead of you." Channing grinned. "I've used that tactic before. Yesterday, in fact."

"I can't wait to hear how it goes."

"Thanks, Kenna." He'd give anything to pull her into a hug—and potentially another kiss. He hesitated, too afraid of losing the ground he'd gained. "I don't care what you said before—we're a good team."

There it was again, that incredible smile of hers. He let himself get lost.

"I should hit the road," she said. "Those wedding favors won't make themselves."

Channing returned the stools to their corner and locked the concession stand door behind them. During the time they'd spent inside, the sun had slipped behind the mountains. Only a fiery, blurry crescent showed above the treetops.

In another two minutes, that would disappear from sight.

"Pretty, isn't it?" Kenna asked as if reading his mind.

"Not compared to you."

The words slipped out before he could stop them, and her expression instantly changed to one of caution.

"Channing."

"I get that you're leaving."

"And you have the arena," she added.

"But you should know, if things were different, I'd pick up where we left off years ago."

Kenna stared at the sunset for several long beats before turning back to him. "If things were different, I'd let you."

Her admission took him aback. He'd expected her to downplay his feelings if not outright dismiss them.

Encouraged, he lifted his hand and cupped her cheek. "Then why aren't we exploring the possibilities?"

"You know we can't."

"No obstacle is too great if we're motivated."

She closed her eyes. "These last couple weeks since I've been home, watching and worrying about Mom and Beau, fighting my attraction to you, talking to Madison, I've learned something about myself. I'm afraid of commitment.

For whatever reason. Losing my dad. Witnessing my mom's relationship train wrecks. Breaking up with my former boyfriend—though, in hindsight, I think that was more me than him."

"I'm willing to wait. I can be very patient."

"I may never come around. As Madison recently pointed out, me being on the road isn't a deterrent to you and I getting involved—avoiding involvements is why I'm constantly on the road." Her shoulder sagged as if her honesty had drained her of energy. "There. I said it."

"I suppose this is the part where I agree with you and wander off into the sunset."

"It's not?"

"I can be patient when what I want is worth waiting for." Channing drew her into an embrace. Before she could spout a string of objections, he cut her off. "What do you say we start with a short trial run?"

"Oh, Channing."

"Hear me out. Let's just hold each other. We'll forget about everything else and every reason why we shouldn't be together and pretend we've resolved all our differences. See how it feels." He tightened his arms.

"Just holding?"

"Okay. Maybe more."

"Hmm…"

"If we don't like it, we can stop."

"You're impossible."

She found his lips with hers, kissing him gently at first and then with increasing eagerness. They were good together. If only the universe and circumstances and their own insecurities weren't stacked against them. If only she'd let down her defenses long enough to see they could find a way if they tried hard enough. If only he could convince her.

Could he? Channing used every second of their trial run to try, alternately kissing her and reveling in the sensation of her face nestled in the crook of his neck.

"This is nice," she whispered.

"Shh. No talking."

Eventually, predictably, she stirred. With tremendous reluctance, he released her.

She sighed. "You're not making this easy."

"That's precisely my intention."

"I don't want to get hurt. I don't want to hurt you."

"I don't want that, either."

"Goodbye, Channing," she said.

"Tell your mom hi for me."

Such mundane parting words, considering the incredible connection they'd just shared.

"I will."

He watched her leave, making sure she got safely to her truck and exited the arena parking area. After that, he conducted his nightly walk of the arena grounds, his mood soaring when he recalled their kiss, only to drop like a stone in a bucket when he thought about her leaving soon.

"ANYONE EVER TELL you you're a big baby?" Kenna dug a carrot piece from her jeans pocket and fed it to Sideways Sam. The rangy buckskin lipped the treat from her fingers with the gentleness of a lamb. "Don't try telling me you were once a champion bronc."

He crunched docilely, making a joke of his former claim to fame.

Kenna waited at the arena's side gate. She'd been about to enter when she got a text from Channing. They were scheduled for another practice session, their sixth in total, but he'd been delayed. A meeting had been moved up from later, or so he said.

Other than the practices with Sam, she hadn't seen much of him these last, sometimes endlessly long, ten days. He'd said he'd been busy with arena business, and she believed him. Besides seeing him coming and going, both Beau and his sister, Jocelyn, had made comments about him having his nose to the grindstone. Even so, part of her worried that he was making work an excuse to avoid her. She had shut him down, after all.

Then again, he hadn't seemed mad at her on the occasions they'd talked. More like distracted. He did have a lot to prove to himself and his family and a lot of responsibility.

There were also wedding-related activities consuming his time. The bachelor party had been the previous Saturday night. Nothing too wild or rowdy—a night out with the boys at a favorite watering hole. On top of that, Channing was helping Beau move his and Skye's stuff into Kenna's mom's house. Most of this moving had occurred when Kenna wasn't there, sadly.

Perhaps their little break had squashed whatever romantic notions had been developing between them. Easier for them both when the time came for her to leave, she supposed. If she had any sense, she'd put Channing—and any potential relationship—out of her mind once and for all.

Feeding Sam another carrot piece, she said, "Guess we won't be practicing today. Can't ride you without a spotter."

Channing had been adamant. Though Sam hadn't come close to throwing Kenna again, she was under strict orders not to get on him without proper safety equipment and another person present, preferably Channing.

Secretly, she preferred him, too. Though, considering the circumstances, a substitute might be in order.

"The women's bull riding is this Friday night," she told Sam. "Channing has to relax the rules before then or you and I won't be showing off for the fans."

She pressed her face into Sam's neck, letting the familiar smell of horse and outdoors soothe her. They'd been training daily. If not riding, Kenna walked and groomed Sam, bathing him one day and cleaning his hooves another. She didn't work him on the lunge line, uncertain how he'd react to that. Better they stick with the tried and true.

As a result, the two of them had become quite the pals. More important, her trust in him was growing. Her goal today had been to ride Sam in the arena, which she hoped would provide a more realistic experience than the practice ring. Well, minus the nerve-racking commotion and intimidating bulls.

Except practicing in the arena had fallen through with Channing standing her up. He hadn't done it intentionally, of course. During one of their chats about something other than Sam, Channing had said several promotional companies had reached out to him regarding hosting events. It seemed with him booking the classic car auction and Honky Tonk Nights concert, word was spreading.

She was glad for him. His vision for the arena's future was coming to fruition and showing enormous potential. She was also curious how his dad was taking the change. Channing hadn't mentioned any progress, whether they were getting along better or if they'd discussed his dad retaining a small role at the arena.

One piece of positive news, Kenna had heard from Channing's sister that tickets for the women's bull riding were nearly sold out. She and Madison had talked and decided on which tricks to perform for their halftime show, Kenna's participation official now that Rocket Man had proved his ability. She couldn't wait to see how he did in front of a crowd. And with Kenna riding Sam during the national anthem, the evening's entertainment portion had come together.

She picked up the flag she'd leaned against the fence earlier, along with her helmet and safety vest. They'd been using the flag while practicing with Sam and so far, so good.

"What if we just hung out for another couple hours?" she asked, directing the question more to herself than the horse. "Madison will be here by then. She can spot me."

Hard to believe the wedding was in four days. Time had flown for Kenna when it wasn't dragging. She didn't have to be a physics genius to see the connection between that and her not seeing much of Channing.

The fact was, she liked him. Walking-on-air, the-world-is-rosy sort of like. He was everything she wanted in a man and husband. What if she'd been wrong to push him away? What if he was her soul mate, like her dad had been her mom's soul mate? What if their obstacles weren't too big to overcome and she was making the biggest mistake of her life?

The questions banged around inside her head like bumper cars. Kenna may think her mom was wrong for always taking chances, but she also admired her mom's bravery. For someone so physically strong and capable, Kenna was an emotional weakling, afraid of a little commitment because, oh, no, she might get hurt.

If she could change that about herself, she would. She'd learned the hard way that, except for gigantic life events like, say, the death of a father, people didn't change. At best, they modified their behavior. Temporarily. Liking someone, even as much as she liked Channing, wasn't sufficient motivation to promote real and lasting change.

Okay, enough already. She had to stop dwelling on Channing and her many annoying personal issues and instead focus on the things that needed her attention, namely riding Sam on Friday night, her and Madison's performance, and her mom's wedding on Saturday.

She and Madison had only tomorrow to practice, though they were old pros and wouldn't require a lot. Starting Thursday, it was full steam ahead. Countless last-minute emergencies were anticipated, and they had another trip to Wishing Well Springs for a decoration delivery, the rehearsal and rehearsal dinner, and a consultation with the hairdresser and makeup artist. Kenna was exhausted just thinking about everything on her to-do list.

Sam nosed her hand, looking for more treats.

"Sorry, guy. Fresh out."

She should take him on a walk at least. If Channing became available, he'd text her. She got only a few steps before Beau appeared, driving an ATV and pulling a flatbed trailer loaded with metal panels used for team-penning practice.

"Hey there, Kenna." He stopped outside the arena and cut the engine, far enough away not to spook Sam, though the horse showed no signs of alarm. "What's up?"

"Sam and I were supposed to practice with Channing. He got delayed with work."

"I'll spot you."

"What about those?" She indicated the load of panels.

"They can wait. Not like they'll grow legs and walk away."

Kenna started to decline his offer and then reconsidered. Why not? Beau was competent and experienced with bucking horses. "Sure, that'd be awesome. Thanks, Beau."

The practice went well. Sam paid no attention to the flag Kenna carried, even when Beau handed it up to her once she was in the saddle. By mutual agreement, Beau drove the ATV to the center of the arena and let the engine idle in an attempt to create a distraction. Sam neither cared nor appeared to notice. He loped several circuits of the arena, his big hooves heavy in the soft dirt.

Kenna bounced in the saddle, the horse's rough gait like trying to sit on a bicycle traveling a washboard dirt road. And he was slow to respond to the bit, requiring every ounce of Kenna's strength to turn or stop him. But he didn't buck. Not once. Growing fat and lazy in his old age had, it seemed, truly mellowed him.

Kenna couldn't have been more pleased, and she smiled brightly when she hopped off near the side gate. Wait until Channing heard. He might be mad at her for practicing without him, but what had he expected, considering he'd stood her up?

"Looking good," Beau said as he sauntered over.

"I really appreciate the help."

"Anytime. We're gonna be family."

That was true, for better or worse. Yes, she was quoting a wedding vow. "Things still okay between you and Mom? No more drama?"

"We've had a couple long talks, and I warned my mom and sister to back off."

"That's good."

Kenna wanted to believe this marriage would be her mom's last. Beau's heart was so obviously in the right place. Except she couldn't help harboring a few lingering doubts.

"If you don't mind me asking..." He shuffled his feet. "Is something the matter with you and Channing?"

"The matter?" Kenna gave an involuntary start. "Why? What did he say?"

"Nothing. He's just been a little out of sorts. And working really hard. Kinda like he's trying to ignore a problem. Gracie says you've been out of sorts, too."

And here Kenna had been commending herself for fooling everyone. "Nothing's the matter with us."

"He's sweet on you, you know. I sorta figure

with you hittin' the highway after the wedding, he's feeling, you know, down in the dumps."

"Sweet on me?" she repeated.

"From where I stand, it appears to go both ways."

"I like him. But, well, the timing's not right."

Once again, she trotted out that tired old line. But she and Beau weren't close, and she was uncomfortable revealing her private self to him. Plus, he worked for Channing, which could make things awkward. Oh, yeah, and he'd tattle to her mom.

"I get it," he said. "You don't want to start something you have no intention of finishing… like Skye's mama did with me."

"Channing and I are strictly friends." The other tired old line she frequently trotted out.

Kenna made a move to leave, wishing Beau would get the hint. She had a sudden desire to return Sam to his stall and dwell on what Channing's moping around really meant. Problem was, Beau blocked her path.

She was about to say something when he interrupted her. *Please, please, don't let this be about Channing.*

"She's coming into town soon." Beau's voice held a funny note Kenna hadn't heard before. Part anger, part bitterness, part frustration.

"Who?"

"Lora Leigh. Skye's mama. Now, don't get me wrong. I love Gracie to pieces. And I'm not interested in Lora Leigh that way. I swear to God. I only wish for Skye's sake, her mama would come around a little more often. Gracie, she's wonderful. Treats Skye like her own flesh and blood. Still, sooner or later, my baby girl's gonna want Lora Leigh in her life. I'd hate for her to grow up feeling abandoned."

"I see what you're saying. And that's not unreasonable."

Those were some deep and meaningful thoughts Kenna wouldn't have expected from Beau. He continually surprised her. More and more, she was seeing why her mom cared for him. He wasn't her dad—not by a long shot. But maybe he could make her mom happy with his thoughtfulness and consideration of others and wanting only the best for the people he loved.

Channing was like that, too. A genuinely decent guy. If Kenna were to risk her tender heart with anyone, there was no better choice.

There she went again, having thoughts that would take her nowhere. Like Beau had said moments ago, Kenna was hitting the highway after the wedding and not returning for two or three months.

But what if she returned sooner? If Madison was agreeable, Piper would join them after her high school graduation for a summer internship. She couldn't replace Kenna. But one of their longtime teammates was capable. With Piper picking up the slack, Kenna returning to Payson in a month rather than two wasn't an impossibility. Heck, it might even be doable.

What would that mean for her and Channing? Was seeing each other a few days a month enough to sustain a relationship? They could squeeze in another day or two if he was able to join her. Some of Hoof Feats' upcoming dates were within a half day's drive. He'd have to be willing to take off work.

"I realize she's just a baby now," Beau continued, "but she'll be a teenager in the blink of an eye. I couldn't stand it if Skye hated me for keeping her mama away."

Kenna had forgotten Beau was there. What had they been talking about? Oh, yeah, Skye's mother. Him wanting her to play a bigger role in Skye's life.

"You're a wonderful dad," Kenna told him. "Why don't you talk to, ah, Lindsey—"

"Lora Leigh."

"Talk to Lora Leigh the next time she's in town. I'm sure if you explain things to her the way you have to me, she'll make an effort to be more involved with Skye."

"I could," Beau mused. "She'll be here this week."

"This week!"

"Tomorrow or Thursday," he said.

"Ooh, that's going to be a problem." Kenna's mom was insecure where Skye's biological mother was concerned. The woman being in town literally days before the wedding might trigger another emotional meltdown like at the bridal shower. "You need to tread carefully, Beau."

"I won't lie to Gracie."

"I know you won't. And she appreciates your honesty. She's been lied to in the past and won't stand for it."

"Oh, she's told me some stories."

"Just choose the right moment to tell her. Emphasize Skye and her needs."

"Yeah," he mused, rubbing his chin. "That's good."

Kenna took a step toward the gate, the urge to leave increasing. "Thanks again. I gotta run. Madison's on her way."

"Have a nice rest of your day." He grinned affably and trotted off in the direction of the ATV.

After returning Sideways Sam to the pasture, Kenna went to her trailer to wait for Madison. Her friend had been to Rim Country enough times that she knew where to park, and the two had agreed to meet there. Like Kenna, Madison traveled in a horse trailer with living quarters, a necessity for nomads like them.

Kenna didn't spot Channing, though she'd searched for any sign of him. Probably for the best, because she wasn't sure what she'd say to him.

Were you serious about dating?

Let's talk. Maybe I can come home more often.

I'm willing to try if you are.

Yes, I'm leery of commitment, but you and I are worth taking a chance.

She'd scared him off after their kiss. That had to be what was going on. But if she said nothing, she'd never know for certain.

Kenna suddenly didn't want to leave Payson without telling him her feelings. Drawing a deep breath, she took out her phone and dialed him. After five rings, his voice mail greeted her. Was he still busy with work or screening her calls? Before she lost her nerve, she left a brief upbeat message saying she was at the arena and asking him to call her.

She ended with, "There's something I need to, um, want to talk about. Okay, bye."

Before she could chew her thumbnail to the quick, he texted her.

You free for lunch?

Lunch. A couple weeks ago, he'd mentioned wanting to take her out to a place that wasn't fast food. She glanced down at her dirty T-shirt and dusty boots. Did she have time to change?

She typed back. I have an hour before Madison arrives.

Meet me in the office.

Kenna didn't give herself time to overthink the situation or change her mind. She quickly typed a response.

On my way.

CHAPTER ELEVEN

CHANNING CARRIED TRAYS of food from his office to his dad's and set everything on the coffee table in front of the sofa. He'd listened to Kenna's voice-mail message twice, his hopes rising one moment and then falling the next. She hadn't sounded mad, though that could be wishful thinking on his part.

He'd missed the practice with Sam. When the opportunity to meet with the food vendor had come up, he should have contacted Kenna immediately. But he'd gotten sidetracked and shut off his phone to avoid interruptions. He'd only recently turned it back on, guilt hitting him when the slew of notifications appeared.

Replaying the message a third time, he attempted to discern a clue about what it was she wanted to discuss. Wedding business, probably, or the missed practice.

Then again, there was that hint of uncertainty in her voice. Could be his plan of giving her space was finally working.

Channing didn't play games with people. On

the other hand, he was an expert with horses. Experience had taught him a gentle approach yielded far better results than an aggressive one. Not that Kenna was a horse, but he knew if he pushed too hard, she'd balk. Whereas if he waited, she'd come to him if and when she was ready.

Bringing in the last load, he studied the array of food on the coffee table—leftovers compliments of the food vendor he'd met with. The idea of inviting Kenna to lunch had occurred to him while listening to her message the second time.

Nothing ventured, nothing gained. What was the worst that could happen? They'd eat and chat about the wedding or Sideways Sam. A better outcome would be they'd cement their friendship and he'd apologize for his recent absence. If that were all, Channing would be satisfied. He didn't want to lose her altogether. But the best outcome? She'd be receptive to taking a step forward in their relationship.

Glancing at the time, he jumped into action. Kenna was due any minute. He went out to the front reception area, where his mom sat at his sister's desk. Jocelyn had left for lunch, and their mom was covering for her, answering the phones and greeting visitors.

"Hey, Mom. Kenna's on her way here. Can you buzz me when she arrives?"

"How nice." Lilian Pearce's still-youthful face bloomed into a wide smile. "I'm really looking forward to her performance Friday night."

Like his sister, Channing's mom supported his efforts to grow the family business. Not just because she wanted his dad to retire and take it easier—she believed in Channing and he loved her for it. He wished his dad felt the same—though, with the women's bull riding almost at capacity and two hefty deposit payments from the classic car auction company and Honky Tonk Nights sitting in their bank account, his dad was giving Channing less and less grief.

Their profits next quarter would be up as much as 4 percent barring any unforeseen circumstances. Not too shabby, if Channing said so himself. If he succeeded in negotiating another deal with one of his recent contacts, their profits would climb higher. He was aiming for six.

Yes, Channing was patting himself on the back. But he'd done a good job. The changes were taking the arena in the right direction. He just had to be careful and not get ahead of himself. The economy this past year had shown that everything could change in an instant.

"I can't tell you how many people have asked about Kenna and Sideways Sam," his mom continued. "I'm surprised, considering we didn't advertise."

"Word gets out. People have seen us practicing."

"Your dad's been telling folks."

Channing almost laughed. "I find that hard to believe."

"He's slowly changing his opinion, not that he'd tell anyone."

"He certainly hasn't told me."

"You know your dad. It's hard for him to admit he's wrong. Especially to his children. You're supposed to look up to him."

"I do look up to him," Channing said, only to mull that over. Maybe he should tell his dad that more often.

"I wish Kenna were staying on after the wedding," his mom continued, changing the subject. "We could hire her as a regular halftime act."

Could they hire her? If they did, Channing would see her more often than every few months—a potential outcome he'd very much like. Many organizations and promotional companies had their own acts, but others looked to Rim Country to provide the entertainment. He could always suggest a talented trick rider with a strong fan base in Payson.

"That's not a bad idea, Mom."

"More opportunity for you and her to get together." She waggled her brows at him.

His mom had always seen right through him

when it came to Kenna. Still, he played dumb. "Get together for what?"

She ignored the question. "The two of you are such a cute couple. I can't wait to see you together at the wedding. You in your tux. Her in her bridesmaid dress."

Inviting Kenna to the office with his mom here might have been a mistake. He went over and sat in one of the chairs.

"I thought you were going back to your office." She stared at him quizzically.

"Nope. Not while there's a chance you'll say something embarrassing to Kenna."

"Me?" She pressed a hand to her heart, a slight smile tugging at her mouth. "You wound me."

"Don't play innocent. You're a meddler."

"What mother doesn't want her children content and settled down? At the rate you're going, you'll never find a wife and start a family. I need more grandbabies."

"I'm not marrying and having kids just to please you."

"You're lonely."

"I'm alone. Not the same thing."

Okay, Channing might be a little lonely. The feeling had disappeared when Kenna came home, only to return these last ten days. More than once, when he sat by himself at night watching some mindless TV show, he'd wondered what it would be like to have her with him.

"You've always liked Kenna," his mom said.

"Do not play matchmaker, you hear me?"

She huffed. "Am I even allowed to speak to her when she comes in?"

As if in response, the office door opened and Kenna entered. She froze, her expression that of someone who realizes she's been the topic of conversation but is too embarrassed to ask.

"Um...hi," she muttered.

"Morning!" Channing stood and flashed his best guileless smile. "That was fast."

His mom stood, too, and scurried out from behind the desk. "Kenna. How's the wedding coming? You need help with anything?" She oozed honey as she dove in for a rib-crushing hug.

"We're fine for right now," Kenna said when she could at last extract herself. "That could change tomorrow, however."

"If it does, you holler. Jocelyn and I will be there in a jiffy."

"Thanks."

Channing rescued Kenna from his mom's clutches and propelled her toward the hall. "You hungry?"

She crinkled her brow. "Aren't we going out to lunch?"

"You have a lunch date?" His mom practically turned cartwheels. "How fun!"

"We are going to lunch." Channing gestured down the hall. "In my dad's office."

Kenna cranked her head to peer around Channing. "Is he joining us?"

"He's at a meeting in town with a livestock broker. It's just you and me."

His mom's lilting voice chased after them. "I'll hold your calls."

He swallowed a groan. Fortunately, Kenna didn't comment on his mom's uncurbed enthusiasm or object to the unusual location of their lunch. Now, if only everything else would fall into place.

KENNA STARED AT the food on the coffee table with surprise and—Channing was relieved to see—pleasure.

"What's all this?" she asked.

"Tacos. And sides." Along with the food, he'd added paper plates, napkins and plastic forks. "I have water bottles. Or if you want something else, I can run to the concession stand for some sodas."

"No, no. Water's fine." She bent and inspected the huge selection of food before lowering herself onto the couch. "Did you rob a taco truck?"

"Not rob, but you're right about the taco truck.

I was meeting with a potential new food vendor, which is why I missed the practice with Sam. Sorry about that."

"It's okay."

He sat next to her, closer than was necessary. He told himself the proximity would make sharing food easier. When she smiled at him, he inched nearer. "These are sample menu items he brought."

She picked through the offerings with interest. "What kind of tacos are there?"

"Beef. Chicken. Pork. Fish. Shrimp. Tofu. There may be some other kinds in there. I can't remember. And about a dozen condiments."

"Hot sauce?"

"Four varieties. Take your pick. We can warm everything up in the microwave." Channing pointed to the mini microwave on a credenza behind the desk—his dad used it for heating the coffee he habitually let get cold.

Kenna laughed. It was nice to hear after a long absence. "I'm not sure where to start."

"Try one of each. There's plenty."

She selected a chicken taco. He liked her liberal use of the condiments. She completely won him over when she added a generous spoonful of jalapeño relish.

"Don't forget the sides." He offered her a plastic fork. "Beans, rice and corn salad."

"This is a feast," she said while heating her loaded plate in the microwave. "Oh, my God, and delicious," she added after reclaiming her seat and taking a bite. "Please tell me the taco truck's coming back."

"For the classic car auction and Honky Tonk Nights. Our concession stand is fine for the usual rodeo and horse show crowd. But we need to elevate the menu for the other events to something classier than hot dogs and frozen burritos. Especially for the concertgoers. We also have to feed the performers and their crews. That's a whole bunch of extra mouths, more than our concession stand can handle. I decided to bring in professional food vendors, which also gives us another service to offer any organizations considering us."

"It's kind of exciting. All these changes." Kenna grinned.

"It is." Channing swallowed a bite of fish taco. "A new era for Rim Country."

So far, so good. The lunch was feeling like old times. Channing didn't ask why she'd called, preferring to continue like they were. A serious discussion might ruin the mood. He'd wait for her to change the topic.

"About practice, I apologize," he said. "The vendor asked to move up our meeting, and I got distracted. You free later? We can—"

"Actually, I did practice."

Channing stopped eating mid-bite. Pieces of shredded lettuce fell onto his lap, and he brushed them off. "We agreed you wouldn't ride Sam without me."

"Beau spotted me. He was delivering panels to the arena for team penning and offered. Don't worry, Sam did great. Not a single misstep."

"Okay."

"You're upset."

"Naw." Channing resumed eating. The only thing upsetting him was the missed time with Kenna. But they were here now and sitting together on the sofa, which was way better than a big arena.

"We tried something new," she said. "Beau let the ATV idle to create a distraction while I rode Sam."

"And?"

"Nothing. He's more than ready for Friday night. I'm still planning on practice sessions tomorrow and Friday morning before the bull riding. If you're busy, I'll recruit Beau."

"I'm free." Channing would make darn sure he was. "We should work Sam extra hard Friday morning. I want him worn out for the bull riding."

"I'll call you after Madison arrives and I have a better idea of my schedule."

He nodded and took another bite of his taco.

"Beau said something earlier." Kenna picked at her corn salad. "Were you aware that Skye's mom is coming to town this week?"

"He mentioned it." Channing had half listened when Beau brought it up, his attention elsewhere. "She shows up periodically to see Skye."

"I wish it weren't right before the wedding. Mom will be upset."

"Yeah." He remembered Kenna telling him about the bridal shower fiasco. "The timing's lousy."

"He's going to talk to Mom. Hopefully that'll go well. It did the last time."

"Did you remind him to get flowers and wine first?"

"I forgot!"

They both chuckled at that, and tensions from the ten-day drought evaporated. It seemed Kenna had only wanted to talk about her practice with Beau and the upcoming visit from Skye's mom. Not any problems between her and Channing. He decided to keep the positive momentum going.

"Does Hoof Feats have any free weekends coming up?" he asked. "Say, in the next three to six months."

"I'd have to check with Madison. She handles our bookings." Kenna pushed her empty plate away and sat back against the sofa cushion. "Why?"

"We might want to hire you. For entertainment. We're always on the lookout for acts and, with larger-scale events in the works, there could be opportunities. You have a following."

"Wow. Really?"

He tried to gauge her reaction but couldn't tell if the prospect thrilled or troubled her. "Would you be interested?"

"Well, sure. If the dates work out. And depending on the rest of the team. Or did you mean just me?"

"Do you ever perform without them?"

"I have. We've all taken individual gigs. Again, everything depends on the contract and our sponsors. For obvious reasons, they have a big say in what we do, and where and when we perform. But I could potentially get away."

"That's great." Channing grinned.

"It's funny..." She hesitated.

"What?"

"I was thinking earlier of ways to come home more than once every couple months. That was the reason for my rambling message."

His pulse spiked. He could hear it drumming in his head. "To see your mom?"

"And...other people."

Easy, boy. Don't rush her. "Like who?"

She spoke carefully, as if each word required deliberation before being uttered. "I know I've given you mixed signals. Kissing you, then pushing you away. That was wrong, and I apologize. Other than Dennis, I haven't dated a lot. Not seriously." Her cheeks turned that pretty shade of pink. "I don't consider myself very experienced."

"If you're looking for someone you can sharpen your skills with, I may have a recommendation."

She glanced away. "I don't want to sharpen my skills."

"Ah." He sighed to cover his disappointment.

"If I date anyone, it'll be for real."

"I see."

When she returned her gaze to his, a tiny sparkle lit her eyes. "About that someone you can recommend..."

"What are you saying, Kenna?" He needed her to be crystal clear—this was too important to risk misunderstanding.

"We have challenges. I'm on the road constantly. I have these pesky commitment issues. Your job is demanding and will only get more demanding when you take over management."

"I like a challenge."

"Yeah?"

"I've missed you the last ten days."

"Me, too."

"This attraction between us, it hasn't gone anywhere for fourteen years, regardless of the obstacles we face or what we put each other through. Frankly, I'm tired of fighting what seems inevitable."

"Agreed." He desperately wanted to reach for her but waited, letting her finish what she needed to say.

"We're already friends, and we get along. We work well together. If you're willing to tolerate my insecurities and idiosyncrasies, maybe we could have that trial run. Longer than a few minutes, of course. But before we start, let's establish a few ground rules."

"Such as?"

"Exclusivity. Who pays for the date, because I feel strongly that whoever does the inviting should foot the bill."

He felt the beginnings of a smile. "I can live with that."

"Now, keep in mind, I may only get back to town once a month. Work comes first. For both of us."

She waited for his response, her face expectant and unsure and incredibly lovely. He longed to take her in his arms and hold her until all her worries ceased to exist.

"Yes."

"That's it?" she asked when he didn't elaborate. "Yes?"

"No, that's not it." Channing cleared his throat and sat up straighter. "I've been doing a lot of contract negotiation lately, and there's a custom."

"Oh?"

"Whenever two parties reach an agreement, they shake on it."

She smiled. "Have we reached an agreement?"

"There are still the ground rules to work out and a few other details."

"For instance?"

"Where we're going for lunch tomorrow," he said, "and then dinner."

"Lunch *and* dinner."

"We don't have much time before you're leaving, and we have to make the most of it. But, yes. We're in agreement."

"Okay." She extended her hand for him to shake.

He pulled her to him for a kiss.

She softened in his embrace. "Why am I not surprised?"

"I've missed you," he said against her lips.

"I've missed you, too."

"We'll figure this out, Kenna. There isn't anything I want more."

"Me, neither."

They sealed that "contract negotiation" with

another kiss. A short time later when Channing walked her outside, his mom beamed at them as if the walls were paper-thin and she'd heard everything.

CHAPTER TWELVE

KENNA FLOATED ON air the entire way from lunch with Channing to where her trailer was parked. Okay, that was an exaggeration. But the sensation did resemble floating, if not flying.

They were a couple. A bona fide couple. They'd sealed their agreement with a kiss, and that made it official.

Her cheeks hurt from nonstop grinning. Madison was bound to notice. She'd been held up in traffic, according to her last text. Kenna couldn't wait to tell her about this latest development with Channing. She was confident of Madison's support. All the Hoof Feats team members dated or had boyfriends, Madison and the others more than Kenna. They navigated the ups and downs with minimal problems.

Carolyn and her current guy were the exception. They were both young, however. Kenna, Madison and the rest were older and wiser and better able to manage conflicts between their professional and personal lives. When Kenna's relationship with her former boyfriend had started to spiral downward, she hadn't missed a single performance or allowed her concentration to wane. No dropped banners for her. It would be the same if she and Channing crashed and burned.

"Wait a minute," she told herself. "Slow down."

They hadn't even started dating, and here she was already planning for the end of their relationship. That was just plain irrational. If today's lunch was any indication, their future looked bright and promising.

Excitement rippled through her. Tomorrow, they'd be stepping out as a couple for the first time.

To keep herself busy until Madison arrived, Kenna tidied her living quarters—cleaning the closet-sized bathroom was her least favorite chore, so she finished quickly. Next, she used a hand vacuum to suck up the worst of the dirt. While wiping down the counters, she heard a trailer pulling up alongside hers. Madison was here!

Kenna's smile increased, if that was even possible. Would her friend be surprised by her announcement? Hardly. She'd been teasing Kenna about Channing for ages now.

Flinging open her trailer door, Kenna hopped down the step and rushed forward, greeting Madison at the driver's-side door of her truck. "You made it!"

The two hugged warmly. They were of similar height and build, though Madison's ginger curls were cut short and freckles covered her entire face.

"Look at you, all giggly and glowing." Madison drew back and gave Kenna the once-over. "I take it things have improved."

"I may have landed a couple gigs here. In Payson. At the arena, actually." Before Kenna could explain and give the reason for the gigs, namely Channing, Madison cut her off.

"No way! I landed us some gigs, too. More than a couple."

Before Kenna could correct her, Madison extracted her phone from her shirt pocket and swiped the screen.

"Take a look at this," she said. "I got the email twenty minutes ago."

She waited, radiating nervous energy while Kenna scanned the email. In contrast, Kenna's excitement dimmed with each line she read.

"Well?" Madison asked when Kenna had finished. "Is that not fan-flippin'-tastic?"

"Yeah, fantastic," Kenna repeated flatly.

Madison continued as if she hadn't heard. "Kingston Saddlery not only wants to extend our contract until next summer, they're designating us as their official rep and adding ten more appearances between now and then. This is what we've been waiting for, girl. Serious backing. I know it's a giant commitment. But, holy cow, Kenna, the money and the exposure!"

"Yeah." Kenna noted the locations of the ten added appearances. None of them were near Arizona.

There went her plan of coming home every month. Should she tell Madison no? Break up with Channing?

Good news wasn't supposed to feel this bad.

"Hey, I thought you'd be jazzed." Madison studied Kenna closely. "This is incredible stuff."

"I am." No, she wasn't. Well, kind of…but also no. "Congratulations. I know you worked hard courting Kingston."

"Why aren't we jumping up and down and squealing? I've seen bloodhounds with happier expressions than yours."

"We'll celebrate. Sorry. It's me. I'm just… surprised." She wouldn't burst Madison's bubble. Not yet. Not until she'd had time to think.

Madison took hold of Kenna's shoulders. "Am I missing something? What haven't you told me? Is there another problem with your mom and Beau?"

"No. Weirdly, they're fine."

"Then what?"

Kenna stalled by giving her friend another hug. "I'm glad you're here."

"I wouldn't miss this wedding for anything."

Madison, Kenna knew, had come to Payson for her, not her mom. She'd been by Kenna's side for her mom's second wedding, the third, and the many various breakups. She deserved a medal for the hours she'd endured listening to Kenna vent and bemoan.

As they walked Madison's horse across the rodeo grounds to the stalls, Kenna attempted to pull herself together. She'd gone from one end of the emotional spectrum to the other in the matter of an hour. She would tell Madison about her and Channing, but later. If she tried right now, she'd start spouting gibberish.

Madison kept the conversation rolling during the drive to Kenna's mom's house. Were there any cute guys attending the wedding? Did Kenna and her mom purchase the hair products Madison had suggested? What time tomorrow were they practicing their tricks for the women's bull riding? Would they have time for mani-pedis before the wedding?

Madison had offered to bunk in her trailer for the five days she'd be in Payson. Kenna wouldn't hear of it and insisted she share the guest bedroom at her mom's. It made sense, after all. Madison had volunteered to be an extra pair of hands, which would be useful as the list of last-minute emergencies was growing by the hour. Madison was also very good with a needle and thread, a talent she'd inherited from her grandmother and that could be useful.

At the house, Kenna carried Madison's dress through the garage door and inside, holding it high off the floor. Madison brought up the rear, grappling with a wedding gift, her laptop, a cosmetic case containing an impressive assortment of beauty essentials and a wheeled weekender suitcase.

"Where's your mom and the kid?" she asked, panting a little.

"Running errands. I think they're dropping decorations off at the wedding barn and swinging by the party store to pay for the table and chair rentals."

"Any food around here?" She eyed the kitchen as they passed through. "I missed lunch because of traffic, and I'm starving."

"I'll fix you a sandwich once we get you settled," Kenna offered.

"You're not hungry?"

"I ate already." *Tacos*, she thought wistfully. With Channing. That now felt like a week ago.

In the guest bedroom, Kenna hung Madison's dress in the closet. Madison dumped her things on the queen bed. This wasn't the first time they'd be sharing a bed, nor would it be the last. In fact, there'd been a few occasions where the five Hoof Feats team members had bunked together in a double-occupancy hotel room with one of them sleeping on the floor.

"So," Madison started, "what gives? You ready to tell me what sent you into a tailspin the second you read the email from Kingston?"

"I didn't go into a tailspin."

"Could've fooled me."

"I'll get lunch ready. You organize," Kenna said, stalling again. "Meet me in the kitchen when you're done."

"I'm expecting answers."

Maybe by the time Madison joined her, Kenna would have some.

She returned to the kitchen, where she ransacked the refrigerator. She and Madison had traveled together long enough that she knew her friend's tastes. A plastic container held leftover fruit salad from last night's dinner. Kenna threw together a Swiss and turkey wrap with lettuce and tomatoes and yogurt dressing. No mayo for Madison, ever. Kenna was pouring them both some iced tea when her friend appeared.

"Looks yummy." She sat at the table where Kenna had placed the food and picked up the wrap. "Soooo, what's going on with you and Channing?"

Straight to the point. Typical Madison.

Kenna sighed. "Is it that obvious?"

"We've been together practically day and night for eight years. If I don't know you by now, I don't deserve to be your friend." She took a giant bite of the wrap. For a small gal, she ate like a line-backer. "Doesn't take a brainiac. There can only be three reasons why you're not thrilled about the new gigs and awesome deal. First, work. But that's going well. Especially now that you have a gorgeous new horse. And I can't wait to see him perform, by the way. Second, your mom, and you just told me that she and Beau are weirdly doing fine. Third, a guy. Which—" she speared a green grape from her fruit salad "—you haven't been upset about since you broke up with that loser horse trainer."

"It wasn't all his fault. I think I was trying to prove to myself I wasn't a misfit or broken inside. That I could have a serious relationship. I wanted to *want* to get married, if that makes sense. When we reached that point and he was close to proposing, I got cold feet. Freezing cold. My commitment issues again." She sighed. "I know what's wrong with me. So why can't I change?"

"It's not easy. Maybe Channing's just the incentive you need. Tell me, is the dry spell at an end? Please say yes."

Kenna smiled. "Yes."

"Yeehaw!"

"We agreed to date."

Madison guzzled her iced tea. "How did you go from zero to dating in, like, hours? As of this morning, you were frustrated with him for missing your practice with Sideways Sam. Yesterday, you were convinced the timing wasn't right and the two of you were destined to always be apart. The day before that, or was it two days, you were afraid to risk getting hurt. Have I got that right?"

"I had kind of an epiphany this morning." Kenna propped her elbow on the table and rested her chin in her palm. "About taking chances. I decided to tell him how I truly felt before I left."

"Okay. Epiphanies can be good. I'm not opposed to you coming to your senses and revealing your feelings."

"Well, right after I had the epiphany, he invited me to lunch. It was like a sign or the stars suddenly aligning. All right, that sounds cheesy."

"Nothing wrong with cheesy." Madison winked at her. "And I've always believed in signs."

"Lunch was…oh…pretty…yeah."

"I bet. And how about the food?"

"Delicious, and we got along like always. Better than always. He mentioned me coming home more, and I said I was already thinking along those same lines. Then he suggested we negotiate."

"Negotiate what?"

"Us dating. The terms. We agreed on a trial run."

Madison wiped her face on a napkin and set it down. "All this business vernacular. Not very romantic, if you ask me."

"It was romantic," Kenna insisted. "Instead of a handshake, we kissed."

"That's better, I suppose. It also explains why you aren't happy about the new gigs with Kingston. Cuts into your dating life."

"I was hoping to come home once a month," Kenna admitted. "Maybe even more often."

Madison twirled her fork. "You missing performances could create a problem with Kingston and some of our other contracts."

"Yeah." Kenna's heart sank.

"Are you thinking of quitting?"

"No!" She sat up straight. "I would never leave you and the others in the lurch." The next second, her shoulders slumped. "Guess I'll talk to Channing. Tell him we can't date." Speaking the words out loud caused a sharp pain in her chest.

"No so fast," Madison said. "Let's brainstorm. It's possible we can find a solution. What about your student Piper?"

"That's what I was initially thinking. Evie could cover for me—the sponsors like her. Piper can pick up the slack."

"Maybe. A lot would depend on if Piper's a good fit. I still need to meet with her and her parents."

Kenna brightened. "She and I could both have trial runs this summer. Piper with Hoof Feats and me with dating Channing. If it doesn't work out, no harm, no foul."

Madison frowned. "I wouldn't say that. There's going to be a lot of harm if it doesn't work out. For all of us."

"I didn't mean it that way." Kenna attempted to backtrack. "Channing and I agreed to ground rules, a trial run being one of them."

"Good grief. Enough with the business terms. Quit depersonalizing your relationship with Channing. You did the same thing with your last boyfriend."

"It helps me to feel less vulnerable and more in control," Kenna admitted.

"Protecting your heart is fine. I get that. Go slow. Minimize risk. And I'm the queen of having an escape plan in place to get out quick if necessary. But there's a difference between that and setting yourself up for failure. Don't enter this relationship convinced it will fail. That's not fair to Channing."

"I'm not," Kenna insisted. "But I need to—

have to—feel safe. For all I know, he could fall out of...out of...like with me in a week and a half."

"He hasn't fallen out of *like* with you in fourteen years."

"Under the best of circumstances, and depending if we get Kingston to agree, Channing and I won't see each other that often. Can we build a relationship on that?"

"If the two of you aren't meant to be, twenty dates a month won't make a difference. On the other hand, if he's the one for you, once a month will be more than enough until you decide to leave Hoof Feats."

Madison made a lot of sense. But rather than a weight being lifted, Kenna felt one pressing down on her chest. The last thing she wanted was to sabotage her brand-new relationship with Channing. Yet, she couldn't make her fears go away with the snap of her fingers. Neither could she forgo ground rules.

So much for floating on air.

Her and Madison's conversation came to an end when they heard the rumble of a car pulling into the garage. Both of them jumped up to welcome Kenna's mom and Skye home.

Kenna put on her best nothing-is-wrong smile, but she fooled no one.

Her mom took one look at her and said, "Kitten, what's wrong?"

Skye burst into loud wails.

"HOW WAS YOUR crab salad?" Channing asked Kenna. They'd decided on lunch at Antonio's Ristorante, one of the nicer Italian restaurants in town.

"Fantastic."

His chicken parmigiana had been the stuff of five-star reviews. "Was the bread too garlicky?"

"No. I love garlic."

"Me, too. Look at that. Our first date and we're finding out all kinds of stuff about each other."

That prompted a smile. Finally. She'd been reserved on the drive to the restaurant and for most of their meal.

"You in the mood for dessert? Tiramisu is my kryptonite."

"Okay." She set her elbows on the table. "What's with all the questions?"

"I'm just making conversation. And trying to figure out what's bothering you."

"Ah."

"I thought things went well yesterday."

They'd kissed more than once, talked and decided to give dating a try. At long last, the timing seemed right for them.

"They did," she agreed.

This was harder than pulling teeth. "Are you having second thoughts?"

She groaned. "I must be the easiest person in the world to read. No lie, you're the fourth one to ask me if I'm okay, counting Skye."

"Skye asked? She talks?"

"She took one look at me and started crying."

"Well." Channing shrugged. "You are easy to read. Never take up acting."

"I'm not having second thoughts," she insisted. "More like the same thoughts. Over and over."

He didn't like the sound of that. "Talk to me."

She straightened as if steeling herself. Channing's meal turned to a doughy lump in his stomach.

"I want us to date and for me to come home more often," she said.

"I hear a *but*."

"*But*...Madison had a surprise for me yesterday. Kingston Saddlery wants Hoof Feats to be their official rep and to add ten appearances over the next year."

"Ten. That's a lot."

"It is."

The lump in his stomach grew heavier. "Congratulations. Kingston is a big name in the horse world."

"I wanted you to know since it affects us."

"You'll be too busy," he said flatly.

He wouldn't force her to choose between her career and him. Certainly not at this early stage. And opportunities like the one with Kingston were rare.

"Well, no. I hope not, anyway. We'll see. Madison and I came up with a tentative plan."

"A plan?"

She reached across the table and took his hand, which had been lying there lifeless. He felt marginally reassured.

"Remember me telling you about my student Piper?"

"Vaguely."

"She wants to be a professional trick rider. Her parents would prefer she attend college, of course."

"Not sure what that has to do with us," Channing said.

"It's part of the plan. We're considering letting her tour with us for six weeks this summer. That is, if everyone agrees. Madison and I are meeting with Piper and her parents after our practice."

"Is she replacing you?"

"Oh, no way." Kenna shook her head. "She's not experienced enough. One of our other team members can, however. Evie, most likely. She's been with us the longest, and the people at Kingston like her. Piper will fill in where possible, which, in turn, will allow me one, perhaps two, free weekends a month. I told Madison this summer could be a test run for both Piper and me."

Allow me one, perhaps two, free weekends.

Amazing how the right phrase and a hopeful gaze from a pair of dark chocolate eyes could dissolve the lump in his stomach. Relief filled him, along with—he was manly enough to admit it—joy.

"I'm not sure about after that," she said.

"Don't worry about that just yet." He brought Kenna's hand to his mouth and pressed a kiss to the soft skin. "Here's to your plan."

"There could still be glitches. Piper's parents have yet to agree and could insist she attend college and not take a gap year. We need Kingston's stamp of approval. If someone gets sick or has a family emergency, I won't be able to get away. Piper's new and untested she could fail."

"We agreed work comes first. I could have conflicts, too. But for now, let's think positive."

"We'll be apart way more than we'll be together," she said glumly. "That's hard on two people. What if we fizzle out?"

"I'd give anything to guarantee won't ever encounter rough patches. Except we will. Every couple does." He kissed her hand again, enjoying the warmth of her skin on his lips and her slight intake of breath. "What I can tell you with absolute certainty is that I care for you and am in this one hundred percent."

"Madison told me you'd say something like that."

"Remind me to thank her." He lowered Kenna's hand but didn't let go, his thumb caressing her knuckle. "Stop overthinking, honey. Let's take this one week, one step, at a time. First, we see how your meeting with Piper's parents goes. Then, we go from there."

"I like your optimism."

"Not to be pushy or anything," he said, "but when's your next trip home?"

"We're performing at a horse show in Utah three weekends from this coming one and in Bakersfield after that. I could maybe stop here for a day, or a day and a half, in between. Depending on Kingston and Piper and everything else."

Channing took out his phone.

"What are you doing?"

He opened his calendar app. "Plugging in the days and giving myself a reminder to schedule time off."

She laughed and took out her phone. "I'll do the same."

"Now..." Channing waggled his brows. "About that tiramisu."

"Ugh. No." She patted her tummy. "All I've

been doing lately is eating. I won't fit in my bridesmaid dress at this rate."

"Are you kidding? You look incredible."

"I'd kiss you if there wasn't a table blocking us."

He started to rise. "I can remedy that."

Her expression turned coy. "Let's wait until we get outside where we don't have an audience."

They did, and the wait was worth it. Eventually, they returned to the arena—urged along by a text from Madison, who was already there.

Channing drove the truck around behind the office where he and the family parked. "Where are you meeting Madison?"

"At the arena. I need to saddle up Rocket Man and Sideways Sam first."

"Sideways Sam? You're not riding him again without me."

"Madison can spot me. You said you have a conference call."

"I'll postpone." He grabbed his phone and opened his contacts. "Me being there when you ride Sam is more important. And besides, you can't handle two horses alone."

"I can. Really, Channing."

"Nope." He didn't budge and insisted on fetching Sam from his stall, which was down the row a short distance from Rocket Man and Zenith. "In case he acts up on you."

"He won't."

The old bucking horse made a fool of Channing. He had to practically drag the lazy good-for-nothing from the stall. And then, when Sam saw Kenna, he ditched Channing, wanting only her. Channing had to admit, the horse showed good taste.

He and Kenna switched lead ropes, with Channing taking Rocket Man. "I'm embarrassed for Sam," he grumbled to the gelding. "He's putty in her hands."

Near the entrance to the horse barn, Kenna stopped and pointed toward the livestock pens, where the bulls milled aimlessly beneath the metal awning. "Is that Beau?"

Channing squinted. Two figures, a man and a woman, stood by the fence, engaged in conversation. "That's him."

"And Skye's mom?"

"Yeah. Lora Leigh. Guess she showed, after all."

"I wonder if Beau ever told Mom. She hasn't mentioned it. Did he say anything?"

Channing adjusted his hat against the sun's glare. "Not to me."

Kenna continued studying the couple, who appeared oblivious to them. "She's young. I mean, I knew that. But I guess I didn't realize how young until now. And pretty. She could be a model."

He wouldn't touch that last comment with a ten-foot pole. "Your mom has nothing to worry about. Beau loves her."

Kenna turned away. "I'm not rocking the boat. If I haven't heard from Mom, then I'm assuming Beau has dealt with the situation."

They hugged and swapped lead ropes again. Kenna jumped on Rocket Man's back. With no tack other than a halter, she trotted the horse to her trailer.

Channing stood and watched until she disappeared around the corner. Man, oh, man, he was one lucky guy.

He took Sideways Sam into the horse barn, where he saddled and bridled the old bronc outside the tack room. Mounting, he rode the Sam to the arena. The stirrups were a little too short, having been adjusted for Kenna.

At the arena, he stopped and climbed off. Kenna and Madison and their horses were already there. All kidding aside, he wasn't taking any chances with Sam and a new situation. Sam wasn't familiar with Madison and her horse. Channing tied the bronc to the fence a respectable distance away and sauntered over.

"Afternoon, ladies."

Madison greeted him with a hug. "Good to see you again, Channing. Heard you and your girlfriend had a nice lunch." She winked broadly at Kenna.

He liked that Madison thought of Kenna as his girlfriend. "It was very nice."

"I'm jealous."

"Have dinner with us tonight," Kenna offered.

Madison held up a hand. "Absolutely not! You two enjoy each other's company while you can. Sunday will be here soon enough."

Channing exchanged glances with Kenna.

For once, her sunglasses were on top of her head and he had an unobstructed view of her face. If he wasn't mistaken, he saw happiness there. Well, that made two of them.

"Sam first?" she asked. "Madison and I need to practice for an hour at least."

"He's ready. Start out slow," Channing warned.

Kenna didn't listen to him. Once she and Sam were in the arena, she urged him into a gallop after a brief warmup. Between this and the trick riding, Channing swore she'd give him a heart attack one of these days.

Fortunately, Sam earned another A-plus, paying no heed to Rocket Man or Madison's horse. Channing's heart was safe for another day.

Who was he kidding? He'd lost it long ago to Kenna. He'd be sorely disappointed if the plan she'd outlined during lunch didn't pan out. Her usual brief visit home every few months wasn't enough. He needed more dates plugged into his phone. Many, many more dates.

With Sam's practice over, Channing collected the old bronc and left the gals to their trick riding. He returned Sam to his stall after unsaddling him, then found Beau at the livestock pens. No mention was made of Lora Leigh by either of them.

The vet had arrived by then for a routine bovine check of the bulls and annual vaccinations. Rim Country prided themselves on the excellent care they gave their livestock, a tradition Channing would continue when he assumed management.

While not close to the arena, he had a view of Kenna and Madison. That was, if he stood at the far east end of the livestock pens and craned his neck. They were currently practicing a doubles trick using Madison's horse, Kenna hanging off the horse's left side and Madison off the horse's right. Both women leaned forward and stretched a leg out behind them like a gymnast performing on a balance beam. Channing refused to move from the spot until they were done.

Next, they each rode their own horse. As the women stood up in their saddles and executed hippodromes, which Channing remembered from when Kenna bought Rocket Man, the two horses loped side by side, shoulder to shoulder.

After a moment, Kenna and Madison reached for each other and clasped hands across the distance. Channing nodded to himself with appreciation. The crowd would go wild when they saw this trick.

More reason than ever for Rim Country to hire Kenna as entertainment for their events. Yes, that was selfish of him, but it was also good for business.

The vet was about halfway done with the bulls when Channing noticed an SUV with a two-horse trailer pulling up to the arena. A couple exited along with a teenage girl. This must be Piper and her family. While Kenna and Madison talked to the girl and her mom, the dad went to the rear of the trailer and unloaded her horse, already saddled.

Ah, decided Channing. *An audition*. Several minutes later, Piper rode into the arena on her horse and performed a series of tricks nearly as thrilling as those of Kenna and Madison.

She rejoined the gathering, and the discussion continued. It was hard for Channing to determine whether or not they'd come to terms, though he figured if Madison or the parents had vetoed the idea, the meeting would have already ended.

At that point, he got sidetracked by the vet. When he next looked over, Piper was loading her horse. She came back around and hugged both

Kenna and Madison. The parents shook their hands. Kenna and Madison waved as the family pulled out and drove away.

Encouraging. Step one of Kenna's plan may have been accomplished. Channing hadn't asked her if she and Madison would talk to Kingston Saddlery before or after the wedding. She'd tell him, he supposed, when she decided.

A few minutes later, the vet finished up. Dr. Lunsford was a short, chubby jovial sort who'd been treating the arena's livestock for over twenty years and was considered the best bovine vet in Payson. On this trip, he'd discovered a few bulls with minor ailments needing tending, from skin lesions to abscesses to lameness. The latter two would prohibit the bulls from being used in competition and require a move to the hospital pen.

"Thanks a lot, Doc, and see you Friday," Channing said.

"I'll be here," the vet replied, climbing into his truck. "Seven a.m. sharp."

Channing was eager to see the vet off so he could go in search of Kenna and learn the outcome of the meeting with Piper and her family. Turned out, he didn't have to—she came hurrying toward him as the vet's truck pulled away.

"Well?" he asked, a bundle of nerves by that point.

Her answer was to throw herself into his arms and kiss him soundly on the cheek.

Channing held her tight, reveling in the moment. Everything would work out for them. He could feel it in his bones.

CHAPTER THIRTEEN

"DO YOU, GRACIE CORDOVA, take Beau Sutter to be your lawfully wedded husband?" When Kenna's mom didn't respond, the minister said, "This is the part where you say, I do."

"Oh, gosh!" She slapped a hand to her forehead, flustered. "I mean, I do. Sorry."

Beau gave a low whistle. "You scared me there for a second."

The minister, a kindly older gentleman, grinned. "This is why we have a rehearsal."

Everyone laughed. No, wait... Not everyone. Kenna surveyed the small gathering in Wishing Well Springs' wedding barn. Beau's mom and sister alone offered only thin smiles.

So much for Beau talking to them. They didn't bother hiding their doubts. Kenna had them, too, though not as many as when she'd first come home. Beau had convinced her that he truly loved her mom and was determined to make the marriage succeed. She supposed her relationship with Channing had something to do with her newfound positivity. If her mom and Beau could conquer their obstacles, surely Kenna and Channing could, too. In comparison to what her mom and Beau were dealing with, a little time and distance impediment felt small.

Her gaze traveled past Beau and his brother, the best man, to land on Channing. He winked at her, and she smiled at him, their private communication giving her the tingles. She imagined him in his tux and melted. The women at the wedding would, too, when they saw him.

The last couple days, since they'd become an official couple, had sped by in a blur. Yes, the many activities contributed to that. Kenna, her mom, Dinah and Madison had been running around nonstop. A button had come loose on the wedding dress—Madison sewed it on. Several guests previously unable to attend suddenly could—Dinah handled that mini-crisis. Kenna finalized the playlist with the DJ.

She and Madison had also been tasked with decorating the tables reserved for tonight's rehearsal dinner at Joshua Tree, the elegant inn and restaurant next door to the wedding barn. They'd accomplished that earlier with the help of the staff. Kenna barely had two seconds to freshen up before the rehearsal and was certain her hair hung limp and her makeup had faded. Channing's appreciative glance said regardless of her appearance, he found her attractive. She beamed at him in return.

Dinah leaned forward and whispered in Kenna's ear. "You and he will be standing there next." She nodded at the altar.

Kenna shook her head. They wouldn't be next. But who knew what the future held? A year from now? Two years? Kenna could dream.

"I now pronounce you husband and wife," the minister said and gestured with his hand. "You may kiss your bride."

Beau pulled Kenna's mom into an enthusiastic embrace, leaning her backward over his arm. More laughs erupted from the family and friends gathered. Twelve of them in total, not counting Wishing Well Springs' wedding coordinator, who was overseeing the rehearsal.

Processional music played from the speakers. Kenna's mom and Beau started walking back down the aisle.

"Maid of honor and best man next," the wedding coordinator said.

Kenna took hold of Beau's brother's arm. She'd rather Channing escorted her, but tradition must be honored. Channing offered his arm to Dinah, who giggled girlishly and proclaimed, "Ooh, lucky me!"

Outside, the group conversed for several minutes. Final instructions were reviewed and questions were answered. Eventually, they headed to the inn. Kenna had ridden with her mom and Madison. Beau had hired a babysitter to stay at his double-wide with Skye since it would be a late night and an upscale dinner wasn't the best place for a baby.

Channing came up behind Kenna and cupped her shoulders. "Ride with me?"

"I'd love to."

She bid goodbye to her mom and Madison. "See you at the restaurant."

They took the long route, driving past the inn where the four-star restaurant was located and then making a U-turn. Amazing, really, how much Kenna and Channing had to say to each other, considering they'd talked four times already today. Kenna had lost track of the number of text messages.

They linked arms as they strolled from the parking lot to the front entrance. Inside, they were escorted to the dining room where the rest of the wedding party and other guests were already seated.

"Here." Dinah patted the empty chair beside her. "I saved two places for you."

"Thanks, Dinah." Kenna slid in beside her.

Channing sat next to Kenna. "We got delayed."

"Oh, I bet you did!" Dinah laughed loud enough to turn heads.

Kenna didn't mind the attention and clasped Channing's hand beneath the table.

"Sorry." Dinah waved to everyone and laughed again.

Dinner progressed pleasantly with lively conversations taking place in pockets around the long table. Whatever concerns Beau's mom and sister had, they kept them to themselves. Beau's dad made a nice, if uninspired, toast once the drinks arrived. The women, other than Beau's mom and sister, delighted in hearing details about the honeymoon trip and wedding dress from Kenna's mom. Beau accepted an abundance of good-natured ribbing.

Kenna and Channing spent much of the dinner in their own little world, answering when spoken to but mostly having eyes only for each other.

Along with dessert, coffee and liqueur orders were placed. The jazz band took the small stage and started their first set. Couples drifted onto the dance floor and swayed to the music, Kenna's mom and Beau being one of the first. His parents, too. When Beau's brother invited Madison to dance, Kenna studied them for any sign of a possible romance.

She turned away when Channing held out his hand to her. "I'm more used to two-stepping, but I can probably manage not to crush your toes if you care to dance."

She placed her palm in his. “I’d love to.”

They’d danced before, during their one date in high school. Like his kissing skills, Channing had improved since then. He spun and dipped her with confidence. Step on her toes? Hardly!

“You and Madison ready for the bull riding tomorrow?” he asked.

“More than ready.”

“Jocelyn sent me a text before the rehearsal.” He grinned. “We’re sold out.”

“You’re kidding!” Kenna squeezed him tight. “I’m so proud of you.”

“This is just the start. I’m contacting the WPRA next week. Now that we have some cred, maybe we can host more women’s rodeo events.” He twirled her in a circle until her head spun and then drew her close. “In a few weeks when you come back to Payson, we could have more to celebrate.”

“Evie’s excited about substituting for me. Madison and I are calling Kingston Saddlery on Monday. Just in case they aren’t on board, which I can’t imagine, we don’t want to spoil the bull riding and wedding.”

Channing kept her on the floor for two more dances. When they finally returned to their seats, Kenna immediately noticed some discord at the table. Beau’s mom seemed to be at the center of it.

"You don't think you should have taken care of the custody agreement first?" she asked. "You're getting married in two days. What if Skye's mom changes her mind?"

"She won't." Beau shifted uncomfortably.

Kenna exchanged looks with Channing. He put a finger to his mouth.

She had no intention of inserting herself. The thing was, she understood the older woman's concern, having expressed the same one to her mom weeks ago. Skye's custody was no small matter. Nothing stopped Lora Leigh from swooping in and taking Skye away from Beau.

"She may not like some other woman raising her daughter," Beau's mom insisted.

"I talked to Lora Leigh the other day," Beau said. "She's fine with the arrangement. We'll get the custody agreement settled after the honeymoon."

His mom's voice trembled when she spoke. "I don't want to lose my granddaughter."

Beau's dad patted her arm. "Now's not the time. Let's discuss this tomorrow."

She paid him no heed. "I love you to pieces, Beau, but you've always buried your head in the sand. Ignoring problems won't make them go away."

Kenna's mom jumped to his defense. "He doesn't ignore problems."

Tension thickened the air, seeming to absorb all the oxygen and background noise.

"I'll talk to Lora Leigh again," Beau said through gritted teeth. "In the meantime, Mom, you need to butt out."

She stiffened. His sister gasped softly. People cleared their throats and blinked with embarrassment. Nearby diners gawked. Their waiter approached only to stop, take one look and turn on his heels.

Kenna wished there were some way to defuse the situation, for her mom's sake at least. She didn't deserve an ugly scene at her rehearsal dinner.

An idea occurred to her. "Is Lora Leigh still in town? Maybe you can meet with her. Mom could come, too, if Lora Leigh is willing. Take a step toward resolving Skye's custody."

Eyes widened in astonishment, including Channing's.

"What did you say?" her mom demanded.

Kenna's stomach clenched, though she'd done nothing wrong. "Skye's…mom. She was at the arena." She turned to Channing for confirmation. "We saw her talking to Beau. By the hay shed."

Kenna's mom swiveled to face Beau. "Lora Leigh was here? And you didn't tell me?"

"Ah, darling. Don't be mad."

"You lied to me!"

He leaned over and attempted to nuzzle her neck. "I didn't want to upset you. Not before the wedding."

She pulled away as if singed. "We promised to always be honest with each other. What else have you lied to me about?"

"Mom," Kenna implored. "I get why you're upset. You have a right. Beau should have told you about Lora Leigh. But his intentions were to protect you, not deceive you. That counts for something."

She looked at Channing. His only response was to give his head a small shake. Her temples began to throb. This was like a scene from a bad soap opera.

"You know how I feel about cheating." Kenna's mom shoved to her feet. "It's the worst form of dishonesty."

Beau stood, too. "I'd never cheat on you. I just didn't tell you about Lora Leigh. After the last time, I figured it was for the best."

Kenna heard a trace of anger in his rising voice. That worried her.

"The last time!" Her mom glared at him.

"Come on, darling," Beau cajoled. "You're making a mountain out of a molehill. We've talked about that."

Not the right thing to say. Kenna's mom's eyes flashed with fury and pain. "If you think something as important as you lying to me is making a mountain out of a molehill, then maybe we shouldn't get married."

"Gracie," Beau pleaded. "Don't say that."

"Mom." Kenna also stood. "Please. Calm down." She wanted to add, *Don't say something you'll regret.*

"Calm down? Let me know how you feel when the man who supposedly loves you lies to you."

Kenna became vaguely aware of the other people at the table. To Beau's family's credit, they weren't smiling with satisfaction. Rather, they wore expressions of genuine distress and dismay, as did everyone else. Several individuals were excusing themselves and discreetly leaving the restaurant. Beau's brother stared after them longingly.

Kenna whispered to Channing, "Any chance you can help me with this?"

"Hey, folks. How about we give Beau and Gracie some privacy?"

Kenna's mom shoved her way out from behind the table. "That won't be necessary. I'm leaving. Madison, can you drive me home?" Swinging her purse over her arm, she glowered at Beau's mom. "Now you won't have to fake a heart attack. The wedding's off." With that, she charged out of the room.

"Darling, wait." Beau hurried after her.

Madison followed at a distance, gesturing for Kenna to call her.

Kenna debated going, too, but then she regained her senses. What could she say? The train wreck she'd hoped they'd avoid this time had arrived, the result of her mom yet again rushing into a relationship with no regard for the consequences.

Thank goodness she wasn't anything like her mom and wouldn't make the same mistake. Madison had scolded Kenna, saying her ground rules were unromantic. Well, they'd have prevented this disaster.

"What was that about you faking a heart attack?" Beau's dad asked his wife.

"I have no idea. She's hysterical."

"Hysterical?" That struck a nerve with Kenna. She was sick of her mom being treated badly by Beau's family. Try as she might, she couldn't remain silent. "Mom overheard you talking at the bridal shower. You said that maybe if you faked a heart attack, Beau would postpone the wedding."

The older woman glanced away.

"Did you?" her husband asked.

"I was joking."

"You need to apologize."

She made a sound of disgust. "Fine."

He motioned to the waiter. When the uniformed man hurried off to ready the tab, the other guests expressed their regrets to Beau's parents and Kenna before leaving. She mumbled what she assumed were appropriate responses.

Her movements jerky, she gathered her mom's spiral notebook and paperwork from the wedding venue. Just as Beau's dad was settling the tab, Beau returned, his feet dragging.

His mom and sister practically fell on him. "Are you okay?" his mom asked. "What happened?"

"It's over." He appeared on the verge of tears. "Gracie called off the wedding."

"Oh, sweetie." His mom wrapped him in a hug. "It's for the best."

Kenna groaned.

The family surrounded Beau and, without any goodbyes, shuffled him through the maze of tables and out of the restaurant.

Kenna ached for him—he was obviously crushed. At the same time, she wanted to berate him for his stupid mistake. He should have told her mom about Lora Leigh, and he should have taken his fiancee's side when his family was unkind to her.

"You ready?" she asked Channing.

They didn't talk much on the drive. Kenna called her mom, who insisted on being left alone.

"She's going to bed and not coming out until

morning," she reported to Channing after hanging up.

"Did she talk to Beau?"

"She won't. Not tonight."

"Was she serious about calling off the wedding?"

"Hard to tell. Could be a knee-jerk reaction. Mom has those. And while I don't usually defend her, in this case she's somewhat justified."

"Calling off the wedding is extreme, though. Beau's crushed."

"I feel bad for him. But he should have told Mom about Lora Leigh. He said he was going to, and then he obviously didn't." Kenna leaned her head back and closed her eyes, wishing the throbbing in her temples would disappear. "I'm exhausted. Aren't you?"

Channing didn't reply.

They pulled into the driveway, and he left the engine running. Kenna wasn't ready to say good night. She'd been anticipating an entirely different end to the evening.

"I'd invite you in, but with Mom being in a state, that might not be the best idea." She inched closer. A kiss would be nice. She needed one after the last hour. And a hug.

He sat stiffly, hands on the steering wheel. "Call me when you know more."

It had been an awkward, difficult evening for

everyone. Kenna wished she could recapture their earlier mood from the dance floor.

"Don't go. Let's talk on the porch. I just need to check on Mom first."

Channing shut off the truck. "All right."

To the left of the front door, a pair of wicker chairs flanked a side table. Their neon green cushions glowed in the moonlight.

Sitting in the farthest chair, he pulled out his phone. "I'm going to call Beau."

"I won't be long."

With a heavy heart, Kenna entered the house. She would have liked to tell Channing she had no clue what awaited her with her mom. Except she did and braced herself.

KENNA TAPPED ON the door to her mom's locked bedroom.

"Mom. Let me in."

"No. I want to be alone." A muffled sob sounded through the closed door.

"Beau's a wreck."

"He lied to me about Lora Leigh being in town. Maybe's he's been lying to me all along."

Kenna knew this was her mom's insecurities talking. She also knew from experience her mom would feel differently once she'd calmed down. Hopefully in time for the wedding.

She tried a different approach. "Do you need anything? A glass of water? Some aspirin?"

"Go away."

"All right. Holler if you need anything."

She wouldn't. This was nothing new. Kenna's mom always refused any help after a breakup.

And, frankly, tonight Kenna didn't have the emotional strength to battle her. She'd much rather be sitting on the front porch with Channing, holding hands, gazing at the stars and planning her return visit in three weeks.

Weary to the core, she turned away. The door to the guest room was closed and no light escaped from beneath it. Madison must be asleep. Kenna didn't disturb her—they could talk in the morning. Instead, she crept down the hall and through the house.

Returning to the front porch, she found Channing where she'd left him, sitting in a chair.

"Whew." She plopped down beside him with a groan.

"How's your mom?"

His serious expression gave Kenna pause. The phone call with Beau must not have gone well.

"She wants to be alone and sent me away."

"I'm sorry."

"She does that when she's upset. Isolates herself. I guess it's her process. She stayed in her room for five days after my dad died and didn't come out until the funeral. My aunt had to handle all the arrangements."

God, Kenna had always hated that word. *Arrangements*.

"That must have been hard on you."

Her eyes misted at the memory. Tonight's events were hitting her harder than she'd thought. "I was never so miserable in my entire life. Even when Mom finally came out of her room, she kept me at a distance. We weren't ever close again. Leaving home was almost a relief."

"Wow. Tough. First you lost your dad, then your mom and then your home."

"Water under the bridge." Kenna forced a dry chuckle past the lump.

"Is it? That kind of stuff can stay with a person."

"I got over it. Survived. I didn't have a choice. Mom's the same with every breakup. Keeps her feelings bottled up until she's ready to go on the hunt again for her next man. It's why I leave. She has no use for me. Not when she's with a man or when they break up."

"Not sure I understand," Channing said. "You leave because she has no use for you or because she pushes you away?"

"Take your pick. They're basically the same thing."

"They're not. Pushing people away is needing

space to cope with grief or solve a problem. No use for them is rejection."

Ow. She hated that word, too.

Pain pinched her heart. This discussion was touching on sensitive areas, and Kenna preferred to leave them be.

She changed the subject. "I hate to say it, but I'm not altogether surprised at what happened at dinner. Mom and Beau have been destined for trouble from the start."

"They have challenges. I wouldn't say they were destined for trouble."

"Really?" Kenna was genuinely surprised at his remark. "Not even after what happened after tonight?"

"They had an argument that was...helped along by others."

"His mom." Kenna gave her head a dismal shake. "I agree, she was way out of line."

"And you."

"Me?"

"You kind of butted in where you didn't belong," he said.

That riled her. "I defended Mom. You'd do the same in my position. Anyone would."

Channing took a moment as if weighing his next words. She didn't like that, either.

"You mentioned that Lora Leigh was in town."

"I didn't *mention* her—we were *discussing* her."

"Beau and his mom were discussing her. You weren't part of the conversation."

"I made a suggestion. Frankly, it was a good one."

Again, he took a moment before speaking. "You told me you had every intention of staying out of your mom and Beau's relationship. Then, you didn't. From an outside perspective, it almost seemed as if you were…stirring the pot."

Kenna's mouth dropped open. "I absolutely was not."

"Maybe it was unconscious."

"I was attempting to help. There was no stirring the pot, conscious or unconscious."

There hadn't been, right? She tried to recall her frame of mind at the moment. Her only thoughts had been of her mother, first smoothing over the tension and then defending her.

"Was you repeating the remark about Beau's mom faking a heart attack also attempting to help?" Channing asked.

"Beau's mom *did* say that, and she accused my mom of being hysterical."

"That might not have been the best time or place to bring up the heart attack remark. You made a bad situation worse."

Guilt stabbed at Kenna, and she deflected by asking, "Does this have anything to do with your phone call with Beau? Is he mad at me?"

"He's upset. And trying to understand what happened. You've been against the wedding from the start."

"I've changed my mind about him lately."

"All right. But what if you were trying to protect your mom from what you perceived as potential heartache by...hurrying the breakup? You've said many times her relationships don't last."

She almost gasped before composing herself. "All right. I admit maybe I spoke up once or twice tonight when I should have kept my mouth shut. But I wasn't hurrying a breakup and I sure didn't cause the problems between Mom and Beau. He did lie to her by not telling her about Lora Leigh's visit. That's on him."

"True. And he regrets it."

Kenna shoved a hand through her hair. "Why are we even arguing about Mom and Beau, anyway? He's your friend and all, but this is their problem to resolve."

"We're not arguing about them, we're arguing about us."

She stared at him. "I'm confused."

"We have a lot of challenges facing us, too," he said. "Are you going to hurry a breakup if we hit a rough patch?"

"What? No. Where's that coming from?"

"You have a fear of commitment that seems

to stem from a fear of rejection or even fear of abandonment. Your mom's. Repeatedly. Your dad's. You've admitted as much."

"My dad died."

"It's another form of abandonment."

She'd realized that long ago—she just hated admitting it.

"Whenever trouble arises, you leave before you're pushed away or rejected. You've been doing it for years. I also think sometimes you attempt to end things before they get bad. With your mom, for example, or your old boyfriend. Why put off the inevitable, right?"

She drew back to stare at him. "Thank you, Doctor Pearce."

"Kenna." He softened his tone. "I'm concerned. You and I are about to jump headfirst into a long-distance relationship. I'm trying to get an understanding of what I'm possibly in for."

"In for?" Invisible fingers pinched her heart.

"Maybe that wasn't the right way to phrase it."

"You make this sound like I alone will be the one responsible for any problems we might face…or any breakup. That's not fair. I'm on the road for work. A lot. But that's not running. I have contractual obligations."

"As do I," Channing countered. "And financial ones. Which is why I have to stay and can't leave to join you."

"You can't miss one weekend?"

"Can you?"

"I'm arranging for Piper to cover for me."

"That's an option I don't have," he said. "Not with Dad retiring. His health won't allow him to run the rodeo for two or three days. The stress would be too much. There's no one else who can do it."

Kenna knew his dad's health was a genuine concern, but that didn't stop her from saying something she knew was petty. "So I should have to be the one to make all the sacrifices if we're to succeed? What happened to two people compromising?"

"Of course you shouldn't be the only one."

"Well, from an outside perspective," she echoed him, "it looks that way."

"I have every intention of joining you when I can."

"Which is when?"

He visibly tensed. "I don't know exactly. It depends how long of an adjustment period we have with Dad's retirement."

She didn't quite buy his answer; a part of it rang true while another part rang of convenient excuses. She should know—she was practically an expert in those.

"Can I ask a question? Why haven't you ever

had a serious relationship? And don't say you've been waiting for me."

"I suppose I haven't met the right person." She'd put him on the defensive, the slight tightening around his mouth gave him away.

"Talking to Madison lately, I've realized I chose a job that keeps me on the road in order to avoid commitment. I'm wondering if you've picked me for the same reason."

"I'm not commitment-phobic."

"No, I'd say you're more commitment-leery. Work comes first for you. It always has, even when you were competing professionally on the rodeo circuit. Getting serious with a woman is a distraction you don't want or need. Girlfriends are also time-consuming and demanding and they have an annoying habit of interfering with plans. Then, here I come along, someone who's only around once every couple months. You get the best of both worlds—a part-time girlfriend who won't compete too much with your job. Better still, she makes the trip to see you, not the other way around."

She could see him mentally chewing on her short speech. Had she gone too far? The invisible fingers pinching her heart squeezed harder. This evening, this conversation, wasn't going like she'd hoped. The complete opposite, in fact, and she was more than a little worried about the outcome.

"I'd like to tell you you're wrong," he finally said, "except I'm not sure you are."

Kenna had been afraid he'd agree with her.

"I care about you," he continued. "That's one hundred percent real. Does your demanding schedule make my life a little easier? Yeah, it does."

She closed her eyes while the wave of hurt passed over her. She'd wanted him to insist she was wrong and promise to come meet her on the road as soon as possible.

"We're both career-focused individuals," Channing said.

"I agree."

"With a lot of issues we both need to work through."

"Yes."

"I guess I have to ask, is this the best time for a relationship?"

The dreaded question Kenna would have given anything not to hear. "Are you calling it quits?" she managed to say around the giant lump in her throat. "Already?"

"I don't want to hurt you."

"Now who's running away?" she bit out. "Or hurrying the breakup?"

"I get how you'd see it that way."

"What other way is there to see it?"

"Maybe all we need is to take a step back."

"A step back?" She peered at him, trying to read his inscrutable expression. "I told you, I don't do causal hookups."

"I was talking casual dating."

"What's the difference?"

"Our feelings for each other is the difference. The potential for more later on."

"Forgive me for being confused. A few days ago, you were all gung ho. Suddenly, you don't like the way I handled myself during Mom and Beau's argument, and we're taking a step back."

"I did rush…us. You aren't here much, and I had limited time."

"No. I don't agree. I think the real reason is I hit the nail on the head—you aren't willing to compromise. The more serious we become, the more pressure from the arena, and you're having doubts. About yourself, not me."

"I have a lot of responsibility."

"And I don't?"

"You have a history of leaving, Kenna. I don't have as much confidence in us as I'd like to."

Oh, to be able to disagree with him. She couldn't, however. Leaving was her response mechanism. Even now, she was clawing to go inside and put some distance between them.

Dear God. She was just like her mom. How

had she not realized that before? The only difference was her mom shut herself in her room and Kenna hit the road. No wonder Channing had suddenly pulled back tonight. He probably thought he'd seen a vision of what was to come in a future with her.

"I'll be honest, it bothered me when we were talking about your mom earlier and you easily dismissed what you went through. Then, when you said she and Beau were destined for trouble, I started to wonder what kind of chance we had."

She couldn't blame him. Why had she ever thought herself capable of becoming involved with a guy?

"Maybe I am a little too damaged right now." The admission caused a rush of pain, followed by her defenses rising. "We were wrong to start anything in the first place and should have followed our instincts."

He was supposed to say they weren't wrong and assure her they were perfect for each other, save a tweak here and there. He didn't.

"Maybe the timing's just not right. Six months could make a big difference. We'll both be under less pressure then."

He was attempting to leave the door open. Was that what she wanted? "What do we do in the meantime? Remain friends?"

"Hopefully."

"Well, it's not like we'll see each other much. With Mom calling off the wedding and us not dating, there aren't a lot of reasons for me to be at the arena." She was assuming any further discussions of her being the halftime entertainment at events were at an end. Also any future classes. "Actually, I'll be by in the morning to get Zenith and Rocket Man. Thanks for boarding them."

"The morning?"

"The sooner I leave, the better for us both. Staying on will only make it harder. I'm not one for long goodbyes, as you well know."

Yes, she was proposing to do the very thing he'd accused her of moments ago: running away.

"Can we meet up again before you go?"

"What's the point?" Now who was hurrying the breakup?

"Kenna, I didn't mean to… This isn't…"

His sorrowful expression was too much for her. Jumping up, she started for the door. "Night, Channing. See you later."

She escaped inside before he could respond. Through the living room's sheer curtains, she watched Channing's truck lights reverse out of the driveway, turn and then disappear. She had an irrational impulse to call him and tell him to come back. That they could work things out. But she didn't.

Rather than wake her mom or Madison, Kenna

went to the kitchen and sat at the table. Covering her mouth with a paper napkin, she let herself cry. She was her mom's child after all, and if she couldn't leave, then sitting alone in the dark was the next best thing.

She'd been right when she said what she did about Channing, hadn't she? He wasn't willing to compromise or put someone he cared about ahead of work. Or had she been lashing out at him because of the harsh, but true, remarks he'd made about her? What if she, and not he, had brought on their breakup?

Tossing down the soaked napkin, she grabbed a fresh one. Sometime later, Kenna sat bolt upright in the chair, suddenly remembering the women's bull riding tomorrow night. She'd told Channing she'd be leaving in the morning. What about her riding Sideways Sam as the halftime entertainment that evening? Should she offer to have Madison replace her? Bite the bullet and stay?

Completely drained and cleaved in two, Kenna couldn't decide. She dragged herself down the hall toward the guest bedroom. She'd talk to Madison in the morning. Together, they'd figure out what to do. In any case, early in the day or later, Kenna was leaving tomorrow.

CHAPTER FOURTEEN

"YOU GOING TO tell me what has you looking like you just lost your best friend, or would you rather leave me guessing?"

Channing turned away from his office window—which he'd been staring out of for the last ten minutes straight—to find his mom standing in the doorway.

"I have a lot on my mind."

She didn't wait for an invitation and meandered in, making herself comfortable in his visitor chair. "A problem with the women's bull riding tonight?"

"No. Yes." Channing debated how much to say.

"Which is it?" she asked. "Is there a problem your dad and I need to know about or not?"

"Everything's under control with the bull riding." That much was true.

"Okay. So why the long face?"

Might as well tell her—she'd pester him until he confessed. "We may have lost our halftime entertainment."

"Oh, no!" She leaned forward. "Is Kenna all right?"

"I'm assuming she's fine. I haven't heard differently." Or noticed her coming by to get her horses, and he'd been watching. "I haven't checked in with her this morning."

He should. He would. Soon.

"A problem with the wedding, then?" his mom asked.

"Yeah." Channing would focus on that and not mention the rest.

"What happened?"

"Gracie called it off. At least, she had as of last night. I've tried reaching Beau but he's not answering his phone."

"The poor boy. He must be devastated."

"He was taking things pretty hard." Channing recounted the Reader's Digest version of the previous night's events, minus the argument between him and Kenna on her mom's front porch. "I hope Beau not answering his phone means he and Gracie are hashing things out. It's either that or he went on a bender."

"Such a shame. Is that why Kenna can't perform tonight? She's taking care of her mom?"

"No. According to her, Gracie locks herself in her bedroom and refuses to see anyone. Kenna's not performing because...she's leaving."

"Leaving! Why?"

"The wedding's off. No reason for her to stay."

"Aren't the two of you a reason?"

"We...broke up," he admitted.

"Already? For pity's sake, what did you say to her?"

"Why do you assume I'm the one who said something?"

"Because you're a carbon copy of your father. Stubborn to the bone and convinced you're right."

"We had a difference of opinion."

"About her mom and Beau?"

"It started that way. I might have accused her of intentionally stirring the pot with her mom and Beau in an attempt to sabotage the wedding."

His mom's jaw dropped. "You actually said that?"

He grimaced. "Not in those exact words, but close enough. It went downhill from there." Exhaling, he gave her a condensed version of his and Kenna's disagreement.

Was it a disagreement? They hadn't fought, not in the strictest sense of the word. They'd had a discussion. An intense one that didn't go well.

"You have to fix this," his mom insisted when he'd finished. "Stop her from leaving."

"What am I supposed to do? Take a switchblade to her tires."

"If necessary."

"I won't force her to stay."

"Then convince her."

He grunted a noncommittal answer, having no wish to discuss his failed loved life with his mom. "The crowd tonight is going to be disappointed with no halftime entertainment."

"We're sold out," his mom said. "And while Kenna and her friend might have attracted a few people, the vast majority bought tickets for one reason—to watch those women ride bulls."

"You're probably right." Channing was the one who'd be disappointed.

"You've done an amazing job this last month. You've landed contracts for two big events and have a sold-out rodeo event. I couldn't be more proud of you."

He wished his dad felt the same. He'd imagined sharing moments like this with his entire family. Kenna, too. Now that dream had gone by the wayside. His fault—he'd been thrown by what happened at the rehearsal dinner, Kenna's revelations about her mom, and her easy dismissal of Beau and Gracie's fight. In hindsight, he should have waited until today to talk to Kenna. Given himself time to absorb the event and better plan what to say to her.

"Here's an idea," his mom said. "Your sister can carry the flag on her horse for the national anthem, and you ride Sideways Sam during halftime. Grumpy Joe's always good for a few jokes and can engage the crowd."

"Maybe."

"Handle it. And with that problem out of the way, you can focus your energy on convincing Kenna to stay."

"Not sure that's possible. Or if I should."

"Why in heaven's name not?"

"She wasn't wrong. The arena does come first. It has to until we're out of this slump."

His mom's features fell. "Sweetheart. The entire fate of the arena doesn't depend on you."

"Doesn't it?"

"You put too much pressure on yourself. It was the same when you were competing."

Kenna had said something along those lines to him last night.

"Your dad went through the same thing when your grandpa retired."

That was news. "Were profits down then, too?"

"No. But we were hit with a huge unexpected bill when the contractor we hired for the renovations bailed on us and we had to hire someone new. The bill was big enough to make us weak in the knees. Your dad was convinced we were going to lose the arena."

"I never heard this story."

"He doesn't like to tell people. He felt responsible. He chose the contractor." She sighed. But even if he could have done a little more research on the contractor before he hired the man, so what? All that mattered in the long run is he pulled us out of the hole we were in, just like you will now."

"Another reason I don't need one more complication in my life."

"Kenna isn't a complication. She could be the best part of your life if you let her."

"We need to have that intervention with Dad." This remark came from Jocelyn, who stood in the doorway. "Not that I was eavesdropping. Okay… I was. But never mind that." She moved farther into the office. "Here's what has to happen. No exception. Dad puts his health first and foremost and retires. Period. And he quits micromanaging Channing. He's had his run at managing Rim Country—it's Channing's turn."

"Your dad will never tolerate an intervention," Lilian said.

"Fine. We'll call it a family meeting. Whatever it takes, we lay down the law. We tell him we want him around for another thirty years, and that won't happen if he refuses to slow down."

"Actually, I was considering asking him to remain on," Channing said.

"What?" his mom and sister blurted at the same time.

"In a much-reduced capacity. It was Kenna's suggestion. I thought maybe he could continue with the city council meetings and manning the booth with Grumpy Joe. Just enough to include him and bolster his morale without overtaxing him."

"That's a great idea," Jocelyn said. "I knew I liked Kenna."

"I haven't said anything yet because I'm not sure he'll be receptive."

"He may not. Which is why we need to move ahead with this family-meeting-slash-intervention? The sooner the better. We can probably convince him if we present it the right way."

The three of them brainstormed the best approach, with their mom providing the most input. Seemed she had a lot of experience getting their dad to cooperate.

"I love the idea, I do," she said when they had a plan in place. "And I'm all for it. Except we've only solved half the problem." She looked to Jocelyn. "Your brother needs to lighten his workload. Enough that he can get a weekend off here and there. How else can he make time for Kenna?"

"Who said I need to make time for Kenna?" he objected.

His mom rolled her eyes. "Men. Do I need to shake some sense into you?"

"Well..." Jocelyn wagged her brows. "I have another idea."

"Will you two stop trying to repair my love life?" Channing grumbled.

"Someone has to," his mom said. "You're doing a terrible job."

Jocelyn ignored them and continued. "I've been wanting to increase my hours. Why don't I help manage the non-rodeo events? There's a lot more I could be doing than I am."

Lilian clapped her hands together. "That's a perfect solution!"

"I agree." Channing smiled. "I also think we should give you a title. Assistant manager." He'd been wanting his sister to play a larger role from the beginning. Here was her chance. "If you're sure, sis."

"I am." Her bright eyes and wide smile confirmed it. "And I've already talked to Dave about this," she said, referring to her husband. "He's very supportive of me working increased hours—and it means he'll get to spend more time with the boys."

"I'm so happy." Channing's mom pushed to her feet and hugged Jocelyn. "I have the best, smartest, most capable children in the entire world. Can't wait for your dad to hear the news."

They agreed on a time later that day to approach Channing's dad, figuring he'd be in a receptive mood when he returned from lunch with his cronies.

Jocelyn hurried back to her desk when the phone rang.

His mom pushed to her feet. “I hate to cut this short, but I need to cut the weekly checks. If not, I’ll have a lot of unhappy vendors.” At the door, she paused, her expression sympatric and motherly. “Don’t worry about tonight. I wouldn’t be surprised if Kenna showed up. She’s a responsible person that way. Takes her job seriously.”

She did. Normally. But Channing couldn’t echo his mom’s expectations.

If he were honest with himself, he’d allowed his own fears to get the best of him. Kenna chose flight over fight, yes—that was her nature. What he hadn’t said last night was he worried that she’d leave at the first sign of trouble and break his heart. Something she could only do because he’d fallen for her.

The thought gave him pause. Maybe he was the one who’d done the sabotaging in order to protect himself.

Grabbing his cowboy hat, he headed out the door. While several tasks required his attention, he strode past the arena and the horse barn toward the livestock pens. The vet had arrived an hour ago for the follow-up visit from Wednesday, and it was now after eight o’clock. Channing had put the head wrangler in charge while he moped, as his mom would call it, but decided to check on the progress. Besides, the distraction would do him well.

He barely noticed his surroundings during the walk, too busy mentally kicking himself. While he was thrilled that Jocelyn would become assistant manager, he was less enthusiastic about the benefits of possible time off.

There'd been at least a dozen better choices he could have made last night with Kenna. And now it was too late. A glance in the direction of the parking area revealed her trailer and Madison's still there. That meant nothing. She could be sleeping in or helping her mom cancel the venue and the caterers and all the other wedding services.

To his enormous surprise, he found Beau at the livestock pens, the man's rubber work boots covered with muck.

"What are you doing?" Channing called out, though it quickly became apparent to him.

"Getting these bad boys separated for Doc. He double-checked the records and we missed a few vaccinations yesterday."

Waving to the vet across the pen, Channing asked Beau, "Need any help?"

"All done." He shut the gate behind the last bull.

Channing ambled over to join him at the fence.

"Why are you here? You're supposed to be off work for ten days."

"That was when I had a wedding to get ready for and a honeymoon to go on."

"Gracie's still mad?"

"Not as much." He shrugged sadly. "But the wedding's still off."

"Sorry, pal."

"We talked up a storm last night on the phone."

"That's good."

"Thought I might've gotten somewhere with her. Seems I overestimated my charm. I'm holding out that she'll change her mind and put me out of my misery. If not in time for tomorrow, then another day."

"No offence, but you don't suppose she overreacted?"

"That's my Gracie for you." Beau's expression was that of an enamored teenager. "One of the things I love best about her. She keeps life interesting."

Channing thought the same about Kenna.

"Gosh, I'm mad at myself." Beau rested his arm on the fence, apparently settling in for a long rant. "I should have told her about Lora Leigh. The very thing I tried to avoid happened anyway, only worse. What's that old saying about the road to you know where being paved with good intentions?"

Channing could sympathize. Hadn't he just come to the same conclusions about him and Kenna?

"Wish I had some advice to give you."

Beau smiled sadly. "I could sure use some."

"Me, too. I messed up with Kenna."

"What? You don't say?"

"We had a disagreement last night after I took her home. A big one."

"That's a shame. Was it about me and Gracie?"

"Started out that way." Like with his mom, Channing relayed the high points—more like low points, actually.

"Aw, man. I'm sure Kenna figured I'd told Gracie about Lora Leigh being in town. Heck, I told Kenna I was going to it. Guess I lied to her, too."

"Believe me, it quickly moved on from there to her relationship with Gracie, her fear of commitment, and my fear of failure and borderline obsession with work." He shook his head, still mad at himself. "I blew it. I spoke without thinking and said some things I wish I could take back. She probably hates me."

"That's funny." Beau looked perplexed. "She didn't mention a word about you and her when she came by a while ago."

"She's here?" He looked around.

"*Was* here. Stopped by to see how I was doing

and to apologize for causing a problem. Left, oh…twenty minutes ago."

While Channing was in his office talking to his mom and sister. "What'd she say?"

"Nothing about you and her. I had no idea you two were on the outs. She and I, we've been getting along better lately. Not so much she confides in me."

"Did she mention where she was going?"

"Nope. Fact is, I did most of the talking. She's a good listener, that one."

Unlike Channing. He was starting to think if he'd done more listening last night instead of talking, he and Kenna would be snuggling over breakfast at the diner right about now. She certainly wouldn't be leaving.

"I need to call her," he murmured more to himself than Beau.

"Sounds like a plan."

He had a lot to tell her, if she was receptive and if it wasn't too late.

"Not that you asked for my opinion," Beau said, "but you'd be a fool to let her get away."

"Got any suggestions?"

Beau knocked his cowboy hat back and scratched his forehead. "I like the direct approach. Forget calling or texting. Track her down. My guess is she's at the house."

"You might be onto something."

A small spark of hope ignited. She'd come to the arena and not loaded her horses. Could part of her want to stay and give them a second chance?

"You in the mood for some company?" Beau asked, flashing a sheepish smile. "I could see if Gracie's softened any toward me."

"Let's go." One thing Channing had learned during his years in business: it was harder to say no in person than on the phone.

While Beau cleaned up and changed into his regular boots, Channing got hold of his dad, who was on his way home from a doctor's appointment. They arranged for him to meet with the vet, freeing up Channing and Beau.

On the way to Kenna's mom's house, Channing sent Kenna a text, asking how she was doing. He didn't want to alert her to his arrival, merely send out a feeler. Depending on her reaction—cool or warm—he'd have an idea of what lay ahead.

She didn't respond, however. He tried not to read too much into it. Her phone could be off. She could be in the other room or with her mom. Not packing. Please, not packing.

When they finally arrived at the house after what felt like a hundred-mile drive, it was to discover an empty driveway. Both Kenna's and Madison's trucks were gone.

"I think we've struck out," he told Beau.

"Mind if I check on Gracie's car?"

Beau hopped out of the vehicle and trotted to the side of the garage. There, he pressed his face to the small window, using his hands to shield the sun from his face. Channing figured from his jaunty return that Gracie was home.

"Her car's there," he told Channing, who had rolled down the driver's-side window. "I'm gonna knock on the door."

"I'll wait. Just in case."

Beau headed to the front door, where he proceeded to both knock and ring the bell. Getting no response, he went to the front window and peered in. By his slumped shoulders, Channing guessed the house was empty.

"She's either not home or refusing to see me," he said, climbing in the passenger seat.

Channing felt for the guy. He was experiencing the same disappointment.

"What do you want to do?" he asked.

"Might as well leave. We can always try again later."

The return ride to the arena seemed to take twice as long. Neither man said much. Once there, Channing sent Kenna another text and, an hour later, when she still hadn't responded, he called. Again, no answer, so he left a brief message.

To his incredible relief, she texted back a few

minutes later. But the single-line response revealed very little and didn't answer the questions banging around inside his head.

I'm with Mom. We're talking.

Channing pushed through the rest of the morning. To be on the safe side, he arranged with his sister and Grumpy Joe to cover for Kenna. Periodically, he stalked the parking area, searching for a sign of either Kenna or Madison. With each unsuccessful sighting, his hopes sunk a little further until he felt like they were wrapped around his ankles.

"Don't let her leave without talking to me," he said, repeating the words like a mantra.

"WHAT ARE WE doing here, Mom?" Kenna asked for the third time. And she'd continue asking until she got a reasonable answer. "And why aren't you locked in your room?"

To her utter disbelief, her mom had emerged from her bedroom shortly after nine o'clock, freshly showered, dressed, her hair styled, and chatty. Kenna had never witnessed a turnaround like this before.

"They have excellent food," her mom said, ignoring the question about her miraculous recovery.

"Is anyone really hungry?"

Kenna had awakened after a grueling and fitful night with no appetite and in a lousy mood. She'd assumed her mom would feel similarly. But no. She was all sunshine and daisies.

"This is like returning to the scene of a crime." Madison's eyes twinkled with mischief as they entered the dining room at Joshua Tree Inn.

Kenna sent her a perturbed look and scanned the immediate area for familiar faces. She didn't want to run into any of the waitstaff from last night or—please, God, no—Beau's brother and sister-in-law, who were staying here.

For reasons that defied explanation, her mom had insisted they *Brunch at the inn*. Kenna had voted for the diner down the road and been overruled.

"Nothing like a little hair of the dog," her mom remarked, which made absolutely no sense to Kenna. Why torture yourself by returning so quickly after a debacle?

The hostess escorted them to a table that was, thankfully, on the opposite side of the large room from where they'd eaten the previous evening. But, as soon as Kenna sat, she wanted to move—their current location gave them an unobstructed view of, as Madison had said, *the scene of the crime*.

Her mom couldn't stop staring. Was she punishing herself? Had that been the reason she chose the inn? Kenna admitted she'd spent a little time on the front porch this morning, reliving her argument with Channing as she sipped her coffee.

Until the moment she'd dropped off from exhaustion somewhere around 2:00 a.m., she'd blamed him for the entire awful argument. The light of day brought with it a fresh perspective, one that placed some, if not the lion's share, of blame at her feet. Why hadn't she admitted he was a tiny smidgeon right and shown him her willingness to work on their differences? Instead, she'd done just what he'd accused her of: she'd headed for the hills.

Make that *would* head for the hills. At some point. She'd gotten to the arena early that morning and, after talking to Beau, returned home, deciding to approach her mom again. But then her mom had emerged from her bedroom a brand-new person, stunning Kenna.

"You're not seriously thinking of leaving today?" Madison demanded of Kenna once they'd placed their food orders. "Yeah, you're mad at Channing, and maybe you have a right, but it's not like you, like *us*, to skip out on a performance. Even one we're doing for free."

"I was thinking you could cover for me. Carry

the flag for the national anthem and perform at halftime?"

"I'm not riding that bucking horse!"

"Your own horse. Or Channing can ride Sam and you can handle halftime."

Madison considered a moment. "I will. Only to protect Hoof Feats' reputation."

"Thanks. I'll let him know."

"After all he's done for you," she grumbled. "Boarding your horses. Helping you with Rocket Man. And still you leave him in the lurch?"

Kenna pressed her fingers to her chest where an ache had lodged. Madison had a point. Kenna had let her emotions get the best of her last night. If only she hadn't gotten so defensive.

"You rodeo women," her mom interjected. "You're all the same."

She was oddly calm for someone who'd canceled her wedding. When would the slew of phone calls start? As of yet, her mom hadn't made a single one. She'd need to alert people—there were a ton—and might try to recruit Kenna, who would then have to stay…

"Just like Lora Leigh," her mom continued. "Leaving at the drop of a hat."

Ouch. That hit a sore spot, and Kenna couldn't help retaliating. "I can't believe you just lumped me in the same category with a person you hate."

"I don't hate her. She's Skye's mama. And she can't help being younger than me."

Kenna blinked in shock. "Then why did you fight with Beau and call off the wedding?"

"A knee-jerk reaction. He lied to me."

"Okay." Kenna almost did a double take. "What brought this on?"

"We talked last night."

"You did? When?"

"On the phone. You were in bed." Kenna's mom sipped her mimosa. "He made me realize I've been my own worst enemy. I was focusing on actions rather than intentions."

Kenna had said as much last night. Apparently, her mom hadn't heard her in the heat of the moment. "That's good."

"I agree," Madison seconded.

"He's a great guy," Kenna's mom continued. "He adores me. I'm lucky to have found him."

Kenna didn't want to pour cold water on her mom's revelation, but she had to ask, "You're not just saying that because you don't want to be alone?"

Rather than get mad, her mom nodded thoughtfully. "I'm not. Don't misunderstand me. I have a long way to go. My insecurities—yes, I have them—haven't disappeared. I'll be a work-in-progress for some time. Luckily, I'll be going through the process with Beau. We're starting couples' counseling after the honeymoon. Probably should have done that first. Better late than never," she quipped.

"Really?" Kenna was amazed. Her mom had never gone to counseling before, not even after Kenna's dad died.

Maybe that was something she and Channing should do. Except now it was too late.

"So…the wedding's still on?" Madison asked.

"Of course it is." Kenna's mom beamed. "I just needed some time to cool off and come to my senses."

"Does Beau know?" Kenna asked. "Because I saw him a couple hours ago and he was in shambles."

"I haven't come right out and told him." She smiled. "I sent him a text with a heart and a smiley face and kissing lips on the way here."

"Mom!" Kenna snapped her mouth shut when the waitress approached with their food, then resumed after she'd left. "Channing and I broke up because of you and Beau's falling-out."

Her mom paused before taking a bite of her quiche. "You most certainly did not. You and Channing broke up because of your own problems."

"She's right," Madison quipped.

Kenna's anger slowly deflated. It was true: her and Channing's problems would have come to a head eventually. If not last night, then later, prompted by something else.

"I'm not like Lora Leigh," she mumbled, trying to take the focus off herself. "Nothing could ever make me voluntarily leave my baby girl." Poor Skye. Kenna would miss her something awful.

"No, you'd just take her along with you," Madison said.

Kenna sat up. She didn't know whether to be insulted or hurt or ashamed. "Does everybody think that of me?"

"You do leave the people you care about," Kenna's mom said. "Me, that horse trainer you dated… Channing."

Something inside Kenna snapped. The misery she'd held inside and never revealed spilled out in a torrent.

"I didn't leave you, Mom. You pushed me away. Over and over and over. After Dad died. Every time you had a new man in your life, every time you kicked him to the curb…you wanted nothing to do with me. Whenever I tried to help you, like last night, you sent me away as if you had no use for me. Do you know how much that hurts? I'll tell you. A lot. It breaks my heart."

If Kenna had thought she'd cried herself out last night, she was wrong. Fresh tears spilled, and she wiped at them with her napkin.

"Oh, kitten." Her mom reached for her hand and squeezed it. Emotion clogged her voice. "I'm so sorry. So very, very sorry."

Kenna stared at her uneaten Belgian waffle. Great, two ugly scenes at the inn in a twelve-hour period. "I guess that's been building for a while."

They were silent for a moment, then her mom said, "When you dad died, I wasn't prepared or equipped to handle my grief. I'd never felt like that before. I retreated—it was my way of escaping. People, they meant well, but their hovering and platitudes and good intentions just kept reminding me of my loss and my pain. I had to insulate myself in order to survive." She swallowed a sob. "I didn't make the best decisions after that. With each breakup, I retreated again. I couldn't stop. I didn't think about what I was doing to you. But I've been selfish and cruel and a rotten mother."

Silence fell over the table for several long moments. Kenna could either accept her mom's apology and attempt to move forward or become estranged from her.

Finally, she spoke. "I understand the part about not being about to stop. Only my problem is avoiding commitment."

"We're products of our experiences."

"Maybe victims."

"Yeah. That's a better term." Her mom squeezed Kenna's fingers again. "We could each use about a hundred hours of counseling."

"And I bet a couple of great guys wouldn't hurt," Madison added, dabbing at her own tears.

Kenna tried to smile but couldn't. The emotional venting had drained her.

"We can't repair the damage I've caused to you overnight," her mom said. "But I promise you this—I won't push you away again. I swear. And if I start to, you have my permission to kick me from here to the moon."

Kenna gave her mom's fingers a return squeeze. "What I want is for you and Beau to be incredibly happy and never have a reason to push me away."

Madison raised her mimosa. "I'll drink to that."

"I love you, kitten." Kenna's mom leaned over and kissed her cheek.

"I love you, too, Mom."

"We're quite the pair, aren't we? Two wonderful men who adore us, and we tried to get rid of them."

"Speak for yourself. You obviously couldn't get rid of Beau if you hired professional kidnappers."

"He is special. And, kitten, you can't get rid

of Channing, either. You haven't yet in fourteen years."

Kenna picked at her food. "Not true. I managed precisely that last night."

Madison chuckled. "Believe me, he didn't spontaneously fall out of love with you."

"He wasn't in love with me to begin with."

"And there are no fish in the sea, either."

"You're in love with him, too," her mom added.

Kenna felt her cheeks redden. "Stop it, you two. Besides, I told him I was leaving."

"Oh, there you go." Madison rolled her eyes. "You can't *possibly* stay in town now, not after *saying* you were leaving."

"Okay, I'm not leaving until Sunday now that the wedding's back on. Doesn't change what Channing and I argued about and how I feel."

"Your aversion to commitment?"

"And the reason for it, which, according to Channing, stems from a fear of loss and rejection and—" she winced "—abandonment. Oh, good grief, I do need that counseling."

"There are no guarantees in life," her mom said. "No one knows that better than me. The truth is, someday you might lose him or others who are dear to you."

"I agree. Which is why I—"

"However, if I believed like you do, I wouldn't have married your dad and enjoyed sixteen of the happiest years of my life. I wouldn't have had you, either." Her mom's eyes misted. "Even knowing the outcome, I'd marry your dad all over again. I want the same for you. A whole lifetime, though—not just a few years. Promise me you'll grab whatever happiness you can, wherever you can. Don't shy away just because it might not last forever."

"It's better to have loved and lost than never to have loved at all," Madison quipped.

Both Kenna and her mom stared at her.

"What?" She looked mildly affronted. "I've read poetry."

"Tell me this," Kenna's mom said. "If you had the chance to reconcile with Channing, would you?"

"I want to talk to him. We've been friends too long to leave things the way they ended last night."

"That's not what I asked."

Kenna peered deep inside herself. She found a lot of fear of loss and rejection that hadn't vanished simply because she'd started coming to terms with it and had a heart-to-heart with her mom. Beneath the fear, however, lay a vibrant layer of hope. She did want what her parents once had, for a year or sixteen years or, God willing, the rest of her life.

"I would," she admitted.

"There you go." Her mom grinned as if she'd won a prize. "We'll drop you off at the arena when we leave."

Kenna panicked. "What will I say to him?"

"You'll think of something."

"What's the old saying?" Madison asked. "Go big or go home."

"I don't think that applies here."

"It does. You need to go big, girl. Get Channing's attention in a way that says you're willing to take a leap of faith with him."

Could Kenna do that? Was she brave enough?

Yes. After all, she hung upside down on galloping horses for a living.

And then, just like that, she knew. "I have an idea, but I'll need help from both of you."

"We're all ears!" her mom said.

"First, I'll text Channing and tell him Madison's covering for me tonight."

"I thought we agreed you're staying for the wedding."

"Channing doesn't know that, and don't let Beau tell him. Keep Channing in the dark. I'll avoid him for the rest of the day, so he won't know what's happening. When the bull riding starts, he'll be expecting Madison to ride up on her horse for the national anthem."

"Only *you'll* ride up on Sideways Sam." Madison smiled wickedly. "I love it."

"I need to get the horses and my trailer. Take them somewhere temporarily so Channing thinks I've left. Maybe Rochelle can help me."

"She's the woman you bought Rocket Man from?"

"Yeah. Mom, your job is to keep Channing distracted. I can't have him looking for Madison or spotting me sneaking in."

"Got it. I'm already thinking of a way. And Beau can help."

"There's one more thing." Kenna smiled. "You still have that old portable sewing machine?"

"In the closet."

"And those tablecloths we bought for the bridal shower?"

"With the reception decorations."

"Madison." Kenna faced her friend. "I have a project for you."

"What kind of project?"

She outlined her plan while her mom and Madison finished their meals. Kenna was too anxious and excited to do more than pick at her food. If everything came together as she hoped, her and Channing's entire lives would change.

With trembling fingers, she composed and sent him the text about Madison. Step one complete. Now on to step two.

CHAPTER FIFTEEN

WOMEN BULL RIDERS were no different from their male counterparts, Channing decided as he manned the gate to the arena. They talked in small groups and studied the bulls while forming strategies. Vented their nervous energy by swinging their arms, kicking posts and pacing. Those who were superstitious practiced their various rituals. Help was requested and given to pin numbers on backs. Waves and whistles were exchanged with friends and family in the bleachers. Comradery abounded, and the air crackled with excitement.

Channing was the one exception. He couldn't muster a single shred of enthusiasm.

His day had gone from bad to worse. It started with him and Beau finding no one home at Gracie's. Next, his only communications from Kenna consisted of two texts, one about her being with her mom and a later one letting him know Madison would replace her tonight. Last, and worse of all, He'd discovered Kenna's trailer and her two horses gone.

She'd left Payson. A heavy fist pressed into his lungs and cut off his air supply whenever he thought of her and what might have been. What could have been. What he *wished* had been.

Why hadn't he fought harder for her? Fought at all for her instead of just letting her go? She was worth it.

He'd been keeping watch on her trailer in case she showed. Then Beau had called right after lunch, begging Channing to come over. He'd been a wreck and needed someone to talk some sense into him, as he'd put it. Channing hadn't been able to tell his friend no. As a result, he'd spent two hours at Beau's double-wide, during which Kenna had come to the arena and gone. He'd missed his one and only opportunity to talk with her and possibly reconcile or, at the very least, say a last goodbye.

But she had a phone. He did, too. People did converse using this modern tool for communication.

His fingers itched to call her. To quell the urge, he shoved his hands into his jeans pocket. What would he say to her, anyway? Don't run? Come back? She'd clearly made her decision. Did he think a too-late phone call would change her mind?

He should apologize. Their friendship was certainly worth saving.

Maybe he'd try again when she next returned to town. Time apart might make her more receptive. Except now that wouldn't be for a couple months, if not longer, instead of the three weeks they'd decided on together.

With the clamoring crowd and nearby conversations filling his ears, he tried in vain to focus. The bulls—the same ones the men used—were in the holding pen and ready to go. The wranglers checked and rechecked equipment. The pickup cowboys, whose job it was to herd the bulls out the exit gate after each ride, leaned forward and rested their forearms on their saddle horns. The bullfighters, in their colorful costumes and face makeup, waited just inside the arena. Not Beau, though. Another man had taken his place.

Feeling a hand gripping his shoulder, he cranked his head around. "Hi, Dad."

"Quite a turnout tonight. I'm impressed. Congratulations are in order."

"Thanks."

The intervention-slash-family meeting that afternoon had gone well. Better than Channing had expected. He credited his mom, who'd stressed how him not putting his health first affected them all. For once, his dad listened. Jocelyn followed up with the financial reports and the recent progress Channing had made. Their dad apparently took this better coming from her and not Channing. And money did talk. Channing ended with the plan for Burle to continue in a small role. He'd liked that idea, especially when Channing insisted he continue sitting in on the weekly company meetings.

"I can admit when I'm wrong, son, and I was wrong about this. Fans are embracing women's rodeo."

"It's here to stay, Dad."

"The world is changing, and we need to change with it. Your mom and I are looking forward to the Honky Tonk Nights concert." He winked. "We're making a date night out of it."

"She'll like that."

Channing did his best to muster a smile. His mom had no doubt informed his dad about Kenna's departure. The last thing Channing wanted was more sympathy. He'd had enough already from his mom and sister to last until next year.

"Sorry that Sideways Sam won't be making an appearance for the national anthem," Channing said.

"That?" His dad dismissed the concerns with a shrug. "I wouldn't worry about it."

"I plan on continuing to rehabilitate the old folks."

Channing would do it, too. In a few weeks. It had been his and Kenna's project. Theirs together. He needed a little time before tackling it alone.

"Absolutely. It's a worthy endeavor." His dad gave Channing's shoulder another firm squeeze. "I'd best get going. Duty calls."

He left, climbing the stairs to the announcer's booth. For as long as Channing could remember, his dad sat in the booth with Grumpy Joe during every rodeo event. Thankfully, that would be continuing for the foreseeable future.

"Hey, Channing."

A trio of young contestants decked out in full gear, including helmets with face masks and safety vests, approached him.

"We just wanted to tell you thanks," the taller one said. "There's almost nothing like this for us gals in the area. We usually wind up driving to Phoenix or Globe."

"Sign us up for the next one," another woman said, "which I hope is soon!"

He chatted with them for a few minutes, amazed at his ability to act normal when that was the furthest thing from what he felt. They left when Grumpy Joe made the usual pre-event announcements. Rim Country's first women's bull-riding event was almost underway.

Channing released a heavy sigh. He'd imagined Kenna here with him, sharing the excitement.

He looked around for Madison. Come to think

of it, he hadn't seen her anywhere. Then again, he'd been distracted. Shading his eyes against the bright glare of overhead floodlights, he searched the immediate area. She was nowhere in sight.

Groaning—he didn't need this—he started to tell the nearest wrangler to watch the gate for him when he ground to a halt. There, strolling toward him and wearing enormous smiles, were Beau and Gracie. They pushed a stroller with Skye, who sat up, wide-eyed and taking in all the sights.

"There you are!" Gracie called out.

"Well, I'll be. This is a change from this afternoon." Channing smiled in return, his first genuine one in the last twenty-four hours. "Something tells me you have good news."

"We do." Beau kissed the top of Gracie's head. She blushed profusely in response. "We wanted to let you know the wedding's back on. You'd better not have returned that fancy tux."

"I haven't. And I'm really glad to hear it. I'd given up hope."

"Well…the wedding was never really off," Gracie admitted.

"No?" Channing sent her a look.

"I had a little tantrum is all."

He swallowed the biting reply that came to mind. Her little tantrum had put Beau through the wringer. Him and Kenna, too.

No, that wasn't right. Channing was a realist. He knew he and Kenna would have had to face their problems sooner or later. But he wished it would have occurred in a less confrontational way. Then maybe they could have talked and found compromises. Learned and grown rather than fought and broke up.

Seeing Beau's exuberant expression and the loving touches he and Gracie shared, Channing kept his mouth shut. At least his friend was happy.

He was about to respond when a thought occurred to him. "What about Kenna?"

"What about her?" Gracie asked, seeming not to understand.

"The wedding's on. She's the maid of honor." A jolt coursed through him. "Is she in town? On her way back?"

At that moment, the wranglers herded the bulls down the enclosure to the bucking chutes accompanied by cheers from the crowd. Stomping and snorting, the bulls made a huge ruckus.

"Sorry, Channing." Gracie held a cupped hand to her ear. "I can't hear you."

"Kenna," he repeated more loudly. "Will she be at the wedding?"

Gracie shook her head to indicate she still didn't hear.

Channing's frustration escalated. If Kenna was in town, then where were her trailer and horses? Had she not answered his calls and texts because she was still mad, or was it for some other reason?

Desperation propelled him to place a hand on her arm and lean in, intending to speak directly into her ear. He drew back when Grumpy Joe's voice blared from the speakers.

"Ladies and gentlemen. Would everyone who can please stand for the national anthem."

The rumble of feet on bleachers was followed by silence. Gracie slipped free from Channing. He opened his mouth to speak, and she shushed him with a finger to her lips. Then she, Beau and Skye disappeared toward the stands. Channing muttered a curse under his breath. It was as if everyone and everything was conspiring against him.

Where was Madison? He looked around again. Still no sign of her.

Thinking he needed to alert his dad in the booth, he reached for his phone in his shirt pocket. Grumpy Joe's voice interrupted him again.

"Folks, you're in for a real treat tonight. Our flag bearer is well-known to most of you. She's a local talent who's made quite a name for herself as a trick rider."

Channing frowned. Madison wasn't from Payson.

"And tonight, she isn't riding just any horse.

She's on a big fellow many of you may know. Former champion bronc Sideways Sam, who is the first successful graduate of Rim Country's own program to rehabilitate former bucking stock into riding mounts."

Chatter erupted from the audience.

"Everyone put your hands together for Kenna Hewitt and Sideways Sam, our very special flag bearers."

Channing's mind grappled to process what was happening as the next several seconds passed in a blur. From around a corner, Kenna, wearing a Hoof Feats costume with lightning bolts down the sides, trotted up on Sideways Sam. Ten feet from the open arena gate, she urged the horse into a full lope, the flagpole balanced in a holster by her side. She thundered by Channing, her gaze aimed straight ahead, her brow furrowed with concentration, her posture straight as an arrow.

Had she seen him? He couldn't tell.

They entered the arena as the first note of the national anthem played. The flag fluttering majestically in the air, she and Sam barreled down the side of the arena to the roar of thunderous applause.

She was a magnificent sight. Yes, Channing had contributed to this amazing accomplishment.

But Kenna had come up with the idea to ride Sideways Sam and then practiced diligently.

Channing's heart swelled with admiration and pride and something more. Love. He finally admitted to himself what he'd been feeling for her from the that first date when they were young. He loved Kenna, and now that she hadn't left, he'd let her know. She must love him a little, too. Why else was she here, riding Sideways Sam?

After one full circuit, she slowed the horse to a walk and guided him to the center of the arena. There, she and Sam waited until the anthem finished playing, her sitting straight and Sam standing still, his shaggy head held high like the champ he was. Even from a distance, Channing could see the beaming smile on Kenna's face.

Well, she had every right to be pleased. She'd not only impressed the heck out of everyone, him included, she'd elevated people's opinion of Rim Country. He wanted to kiss her more in that moment than ever before.

With a laugh, he realized Gracie and Beau must have known all along that Kenna was riding Sam. That was why Gracie hadn't answered his questions. His dad and Grumpy Joe must have been in on it, too. Channing was the only one left in the dark. Fine by him, he'd take surprises like this any day.

He wanted to ask her what it meant, her returning to ride Sideways Sam. But he'd have to wait. With the final notes of the song hanging in the air, Kenna trotted Sam back toward the gate.

"You'll be seeing more of this lovely lady at halftime," Grumpy Joe said, "along with her partner, Madison. Until then, show her and old Sam there what you think of them."

Applause, louder than before, filled the arena. Kenna rode past Channing still wearing her smile. His own face felt ready to crack in half, his grin was that big.

"Kenna. Kenna!" He started after her. "Wait."

She stopped and glanced over at him but didn't dismount. Her smiled dimmed, and her eyes shone with uncertainty. "I have to warm up Rocket Man for halftime."

"Can we talk?"

"After halftime. If you still want to."

If he still wanted to? Channing didn't understand.

She swung Sam around then and headed toward the horse barn. He considered going after her, but one of the wranglers hollered to him about helping with a cantankerous bull acting up.

Channing returned to the chutes, confused and agitated and baffled. Kenna showing up unannounced. Her cryptic remark. What did it all mean?

KENNA RODE SAM around the horse barn and to the outdoor stalls where Rochelle waited with Kenna's truck and trailer. Rocket Man, already saddled and bridled, stood tied to the side. They'd snuck in earlier with Beau's help, using a private rear entrance. He'd assured Kenna that Channing was too busy with the bull riding to notice them.

Rochelle had helped Kenna carry out her plan by keeping Zenith and Rocket Man at her place for the afternoon. An hour ago, in response to Kenna's all-systems-go phone call, she'd driven Rocket Man to the arena, meeting Beau at the private entrance.

"Well?" Rochelle called out as Kenna approached. "How'd it go? I heard the cheers and applause from here."

"Fantastic. Couldn't have asked for better."

Elation filled Kenna's heart at the memory of her and Sam riding into the arena. The feeling came close to the first time she'd performed with Hoof Feats.

"And Channing? What did he think?"

Hopping off Sam, Kenna tied him to the side of the trailer. The former bronc would be fine there in the shade until after the halftime show.

"I'm not sure. I think he was smiling. But then..." Doubts assailed her. "He hollered to me that he wanted to talk. He looked serious and sounded intense."

"Mad intense or *glad* intense?"

"I don't know. He might not like that I didn't work with Sam this morning and tire him out ahead of time."

As if reading her thoughts, Rochelle said, "You can't back out now. You've come this far."

Go big or go home. Well, Kenna was going big.

"Madison's waiting for you in the practice ring," Rochelle said and patted Sam's nose. She'd taken a shine to the old bronc, and vice versa.

"Okay." Kenna rechecked the saddle and bridle before mounting. Rocket Man pawed the ground impatiently, raring to go. He'd have his chance in a minute. "You heading to the arena?"

"You kidding? I wouldn't miss this for anything. Good luck, sweetie."

Kenna would need it. She accepted the bundle Rochelle handed her and gave Rocket Man a gentle kick.

At the practice ring, Madison asked the same questions as Rochelle, but added a couple more to chide Kenna.

"Why didn't you talk to him?"

"I got flustered. His eyebrows were knotted together like when someone says something he doesn't like."

Second, third and fourth thoughts marched in a parade across Kenna's brain. The idea that had her rallying the troops this morning now had her ready to retreat. A million things could go wrong, including her making a complete and utter fool of herself.

"Let's get this show on the road," Madison announced.

Kenna struggled to calm her jittery nerves.

They began their warmup on Madison's horse, executing the double one-foot stand they'd practiced this week. Rocket Man was still too inexperienced for such an advanced trick. An hour later, muscles limber and kinks worked out, they made their way to the arena. Every cell in Kenna's body tingled with anticipation, and the rolled bundle she'd secured to her saddle felt like it was shooting sparks.

Hearing a sharp whistle and her name, she located her mom and Beau in the front row along with Skye in the stroller. Her mom blew kisses. Beau gave her a thumbs-up. Kenna waved in return, too on edge to do more.

Channing stood at the gate where she'd seen him earlier. She tried not to look at him, refusing to take any chances. In her version of what was about to happen, he'd be grinning from ear to ear. Reality could be vastly different.

"Relax, will you," Madison said. "He's going to freak."

"Or freak out."

"The man loves you. This isn't a mistake."

Kenna could resist no longer. She snuck a peek at Channing out of the corner of her eye. And then their gazes connected.

Pow! The impact hit her with a shower of starlight. Kenna felt the emotion coming off him as if the thirty feet separating them was only thirty inches.

She smiled. He did, too. She could have sworn birds started singing and bells were ringing, but that was impossible.

"We're next." Madison gave her arm a jiggle just as Grumpy Joe announced the end of the first half and tonight's entertainment.

Kenna looked away from Channing, then ahead, then back at him again. Yep, birds singing and bells ringing. Possibly a full orchestra playing.

"Ladies and gentlemen." Grumpy Joe's voice carried across the arena. "Like I promised you earlier, we have some mighty fine entertainment in store for you. Let's give a big Rim Country welcome to Kenna and Madison, stars and founders of Hoof Feats. The first trick they're performing for you tonight is a sidesaddle layout."

Kenna cued Rocket Man into a lope and entered the arena, Madison right behind her. They both executed the same trick simultaneously, matching each other's movements with exact precision. Even over the din of Rocket Man's pounding hooves, Kenna could hear the audience cheering. Next, Madison performed a flawless side backbend. They took turns in rapid succession—three solo tricks each—and finished with Kenna climbing on with Madison for their double one-foot stand.

Then the moment Kenna had been planning for all day arrived.

"Go get 'em, girl," Madison said.

Kenna nodded, her throat too dry to speak. Once in the saddle, she untied the bundle and tucked it under her arm.

Loping into the arena, she waited until Rocket Man's gait reached a steady rhythm. She then stood up in the saddle, executing a hippodrome. Channing recognized it—she could tell from the smile he wore when she rode past.

On her next circuit, anticipation rising like an ocean wave, she removed the rolled-up banner Madison had sewn for her from the tablecloths and unfurled it. Holding the end with both hands, she raised it high over her head, letting the entire six feet unfurl. Whoops and hollers filled the stands as the crowd read the message.

Kenna <3 Channing.

Her arms trembled as she finished the circuit, lowered herself down into the saddle and gathered the banner. She barely heard Grumpy Joe saying something like, "Wasn't that special?" and "There's never a dull moment at Rim Country."

Kenna flew through the gate having no clue what to expect. Rocket Man must have had his suspicions, for he gathered his legs beneath him and scrambled to a bumpy stop without Kenna having to pull back on the reins.

She hopped off and spun just as Channing reached her. The banner floated from her hand and fell in a soft heap at her feet as he hauled her into his arms and planted a hard kiss on her mouth. She responded by melting against him. How could she not when she'd been hoping for, dreaming of, this reaction from him? People around them clapped. Someone said, "Congratulations," and another, "I love being right." Was that Madison?

"You stayed," Channing said, parting from her.

The small statement carried a lot of weight, and he knew it. She could tell from the timbre of his voice.

"I stayed."

"What changed your mind?" he asked.

"Something Mom said at brunch. She was telling Madison and me about my dad. How she'd marry him again even knowing the outcome just to have those sixteen years of happiness. It sounds sad, but it wasn't. I realized I wanted that kind of happiness, too, and that to get it, I would have to take some risks."

"Must have been some brunch."

"It was. For a lot of reasons. I'll tell you more later, but Mom and I had a good talk."

"I'm glad."

Rocket Man tugged on the reins still tangled in Kenna's fingers.

"I should put him away."

"I'm coming with you," he said and called to the wranglers.

He and Kenna walked together hand in hand to her trailer.

"Was the banner your idea?" he asked.

"Madison suggested I do something that would get your attention."

He laughed. "You did."

"And something that would show you in a big way I'm through running and avoiding commitments."

"Yeah?" He grinned at the teasing way she stressed *commitments*.

"We said a lot last night. Some of it was pretty hurtful. But sometimes painful truths can set us free. I had to unload a busload of baggage before I could move forward."

"I came to some realizations, too. You're right. I have used work as an excuse. And I have a raging fear of failure. Which, in hindsight, I might have gotten from Dad."

"We are products of our environments," she said, repeating her mom's words.

He cradled her cheek. "We're making changes at the arena. I have a lot to tell you, too. Most importantly, Jocelyn's going to be assistant manager and take over the non-rodeo events."

"That's awesome!"

"I should be able to get away once in a while."

"Seriously?"

He stroked her skin with the pad of his thumb. "If you're willing to have some company on the road, I promise not to spend the entire time on my phone."

She snuggled him, unable to resist. "We can make this work."

"Absolutely."

"A year at the most. Our contract with Kingston will be done by then. Who knows what will come after that, but whatever it is, I'll come home more. A lot more."

"I like the sound of that."

They stood holding each other until the horses grew impatient, Rocket Man bobbing his head and Sam tugging on the lead rope.

"Come on, boys," Channing said, releasing Kenna. "Let's go." They quickly unsaddled the horses and led them to their stalls, once again walking hand in hand. “Where’s Zenith?”

“At Rochelle’s,” Kenna said. “She let me keep him and Rocket Man there so you’d think I’d left town.”

“It worked.” He gave her a swift kiss. “Don’t ever do that again. I nearly had a stroke.”

Once the horses were settled in, they shut and latched the stall doors. Kenna leaned against Rocket Man’s stall. Channing sidled up beside her and rested an arm on the door. With his other hand, he toyed with a strand of her hair.

She sighed. “I should tell you, I have a few ground rules before we start.”

“Do tell.”

“Even though we’ll only see each other a couple weekends a month, we’re not casually dating. No friends with benefits.”

“Agreed. One hundred percent.”

“And we’re exclusive despite the long distance.”

“I wouldn’t have it any other way.” He leaned in and touched his forehead to hers. “I love you, Kenna Hewitt. I have since I was fourteen.”

“I love you, too. But I guess you already know that.”

“Honey, everyone here tonight knows it. And by tomorrow, half the town will, too.”

She grinned. “You really liked the banner?”

“What do you think?” He wrapped an arm

around her waist and tugged her against him. "You made a commitment to me. A big one."

"Ooh." She pursed her lips in thought. "I suppose I did."

"In front of all those witnesses, too. No backing out now."

"I don't want to back out." She pressed her lips to his, sealing her commitment with a kiss. "You're stuck with me."

"Promise?"

"I'm done running, Channing. I may be on the road for the next year, but I'm always coming home to you, as often as I can."

Neither of them heard the final ride of the evening or the announcement of the winners. They were too lost in each other and the love they'd almost let slip away.

CHAPTER SIXTEEN

KENNA SIPPED HER CHAMPAGNE, letting the bubbles dissolve on her tongue. She chased the drink with an after-dinner mint swiped from a crystal serving dish.

Dinner had finished an hour ago, served buffet-style in front of Wishing Well Springs' gloriously decorated wedding barn. It had been followed by cake, revelry and multiple toasts. There was one from Beau's brother, and Dinah got up and recited antidotes that had everyone in stitches. Beau's mom gave a surprisingly sentimental speech.

Between the night of the rehearsal dinner and today, Beau's family had made peace with his choice for a wife. They'd apologized to Kenna's mom, and she'd graciously accepted. Kenna didn't question what had prompted the turnaround—she was simply glad and grateful.

After the cake and toasts, the DJ had fired up the music. Everyone clapped when Beau and Kenna's mom glided onto the portable dance floor. Guests joined them and before long there wasn't one square inch of available space. Kenna had given her first dance to Beau's brother, as was often custom for the best man and maid of honor, and her second dance went to Beau. After that, Channing had claimed her until Madison cut in.

It was then Kenna had decided on another glass of champagne. As she returned to the festivities, the folds of her pink bridesmaid dress fluttered around her ankles. To her relief, she'd not tripped once in her three-inch heels, though the walk up the aisle had been daunting.

After seeing the appreciative glint in Channing's eyes when he'd stared at her across the altar, she'd contemplated dressing up again soon. He'd made a yummy sight himself in his Western-style tux. If she hadn't already been in love with him, she'd have fallen in that instant.

But she was in love with him, as everyone here knew, along with about seven thousand people on social media. Someone in the stands had filmed her last night during her unveiling of the banner and posted the video. The person had tagged Hoof Feats' page and, while not going viral exactly, there'd been a lot of "likes" and "hearts" and shares. The number was increasing hourly. Kenna's phone had been blowing up. When she answered the door for the mailman—he'd had packages for her mom—he'd asked Kenna about it.

Rather than being embarrassed, she owned the

attention. The story would be a great one to tell her and Channing's children someday.

Oops! Kenna was getting ahead of herself there. Must be the champagne talking.

She meandered along behind the cluster of dining tables, her gaze taking in the lovely sight. Over the tops of heads, she watched the dancers, seeking the familiar face that was now very dear to her, and suffering a pang of disappointment when she didn't find it. In the trees above, light from multicolored lanterns cast the scene in a fairy-tale glow. The photographer darted in and out, capturing moments to be shared and cherished and brought out year after year on anniversaries.

Bits and pieces of conversion drifted to Kenna over the music and merriment. Most were what one would expect at a wedding: old friends catching up; children being reminded to behave; a recounting of the ceremony. But Kenna went still as the words from two women she didn't know penetrated the lovely haze surrounding her.

"Can you believe that dress?" the one in blue said. "Snow white for a *fourth* wedding? And there must be ten yards of fabric in that train alone."

"Well, it is a lovely dress," the blonde answered.

"How much older is she than Beau? Twenty

years?" The woman in blue didn't bother lowering her voice.

"Thereabouts."

"Just imagine their tenth anniversary. If they last that long. He'll take one look at her and wonder what he was thinking."

"Gracie's very attractive."

"She is *now*."

"There are a lot of beautiful mature women." The blonde named several celebrities.

"They can afford plastic surgery and enhancements. Gracie works part-time and she isn't marrying money."

Ice and then heat coursed through Kenna. This might have been her not long ago, sitting at the table and having a similar conversation. No more and not ever again! She could say her mom and Beau's relationship had changed her, given her a new and better perspective, but the truth was that Channing had changed her. He'd shown her what mattered most in a relationship, and it wasn't age or money or looks.

She squared her shoulders and approached the two women from behind, putting a hand on each of their shoulders.

Leaning forward, she said, "I can imagine their tenth anniversary. They'll be every bit as happily married as they are today."

The women twisted around with a start. The blonde swallowed a gasp.

"Age is just a number," Kenna continued. "If they had let something that insignificant deter them, they might not have found the kind of love worth waiting for."

"We...we're sorry," the blonde said.

Her companion madc a derisive sound and averted her gaze.

Kenna shook her head. Nothing she said would change the woman's thinking. Rather than let the encounter spoil her mood, Kenna wandered off in search of Channing. He'd apparently left the dance floor. Where could he have gone?

As if her thoughts had conjured him, he emerged from a small group of people gathered near the entrance to the barn.

He circled her waist with his arm when he neared, and the fairy-tale glow returned.

"You all right?" he asked.

"Fine." She described her conversation with the two women, ending with her parting declaration.

"Good for you speaking up. You're a good daughter. A loyal friend. You defend the people you love."

"I've learned a lot this past month. Not just about myself. About my mom and my past, too. You helped me."

“We’ve both learned some things.” He took her hand in his. “Come on. Let’s dance.”

Without waiting for her reply, he pulled her through the maze of tables and past the crowd. They claimed a small open space on the edge of the dance floor but soon worked their way toward the center.

How different tonight was from the rehearsal dinner, Kenna thought as she relaxed into Channing’s strong embrace. No trouble loomed on the horizon. Only joy filled her heart. The fears that used to compel her to leave had vanished, replaced by excitement and anticipation for the future.

“Here we are again,” he said in her ear. “On the dance floor where it all started fourteen years ago.”

“Seems fitting. I feel more like the person I was before my dad died than I have in a long, long time. A little older, of course. And wiser.”

“I’m going to miss you when you leave on Monday.” He pressed his cheek to hers.

She loved the scent of him. Even in a tux, he still smelled of leather and outdoors. “I’ll be home in three weeks.”

“The longest three weeks of my life.”

“I’ve made a decision,” she said.

“What’s that?”

"I'm quitting Hoof Feats when the Kingston contract is up."

He stopped and stared down at her. "Are you sure that's what you want?"

"Very sure. I'm ready to settle down." She grinned. "My priorities have changed recently. You're looking at someone who embraces commitment. I'll probably adopt a rescue dog. And a cat. Two cats."

He laughed and planted a soft kiss on her forehead. "What are you going to do? Teach?"

"That's the plan," she mused. "I'm hoping to have regular monthly classes. More if I can swing it. And give private lessons. A few of the parents have asked me about that already. Eventually, I'll train horses like you suggested. For clients and, once I save some money, I'll buy one or two of my own to train and sell. Rochelle has already given me the name of someone interested. She and her husband have a lot of connections in the horse world."

Kenna paused and studied Channing's face again. "There's just one minor hitch."

"Which is?"

"I need a permanent facility to partner with. One with the right equipment, and it'll have to be conveniently located. Don't suppose you can think of one."

Channing anchored her more firmly to him.

"As it happens, I may know a soon-to-be rodeo arena manager who's looking for the right person to partner with. In more ways than one."

"Maybe you can give me his name." She beamed a smile at him. "You were right about Rocket Man and the buyer for Snapple."

"We'll discuss it later. When I get you alone."

She was looking forward to that.

Channing slowed their steps when the DJ play a country love song. "That soon-to-be rodeo arena manager I mentioned is always looking for a halftime act. If you're interested."

"I am. I also want to keep working with the old folks. If you're agreeable."

"After your ride on Sam last night, even Dad's agreeable."

"I found a place to live, too. When I'm in town."

"Where's that? Nearby, I hope."

"*Very* nearby. Beau's old double-wide. If I can get the man smell out." She wrinkled her nose, which earned her a chuckle. "With Beau and Skye moving in with Mom, I don't want to be underfoot. Not that I relish living in a double-wide, but it's only on weekends. For now. And there's a place to park my horse trailer, which is good. Once I'm no longer with Hoof Feats, I'll figure something else out. Oh, and I'm also increasing my class load at Eastern Arizona College and finishing my AA degree."

"That's a lot of changes. Are you ready?"

"More than ready." The love she felt for Channing bubbled up and spilled out in a gentle sigh. "I can't wait for what comes next."

She and Channing would manage during the coming year and overcome the distance obstacle. She didn't have a single doubt.

"For the record, I was never letting you go," he said, his voice husky. "Especially not after you rode in on Sam. You took my breath away, honey. Me and half the guys in the stands."

"I only cared about one guy." She rested her cheek on his chest.

Several seconds passed before Kenna and Channing realized the music had stopped. Dinah was making her way to the front of the gathering, portable microphone in hand.

"It's that time of the evening, ladies. Our gorgeous bride is throwing the bouquet. Get yourself over here, Gracie." She motioned emphatically with her arm.

Kenna and Channing, along with the other dancers, stepped back to clear the floor. Her mom, celebrating over on the side with Beau's grandparents, gathered her long train and, with Beau's help, joined Dinah. She must have known this was coming, for she clutched her bouquet of peach-colored roses.

"All you single ladies out there," Dinah exclaimed, "hurry yourselves over here!"

"You going?" Channing tipped his head, a gleam in his expression.

Kenna started to say no. In the past, at her mom's previous weddings and those of friends and families, she'd always tried to wheedle out of this part. When forced to, she'd stood at the very back, expending no effort to catch the bouquet.

She hadn't wanted to, having a lousy opinion of marriage. That had changed, however. She now found the idea of entwining her life with someone special appealing.

Madison came up from behind Kenna and grabbed her by the arm. "What are you waiting for? Let's go!"

What *was* she waiting for?

Tossing a smile over her shoulder at Channing, she eagerly joined the group of women gathered in a semicircle in front of her mom. There were participants of all ages, including Beau's sister. Beau stood near the DJ, holding Skye and waving her arm like Kenna's mom did. She'd be babysitting while Kenna's mom and Beau were on their honeymoon.

"Can someone please give us a drum roll?" Dinah asked.

Several guests obliged, banging their fingers on tables. Cheers and whistles went up. The photographer stationed himself at a good vantage point.

"Gracie, my dear," Dinah said. "Whenever you're ready."

Kenna's mom made a few teasing remarks to some of the single ladies in the front that elicited peals of laughter.

"We won't catch the bouquet way back here," Madison complained to Kenna.

"I'm not fighting my way up front."

Finally, her mom turned away and presented her back to the gathering. The drum rolls increased in volume. People started chanting. Raising her arm, she flung the bouquet backward.

It sailed over the heads of the ladies as if in slow motion. A scramble ensued, and shrieks erupted. Kenna watched in amusement…and then with mild shock as the bouquet flew straight at her with the precision of a heat-seeking missile.

With a will of their own, her hands opened and her arms stretched up. The next second, her fingers closed around the bouquet. All around, the chaos slowly calmed.

"You caught it!" Madison squealed. "You know what this means. Here comes the bride," she sang.

Kenna didn't want to, but she couldn't help herself and sought out Channing. He stood right where she'd left him, grinning like a fool.

Suddenly, Kenna's mom was there. "Oh, kitten, I'm so happy for you." She squeezed Kenna hard enough to expel the air from her lungs.

Beau also appeared, Skye in his arms. "Well, look at that," he boomed, pulling Kenna and her mom into a giant embrace with Skye between them. "Family hug."

Kenna didn't resist. They *were* kind of a family, and that was all right with her.

"Kenna caught the bouquet," her mom said when Beau released them. "She'll be the next one to get married."

"That's just an old saying," Kenna insisted.

"It's tradition."

"That's what I've always heard."

The remark came from Channing, who'd suddenly materialized beside her.

Whatever air remained in Kenna's lungs escaped in a rush when he stole her away from the others and guided her to a semiprivate corner.

"Consider this fair warning," he said. "I love you, Kenna, and what I want more than anything in the world is for us to be together."

"I want that, too."

She swore the singing birds and ringing bells from yesterday were back, along with the orchestra. But it was probably only the DJ playing music.

"It won't be today..." Channing lowered his mouth to hers close enough that his words landed on her lips. "And maybe not until you retire from Hoof Feats. I figure you need some time to adjust to the idea. But I have every intention of proposing to you. No way are you getting away from me again."

She looped her arms around his neck. "You have nothing to worry about. I'm done running. For good. For always. Forever."

He kissed her then, and Kenna knew with absolute certainty she was home at last.

* * * * *

Get 4 FREE REWARDS!
We'll send you 2 FREE Books
plus 2 FREE Mystery Gifts.
LOVE INSPIRED SUSPENSE
Desert Rescue
LARGER PRINT
LOVE INSPIRED SUSPENSE
On the Run
VALERIE HANSEN
LARGER PRINT
Love Inspired Suspense books showcase how courage and optimism unite in stories of faith and love in the face of danger.
FREE
Value Over
$20
YES! Please send me 2 FREE Love Inspired Suspense novels and my 2 FREE mystery gifts (gifts are worth about $10 retail). After receiving them, if I don't wish to receive any more books, I can return the shipping statement marked "cancel." If I don't cancel, I will receive 6 brand-new novels every month and be billed just $5.24 each for the regular-print edition or $5.99 each for the larger-print edition in the U.S., or $5.74 each for the regular-print edition or $6.24 each for the larger-print edition in Canada. That's a savings of at least 13% off the cover price. It's quite a bargain! Shipping and handling is just 50¢ per book in the U.S. and $1.25 per book in Canada.* I understand that accepting the 2 free books and gifts places me under no obligation to buy anything. I can always return a shipment and cancel at any time. The free books and gifts are mine to keep no matter what I decide.
Choose one:
☐ Love Inspired Suspense Regular-Print (153/353 IDN GNWN)
☐ Love Inspired Suspense Larger-Print (107/307 IDN GNWN)
Name (please print)
Address
Apt. #
City
State/Province
Zip/Postal Code
Email: Please check this box ☐ if you would like to receive newsletters and promotional emails from Harlequin Enterprises ULC and its affiliates. You can unsubscribe anytime.
Mail to the Harlequin Reader Service:
IN U.S.A.: P.O. Box 1341, Buffalo, NY 14240-8531
IN CANADA: P.O. Box 603, Fort Erie, Ontario L2A 5X3
Want to try 2 free books from another series? Call 1-800-873-8635 or visit www.ReaderService.com.
*Terms and prices subject to change without notice. Prices do not include sales taxes, which will be charged (if applicable) based on your state or country of residence. Canadian residents will be charged applicable taxes. Offer not valid in Quebec. This offer is limited to one order per household. Books received may not be as shown. Not valid for current subscribers to Love Inspired Suspense books. All orders subject to approval. Credit or debit balances in a customer's account(s) may be offset by any other outstanding balance owed by or to the customer. Please allow 4 to 6 weeks for delivery. Offer available while quantities last.
Your Privacy—Your information is being collected by Harlequin Enterprises ULC, operating as Harlequin Reader Service. For a complete summary of the information we collect, how we use this information and to whom it is disclosed, please visit our privacy notice located at corporate.harlequin.com/privacy-notice. From time to time we may also exchange your personal information with reputable third parties. If you wish to opt out of this sharing of your personal information, please visit readerservice.com/consumerschoice or call 1-800-873-8635. Notice to California Residents—Under California law, you have specific rights to control and access your data. For more information on these rights and how to exercise them, visit corporate.harlequin.com/california-privacy.
LIS21R

COMING NEXT MONTH FROM

HARLEQUIN

HEARTWARMING

Available May 11, 2021

#375 ROCKY MOUNTAIN BABY

The Second Chance Club • by Patricia Johns

Taryn Cook is pregnant with her own miracle baby...but she hadn't anticipated that the father, Noah Brooks, would want to be part of her baby's life. Can a man who never planned on being a dad truly be the father this baby needs?

#376 AN ALASKAN HOMECOMING

A Northern Lights Novel • by Beth Carpenter

To fix a family matter, Zack Vogel wishes he were married. His old friend Rowan O'Shea is happy to help him out...and the closer they get, the harder it is to imagine a future without one another.

#377 A FAMILY FOR THE FIREFIGHTER

Polk Island • by Jacquelin Thomas

After rescuing a toddler, firefighter Leon Rothchild faces the flames of his past. Finding himself drawn to the child's mother, Misty Brightwater, he has to decide if his attraction is worth tearing down walls he's spent years building.

#378 HER RODEO RANCHER

The Montgomerys of Spirit Lake

by M. K. Stelmack

When rodeo celebrity Will Claverley persuades city girl Krista Montgomery to become his fake girlfriend for a few days, old emotions flare up. Is there any way these two opposites could attract...and develop lasting love?